A JACK RYDE

SLIP OUT THE BACK JACK

THE MILLION-COPY BESTSELLING WRITER

WILLOW ROSE

Books by the Author

HARRY HUNTER MYSTERY SERIES

- ALL THE GOOD GIRLS
- RUN GIRL RUN
- NO OTHER WAY
- NEVER WALK ALONE

MARY MILLS MYSTERY SERIES

- WHAT HURTS THE MOST
- YOU CAN RUN
- YOU CAN'T HIDE
- CAREFUL LITTLE EYES

EVA RAE THOMAS MYSTERY SERIES

- DON'T LIE TO ME
- WHAT YOU DID
- NEVER EVER
- SAY YOU LOVE ME
- LET ME GO
- IT'S NOT OVER
- NOT DEAD YET

EMMA FROST SERIES

- ITSY BITSY SPIDER
- MISS DOLLY HAD A DOLLY
- RUN, RUN AS FAST AS YOU CAN

- Cross Your Heart and Hope to Die
- Peek-a-Boo I See You
- Tweedledum and Tweedledee
- Easy as One, Two, Three
- There's No Place like Home
- Slenderman
- Where the Wild Roses Grow
- Waltzing Mathilda
- Drip Drop Dead
- Black Frost

JACK RYDER SERIES

- Hit the Road Jack
- Slip out the Back Jack
- The House that Jack Built
- Black Jack
- Girl Next Door
- Her Final Word
- Don't Tell

REBEKKA FRANCK SERIES

- One, Two...He is Coming for You
- Three, Four...Better Lock Your Door
- Five, Six...Grab your Crucifix
- Seven, Eight...Gonna Stay up Late
- Nine, Ten...Never Sleep Again
- Eleven, Twelve...Dig and Delve
- Thirteen, Fourteen...Little Boy Unseen
- Better Not Cry
- Ten Little Girls
- It Ends Here

MYSTERY/THRILLER/HORROR NOVELS

- Sorry Can't Save You
- In One Fell Swoop
- Umbrella Man
- Blackbird Fly
- To Hell in a Handbasket
- Edwina

HORROR SHORT-STORIES

- Mommy Dearest
- The Bird
- Better watch out
- Eenie, Meenie
- Rock-a-Bye Baby
- Nibble, Nibble, Crunch
- Humpty Dumpty
- Chain Letter

PARANORMAL SUSPENSE/ROMANCE NOVELS

- In Cold Blood
- The Surge
- Girl Divided

THE VAMPIRES OF SHADOW HILLS SERIES

- Flesh and Blood
- Blood and Fire
- Fire and Beauty
- Beauty and Beasts
- Beasts and Magic
- Magic and Witchcraft

- WITCHCRAFT AND WAR
- WAR AND ORDER
- ORDER AND CHAOS
- CHAOS AND COURAGE

THE AFTERLIFE SERIES

- BEYOND
- SERENITY
- ENDURANCE
- COURAGEOUS

THE WOLFBOY CHRONICLES

- A GYPSY SONG
- I AM WOLF

DAUGHTERS OF THE JAGUAR

- SAVAGE
- BROKEN

There must be fifty ways to leave your lover

~*Paul Simon 1975*

Prologue

Four bodies cast four shadows on the barren walls behind them. The scarce glow from the candle placed on the table in the middle lights up their faces. They take turns with the knife, cutting their thumbs open. A drop of blood lands on the dark wooden table. Eyes meet across the room. Determined eyes. All four thumbs are pressed against each other, one by one. Blood is shared, secrets buried. The pact is made. The four of them know that there is no way back from here.

THIS IS WHERE IT BEGINS.

1

November 2009

"Hurry up. We're going to be late."

Maggie Foster's daughter looked impatiently at her mother. Maggie was getting her two year-old out of the Toyota. "I'm doing this as fast as I can," she groaned.

"We'll miss the movie," her daughter continued. "We need to get popcorn too."

"Hey," her father, Dan, said. "You be nice to your mother or we're not going to the movies at all."

Maggie sent her husband a friendly smile. Her oldest daughter had been giving her mother a hard time lately. She was fifteen and acting like a real teenager. Maggie often wondered if it was just due to the fact that her baby sister took up a lot of the attention that she was used to getting or if it was just an age thing.

Her oldest daughter groaned and rolled her eyes at her father.

"Watch it," he said.

Maggie managed to get the baby out and put her on her hip, while Dan took out the stroller from the back. It was late Friday after-noon. The parking lot was already packed behind the mall. There were a lot of people that—like the Fosters—had chosen to spend their

Friday night at the mall. Maggie hoped not all of them were going to the movies. A two year-old made a lot of noise and had a hard time sitting still, even if it was *The Princess and the Frog*. Hopefully, there would be other young kids present, so they wouldn't be the only ones destroying it for everyone else.

It was the first time Maggie had taken her youngest to the movie theater. And she did it only to please her oldest daughter, who constantly complained that they never did anything fun anymore— not since *the baby* came into their lives. Maggie wanted to prove to her daughter that they could still do the same things as they used to.

Now, as she walked towards the colorful building housing the mall and movie theater, she wasn't so sure it was a good idea anymore. She had this feeling in the bottom of her stomach that wouldn't leave.

Maggie stopped as they reached the front doors of the mall. The baby was already fussing in her arms. She was sweating from holding her. It was another hot afternoon in Boca Raton, north of Miami. Usually, Maggie loved the heat, but today it had been bothering her. Maybe she was coming down with something.

"Maybe we shouldn't..." she said.

Her oldest daughter growled. "I knew it!"

Dan looked at Maggie. "Are you not feeling alright?"

"But...but, you promised!" their daughter whined.

"I know, sweetie," Maggie said.

"You can't break a promise. You just can't." Their daughter was holding it together, but Maggie could tell she was about to crack. She looked at her husband. Everything inside of her screamed that she didn't want to do this, that she had to get herself back into the car and drive home, but how could she? How could she break her daughter's heart like that?

"I won't," Maggie said, sounding as reassuring as possible. "I'm just tired. It's okay."

Her daughter's eyes lit up. "So, we can go see the movie?"

Dan looked at Maggie. She smiled to convince him it was all

right. He would cancel the entire thing if he suspected she wasn't well. The baby was crying. Maggie shushed her to make her calm down, and then gave her the binky. It was going to be hard with her inside the movie theater, but she was going to do it. For her daughter's sake.

"Are you sure?" Dan asked.

Maggie forced a smile and grabbed the door. "I'm sure. Let's go. I can't wait to watch this movie."

2

November 2009

THE MALL WAS CROWDED, as always. Teenagers were everywhere, hanging out in the food court and by Claire's. Brad Schmidt remembered when he used to be one of those teenagers, hanging out on a Friday night, looking at the girls. He still liked to look every now and then at the young girls, but made sure his wife didn't notice.

"You want more?" Gabby asked their daughter, Ally.

Ally shook her head.

"Eat the rest," Brad said.

"I'm full," Ally said.

"We paid for this sandwich, so you eat the rest," Brad continued.

"But..." Ally looked at him, but he wasn't going to cave. And she knew it. Brad felt his face turning red in anger.

"Eat it," he said, raising his voice.

Ally looked into her father's eyes and knew there was no way she was winning this. She looked at her mother, who turned her face away, avoiding the glare of the other people in the food court. Brad clenched his fist under the table. He couldn't believe she would defy him like this in public. She would have to hear about this later.

Ally picked up the sandwich and took another bite.

Brad felt the blood calm in his veins. He took in a deep breath and smiled.

"Good girl," he said.

When she was done, Gabby crumbled the Subway wrapper and threw it away. Brad swallowed the rest of his sandwich and washed it down with his Coke. He was looking forward to an evening in the movie theater, just stuffing his face with popcorn and soda. He would probably get a candy bar or two as well, while he was at it, and hopefully without Gabby seeing it. She hated how much weight he had gained over the last couple of years and was always on his case about it. He didn't mind too much. After all, he had nailed the girl, he had a great job where he didn't have to move much, but could stay behind his computer all day, and he had a beautiful daughter. He was happy and wanted to enjoy life. It wasn't like Gabby was that slim anymore either.

They got up and threw away the trash, then walked towards the theater that was already packed with people. They got in line, and when it was their turn, showed the usher their tickets to *The Princess and the Frog*, the movie Ally had been asking to see for several weeks now. Brad didn't care what movie it was, as long as he could sit in the dark and eat without anyone demanding anything of him.

"Anyone need to pee?" Gabby asked, looking at their daughter. Ally nodded. "Good. Come on," Gabby said, and pulled her daughter towards the restrooms.

Brad sat down on a bench to wait. He looked at his watch, wondering if he should just go inside and get some seats while there were still some good ones left. He looked at the popcorn boxes and drinks that Gabby had put down on the bench next to him. He could hardly carry it all on his own, and there was no way he could leave it out here. Someone might take it. No, he had to wait. They would be quick if the line wasn't too long in there.

Brad grabbed his phone and silenced it. Might as well do it right away. A couple walked past him and smiled. He nodded.

"How're you doing?"

A couple of teenagers giggled as they walked past him and disappeared into another movie. Brad wasn't looking forward to his daughter reaching that age. He couldn't bear to think of her as this monster, this erratic creature who would hate her parents and the world they lived in. He hadn't been too good himself, the way he had behaved back then. But she wouldn't be like that. Not his Ally. He had raised her better than that...with tough love, the way his own parents had raised him. It was for her own good. To keep her out of trouble later in life.

Brad's eyes met those of his daughter as she walked out of the restroom. His heart melted. No, Ally wasn't going to be anything like those girls. She was Daddy's girl. She was going to remain that way always.

She bumped into him and almost made him drop his candy. He felt the anger rise in him and was about to yell at her for being so clumsy, but controlled his anger for once. This was not the time or the place.

He looked up and his eyes met with Gabby's. She was always on his case about him being too harsh on Ally, but she knew he loved her.

"Let's go watch the movie," Gabby said, and grabbed the boxes of popcorn in her arms. Ally took her own box and soda, while Brad grabbed the rest. He followed them inside the theater, where Gabby found seats next to a family of four. Brad grumbled a little when he saw the girl in the seat next to him, who could be no more than two years old. The theater was almost empty, why did they have to sit right next to them? Young children were always trouble in a movie theater. Why did people even bring them? They didn't watch much of the movie anyway. It was a waste of money, in his opinion. Now, he just hoped the little girl in the seat next to him wasn't going to ruin it all for him.

"How are you doing?" he said, and nodded to the parents who seemed vaguely familiar. A daughter who looked like she was teenager peeked over as well. He smiled at her. She didn't smile back.

Kids today, Brad thought to himself, and grabbed his first candy bar as the previews came on. Brad smiled and leaned back in his seat as the chocolate melted on his tongue. He felt good at this moment. He had everything under control. He was doing okay for himself, his company was booming, and he had a beautiful family. Life was good.

He had exactly thirty-five minutes left to enjoy it.

3

November 2009

As SUSPECTED, the baby couldn't sit still for long. She kept crawling into Maggie's seat and making loud noises. It was exhausting, and Maggie didn't get to watch much of the movie. The man in the seat next to her seemed to be annoyed by the baby crawling up and down in her seat. The theater was almost empty, and Maggie wondered if she should take the baby up to the back row and sit with her there. But she would still make noises. Maggie closed her eyes and wished she were at home, where the baby could be as noisy as she wanted to and she didn't have to shush her constantly.

"Sit down," she whispered.

The baby whined and pushed her hand away, then continued to crawl up on the seat, then down on the floor, then back up. The seat squeaked every time, and people behind them were clearing their throats. The baby crawled up on the seat and jumped in it while laughing loudly. She stared at the people sitting behind them. They shushed her. Maggie felt embarrassed and pulled her down. As she did, she felt her diaper. She turned and looked at her husband.

"I need to change her," she whispered in his ear.

Dan nodded, while stuffing his face with popcorn. He was all into the movie, unlike Maggie, who had hardly seen anything. She was just waiting for this entire thing to be over so she could go home.

Maggie grabbed the bag and swung it over her shoulder, then grabbed the baby, who started crying, since she wanted to keep jumping in her seat.

"Excuse me," she said to the big man next to her. He pulled his leg to the side with an annoyed sigh and let her pass. The baby was crying loudly now, and Maggie hurried as fast as she could to get out of the theater. Once the door shut behind her, she breathed a sigh of relief. Finally, she could relax. Her shoulders came down and she held her daughter tightly in her arms. It would probably have been better if her oldest daughter had gone alone with her father. They would do that next time. There was no way Maggie was doing this again.

She took the baby to the restroom and put her on the changing table. She didn't want to lay down, so she had to hold her with force. It had been like this a lot lately. She had started to get a will of her own and never wanted to do as her mother told her.

"Lay still," she said with sweetness in her voice.

But the girl was still fussing and moving around while she pulled off her diaper. It was heavy with pee. She changed it quickly, then tickled her tummy and kissed her before she put her clothes back on. The baby laughed and grabbed her hair and pulled it. It hurt, but Maggie didn't mind. She enjoyed these moments so much. It was completely different than when she had her first child. Back then, she had been so young, so constantly anxious about doing the wrong thing, it had made everything so hard for her. Plus, she had to deal with a mother-in-law who constantly implied she wasn't doing anything right, with the result that her husband never thought she could do anything right either. Neither could their daughter, come to think of it. Lately, Dan had been on all of their cases, and it was exhausting.

Maggie decided she didn't care about watching the movie and that she would take a stroll with the baby in the mall instead until the movie was done. Maybe the baby would take a nap. Give Maggie a little break.

She grabbed her bag and walked towards the theater. First, she needed to go back in and tell Dan her plans, and then get the stroller, of course.

The baby was laughing and hugging her head, and Maggie felt so cheerful as she opened the door to the theater, where the sounds of pure hell met her. At first, she thought they were laughing. She thought people in the theater were just laughing. Like laughing hysterically, but as she walked up the ramp, she realized the movie hadn't made the audience laugh; it was something else that had made them scream in terror. The deafening sound of shots being fired made her realize the horror that was taking place.

Maggie's heart stopped and she rushed inside, just in time to see her oldest daughter and Dan fall to the floor. By the exit stood the shooter, still firing into the crowd again and again while people tried to escape. Bodies were dropping to the ground like flies. Maggie stared at the shooter and the fire in this person's eyes that seemed to be beyond this life. At first, Maggie couldn't move. She couldn't speak, she couldn't even scream. Instead, she grabbed her youngest daughter and held her tight as she turned around and ran out the same way she had come in.

Part One

MAKE A NEW PLAN

4

March 2015

THE NOISE WAS UNBEARABLE. Stanley Bradley had always hated Disney World more than any place he could think of. But the light in his granddaughter Elyse's eyes when he took her there made it all worth it. Even the waiting in long lines while sweat ran from his forehead and stung his eyes, even the tasteless hotdogs they ate for lunch, even the constant music coming from everywhere and people cheering almost hysterically at the parade in the afternoon.

Just seeing her smile made it worth it.

It wasn't often Stanley got to see his grandchild and spend time with her, since her mother, Stan's only daughter, lived upstate and rarely came to visit.

"You never have time for me anyway," she always grumbled on the phone. "Like you never had time for me while I was growing up."

"It wasn't that bad, was it?" Stan asked.

"Maybe not. But you have always been married to your work. Even when you were home, you always had your nose buried in some research material or some new article published in *The Scientist*. I think I saw the front cover of that magazine more than I saw your eyes, growing up."

Tina always knew how to make him hurt. He hated that she blamed him for not being around enough in her childhood. Especially when the fact was that it was her mother who kept him away from her. Nothing he did was ever good enough for her. It began when she was just a newborn baby. Stan had wanted to change a diaper every now and then, but if he suggested it, Melanie would simply laugh and tell him he was too distracted, that the baby would roll from the changing table while Stanley was lost in some thought or just remembered something he needed to write down.

"You leave this to me," she had told him. "This isn't rocket science." Then she would laugh and take the baby from his hands. Later, when she was older and Stanley wanted to take her places, Melanie would always come up with some excuse for her not to be able to go.

"She needs a nap," she would say or, "no girls are interested in space ships."

"It's a shuttle," Stan would correct her, but it was no use. Twenty-five years Stanley had worked at Kennedy Space Center, and never once had he been able to take his little daughter there. Or the son who came later in life.

"She'll be bored to death," Melanie would say, and take the girl away from him again.

In the end, Stanley finally stopped trying. He immersed himself in his work and his research and let Melanie bring up the children. According to Melanie, it was for their own good. It was what was best for them.

Now, Stanley felt like he had gotten a second chance with his granddaughter. It was all part of his plan to try again. To make up for what he had lost. He only saw Elyse once a year, when Tina came down over spring break. But it had quickly become his favorite time of year, and the visit to Disney his favorite event. Elyse was now four years old and so delightful he caught himself hoping she would never grow older.

"Don't grow up and get angry and mean like your mother and

grandmother," he would whisper, when she ran to Mickey Mouse and gave him the biggest hug in the history of hugging, still smiling from ear to ear, even after waiting an hour in line to get inside of his house.

"Look at me, Grandpa!"

Stanley looked and took her picture while Mickey put his arm around her. While looking at her on the screen, he shed a small tear, thinking how he had dreamt of doing something like this with Tina when she was young. Elyse had the exact same smile as her mother. It was captivating.

So much time had been wasted, so much lost.

5

March 2015

THE SUN SHONE through the windows at my condo, cruelly exposing the salt covering the glass on the outside like a filter. It had been blowing from the east for a few days in a row, and the layer of salt in the air from the ocean lay thick on my windows. The salt was like a mist. Now, the wind had finally settled and it was quiet again outside.

Inside my condo, it had become quiet since my parents moved back home when the forensics techs finished their work on the motel, and since Shannon King had decided to move into an apartment I helped her find in the same building as mine. She didn't want to keep imposing on my family and me, even though I told her she could stay for as long as she wanted. She needed time and space to find out what she was going to do. Joe had promised her he would drag her through a custody battle when he left Cocoa Beach to go back to Nashville. I was certain he wasn't bluffing. A guy like him never bluffed.

Meanwhile, the kids and I had gone back to normal. As normal as it gets when you work as a homicide detective. Shannon and I were still seeing each other, and she and Angela often came down to the motel and ate with us. On weekends, we all hung out together at my parents' place while I helped them out.

"Dad?"

It was Abigail. She was standing in the living room rubbing her eyes. It was almost time to get up. I always woke up at sunrise. It was my favorite moment of the day...standing in the living room and watching the sun come up over the quiet Atlantic Ocean. The waves were glassy this morning and I wanted to go surfing as soon as I dropped the kids off at the bus.

I put my arm around her shoulder and pulled her close. "You sleep well?"

She nodded and stretched.

"Are you looking forward to spring break?" I asked. Today was the last day of school before break. I had signed both kids up for surf camp all week.

Abigail nodded. "I can't wait to go surfing."

"I don't want to go surfing." Austin had come out of their room too.

I smiled and kissed him. "I'm sure you'll want to once you get there," I said. "It's going to be fun."

Austin groaned. "No, I won't." He crossed his arms in front of his chest and looked at me angrily. He was always grumpy in the mornings and made a big deal out of small things. Mornings were the worst for him. He wasn't a morning person like Abigail and me.

"This is not the time to be discussing this," I said. "Get dressed. Grandma is waiting with breakfast at the deck."

They both sighed, then turned to their room where I had put out clothes for them to wear. Today was a big day at the school. There was an awards ceremony to mark the end of the quarter, and both kids were up for an award. I couldn't be prouder. I had told Sheriff Ron I was going to come in late today. I wanted to be there and take pictures of my babies.

I looked at the clock. It was a quarter till seven. I walked to Emily's door and knocked. "Are you up, sweetheart? I don't want you to miss school."

There was a sound and someone grunting something behind it

and I figured it was her. She wasn't a morning person either, but it hadn't always been like that. I guess most sixteen year-olds weren't morning people. When she was younger, Emily would always be the first one up, jumping on my bed. Now, she hardly spoke a word to me till the afternoons. She went quiet behind the door and I knocked again. "Don't fall back asleep, honey." Abigail and Austin came out from their room all dressed and with their backpacks on. "We're leaving for Grandma's now," I said.

"Fine," Emily yelled from behind the door.

"See you this afternoon, sweetheart."

She answered with another grunting sound, and I hoped it meant she was awake enough to get herself into that car of hers and make it to school on time. I had long ago decided she needed to take responsibility for her own life and hoped it was working. I wasn't going to be the kind of dad that checked up on her constantly. I wanted her to know I trusted her.

6

December 2002

SHE WAS A CHRISTMAS CHILD. A true blessing for Dottie and James West, as were the three previous girls. But this one was special. Dottie knew she was. Not just because she was born on Christmas night. There was something about her that made Dottie love her more deeply than she had the other three, who were four, six, and nine at the time of little Elizabeth's birth. She knew right from the beginning when she looked into those very blue eyes of her newborn that this one was different than the rest. Just the way she felt while lying in her arms was different. Her body felt different.

When Dottie took her daughter home, she wondered why she hadn't heard her baby cry yet. With the previous three girls, they had cried from the moment they could breathe, but not Elizabeth. She was just lying there, quietly staring at her mother.

"Do you think she's alright?" Dottie asked the next morning, when she woke up and the baby hadn't cried all night. The baby was in her crib staring at her mother without making a sound. "She's so quiet," Dottie said, looking anxiously at her husband.

James shrugged. "I'm sure she's just fine. She's just quieter than the others. That's all." James took a shower, then got dressed. All the while, Dottie tried to feed her baby. But Elizabeth didn't want to suckle. It frustrated Dottie, who kept trying to get her to take the bottle.

"She hasn't eaten at all," she groaned in desperation.

James pulled out a pair of pants from the walk-in closet and put them on. He grabbed a shirt and a tie.

"You think she's alright?" Dottie asked again.

James sighed. "You've asked that seven times since we brought her home. Yes, I believe she is just fine. Just like the three previous were fine."

"She just feels so...so different," Dottie said.

"Different how?" he asked.

"Floppy," Dottie said, and looked at her husband. She kind of liked the way Elizabeth felt in her arms. She was so soft, but she worried that something could be wrong.

James smiled, and then leaned over his wife. He kissed her on the forehead with a light chuckle. "Remember when we had Anna? You thought she had a tumor because of that big birthmark she had on her forehead. And what about Dana? She had little spots all over her body that turned out to be hormones or something. And what was it that was wrong with Tiffany?"

Dottie smiled. "She cried all night two nights in a row and I thought she had colic."

"Now did any of these beautiful girls ever die or have anything wrong with them besides what was going on in your mind?" James smiled and kissed her again.

Dottie drew in a deep breath. He was right. She had felt the exact same way with all of her children. It was only natural for a mother to worry about her baby. The truth was, all four children had been different. No two were alike, so it was silly to compare them in the first place.

"Now, if you'll excuse me, I have to go to work," James said.

"I wish you didn't have to," Dottie said.

James smiled again. "I'll be back tonight. Try not to spend all day worrying. Try to enjoy our newest little family member while I'm gone."

"But, what if she doesn't eat anything?" Dottie said anxiously.

"She will. All children eat when they get hungry enough. Let her settle to this new reality first, then you'll see. It's all a little much right now."

Dottie felt emotional and overwhelmed. She was about to cry. It was the same every time she brought a child home. It was such a sensitive time. She always spent at least one whole day crying afterwards.

James grabbed his briefcase. Dottie could hear the other kids in the hallway now. It was time to get up and get them to school. Luckily, it didn't seem like Elizabeth would demand much of her mother's attention this first day at home. She could still attend to the needs of the others. Was it just this simple? Was Elizabeth simply just an easy child?

James leaned in over Dottie and kissed her again. He looked deep into her eyes. "She'll be fine. Do you hear me? She'll eat when she gets hungry."

7

March 2015

SHANNON LOOKED at her daughter in the back seat. It was the last day of school before spring break, and they were both looking forward to some time together. Angela had started at Abigail and Austin's school, not in the same class, but they still saw each other every day at recess. But it had been a rough couple of weeks for her daughter. Starting a new school in a strange new place was a lot for a six year-old. But she had handled it well. She was a tough cookie, Shannon was happy to realize.

"See you this afternoon," Shannon said, as they reached the drop-off line and it was their turn. A teacher helped Angela get out of the car. Shannon had been driving her every morning, even though she knew Angela could go on the bus with Jack's kids, but Shannon wasn't ready for that yet. It was hard for Shannon to let her daughter go...ever since she was kidnapped, but life had to go on, and especially Shannon needed her life to move on.

Things were getting harder with Joe, who was building his case against her. Shannon had her lawyer working to build her case, but she was terrified of how this would end. Plus, Angela missed her dad and kept asking when she was going to see him, and that didn't make things easier. All Shannon wanted was for her daughter to have as ordinary a life as possible.

"Love you, Mom," Angela said and slammed the door.

"Love you too," Shannon said, and watched her daughter spring after the other kids inside the yellow brick building. Shannon had come to love Roosevelt Elementary. The entire atmosphere was just what her daughter needed right now. It was a safe environment and there was a lot of warmth. The only thing Shannon worried about was the press. As she drove past the entrance and back onto Minutemen Causeway, she spotted two photographers in the bushes outside of the school. They had been there waiting for their photo-op ever since Angela had started at the school. The school knew about it, and so did the local police, so they made sure they didn't get onto the school's property, but had to stay outside. They still managed to get pictures now and then of her daughter when she was dropped off and picked up, but that was all.

Shannon knew they were trying to get pictures of her and Jack together. They had already succeeded and had plastered the photos all over the magazines. The cover of one of them this week read *Shannon's New Bad Boy* and then they had printed a picture of Jack in his board shorts coming out of the water. It had made Shannon so angry, but Jack had been really cool about it.

"It's the price you pay for dating a celebrity," he had simply said and kissed her. It had been such a relief for Shannon. She was afraid the press would end up destroying the healthiest relationship she had ever had. But Jack was a cool guy. He wasn't so easy to shake. Not even when they teased him at work.

"They'll grow tired of us eventually," he said, the last time photographers had jumped out of the dunes while Shannon and he were walking on the beach together. "I'm hardly that interesting."

He had a way of making Shannon laugh, even when things were bad. She adored him for that. Shannon had decided to stay in Cocoa Beach, to be close to him and his family, who had welcomed her so warmly. Both she and Angela seemed to be thriving here, and except for the photographers, it was as close to paradise as she had ever been. Bruce, her manager, kept asking when she was going back on tour, but she hadn't been able to give him an answer. The papers wrote about her custody battle and divorce and then about her new lover, and she needed time, she kept telling him.

"I can't hold them for much longer," he kept saying. "The label is getting anxious. They're afraid of losing money. But I'll try."

Shannon didn't care much about her career lately, or her label for that matter. Now was the time for her to heal her wounds. And it was time to focus on Angela. Plus, she had started to learn how to surf. Jack had been teaching her and she had to admit it was hard, but she quite enjoyed it. There was nothing like starting the day on the ocean among pelicans and dolphins. She wasn't going anywhere now.

Shannon stopped at a red light in downtown Cocoa Beach. She smiled when she saw two young guys with surfboards under their arms. A sign told her the street would be closed later in the afternoon because of Friday Fest. She was going there with Jack, while his mother had promised to take care of the kids. Sherri was so sweet. She really liked Angela, Shannon could tell.

Shannon picked up her phone and scrolled through her emails. She received hundreds of those daily from her fans. Mostly praise for how much they loved her music; some of them were haters, who asked her to drop off the face of the planet and hoped she realized she was going to hell for living her life in sin. Over the years, Shannon had gotten good at ignoring them and only read the good ones. Those that made her feel good.

Today, one of the emails made her pause and forget about the light that now turned green. In the subject line it said.

I'm sorry for what I have to do.

8

March 2015

KATIE MUELLER STARED out the window of the mini-van as the countryside passed by. They had almost reached Orlando and were less than an hour from their destination. It was the first time Katie was going to spend spring break without her parents. She was going to Cocoa Beach with some people from her college. She had heard about how everyone went to Florida for spring break since she was a child, but never thought she would actually go there herself. It wasn't exactly her type of thing. She wasn't a party-girl like the others in the mini-van. Not like Leanne or Britney, who were already drinking beers and taking shots up in the front of the car.

As the mini-van hit 520 towards Cape Canaveral and the bridges leading to the island, the girls were singing loudly and laughing, while the three boys that had come along on the trip enjoyed watching them. Katie wondered what she was even doing there.

It was Greg that had convinced her to come. Greg was a history major like Katie. He was the one driving the car. Katie'd had a crush on him since the beginning of the school year. So, naturally, when he asked if she wanted to come, she had said yes. Her parents were thrilled to hear that she was going.

"Finally, you're getting out a little," her dad had said. "I'm glad you're making some friends. College is supposed to be a fun time. I know mine was."

Katie wasn't going to have fun. She couldn't tell her dad that, but that's what she had thought to herself. She was going because she thought she might get to spend some time alone with Greg. She hadn't realized she would also have to endure the perkiness of Leanne and Britney.

"How are you doing back there," he asked, looking at Katie in the rearview mirror.

Leanne and Britney giggled.

Katie smiled. "I'm good, thanks."

Greg smiled. "Good. We're almost there. I booked us all rooms at a small motel. It's right on the beach. I'm sure we're going to have a lot of fun. Girls stay in one room, boys in another."

They were seven in total. The last girl, Irene, wasn't part of the party-troop either. Still, she wasn't the type Katie saw herself hanging out with either. She couldn't stop staring at her fake mega-boobs. And the fact that she always wore those small tank tops that didn't seem to hold anything inside made her look ridiculous, like a porn-star in some bad movie. She didn't think she had anything in common with this girl, who at the age of twenty-one, insisted on having something altered on her face or body at least once a year, paid for by her parents, naturally.

Katie watched the swampy marshland as they drove towards the water, looking to see if she could spot an alligator somewhere, since everyone said there were alligators in all waterholes in Florida. Until now, she hadn't seen any. A couple of cows were eating grass behind a fence, but that was hardly spectacular. An armadillo had been hit by a car and was lying on the side of the road. Big billboards told her Ron Jon's, the world largest surf shop, wasn't far away. Katie wasn't very fond of the ocean or the beach. She hated to get sandy, and certainly didn't enjoy the way she looked in a bikini. Yet, she had still found herself shopping for a new one for the trip after Greg had asked her to come along. She didn't exactly look forward to showing off her winter-pale pillars of legs. Not when she was going to be next to those long-legged beauties and the Barbie-doll. Katie was short and slightly overweight. She wasn't so sure Greg would enjoy that sight. She had bought a long beach-dress that she could wear to cover herself up until she could lay down in the sand. The worst part was walking or standing. Lying on a towel, she could do.

"We're here!" Greg exclaimed.

Katie looked out the window and spotted the sign. "Motel Albert's?" she mumbled. It sounded like the motel from a horror movie. *Psycho*. What was the name of that motel again?

Bates. That's it Bates Motel.

"A boy's best friend is his mother," she said with a scary pretend-chuckle, as she exited the van and looked at the front of the old motel that looked like it had been built in the sixties, with the red *Motel* sign on top. Greg smiled and looked at her.

"We're going to have so much fun here," he said.

9

March 2015

Stanley Bradley felt sick to his stomach. He sat up in the darkness, leaned to the side, and threw up. He had no idea where it landed, but didn't care either. It was so dark, and all he cared about was the fact that he felt terrible. Not until a lot later, when the worst nausea had subsided, did he start to wonder where he was. The realization hit him like a blow to his face.

"Elyse," he whispered into the darkness. Where was Elyse? She had been with him. They had been at Disney World. Then what? They had walked back to the car in the parking lot. The car had been parked by Pluto, he remembered randomly for some ridiculous reason. They had driven out from there. They had been in the countryside, singing...yes, they had been singing one of Elyse's favorite songs. What was the name of it again? The one from *Frozen*? How did it go again?

The cold never bothered me anyway.

Yes, that was one of the lines, Elyse's favorite line in the song. *Let it go*, was the title of the song.

Then what? What had happened? Where was he now? Where was Elyse?

The car. Something happened to the car. There was something in the road. Something that made the car drive off the road. The tires punctured, he remembered. The car screeched; Elyse was screaming. Then what? Then it all went black.

There was a sound in the room; it sounded like a door opened, the light was turned on, and Stanley covered his eyes.

"Oh, good, you're awake," a voice said.

"Where am I?" Stanley asked with a trembling voice. "Where is Elyse? Where is my granddaughter?"

As his eyes got used to the light, he realized he was looking directly into the barrel of a gun. He gasped and fell back into the bed.

"Now, lay still, Mr. Bradley," the voice said. "It's for your own good. You hurt yourself badly in the accident."

Stanley looked into the barrel with his heart pounding in his chest. "Am...are you holding me prisoner here?"

"You can call it whatever you like," the voice replied. Something was put in his hands. It was a plate of food.

Stanley stared at the steak and potatoes with thick gravy. It looked delicious, but he still felt nauseated.

"I'm not hungry. I demand to know what happened to my grand-daughter."

"Eat," the voice said adamantly. The gun was pushed closer to his face. "Eat or your granddaughter dies."

Eat or your granddaughter dies? What kind of an ultimatum was that? How was that threatening?

Stanley shrugged, then grabbed the knife and fork and started eating. As he sunk his teeth into the steak, he realized he was actually quite hungry, and this was good meat. The potatoes were slightly overcooked for his liking, but he ate them anyway, while this strange person kept staring at him while holding the gun.

"It's quite good," he said, still wondering why this person wanted him to eat so badly. Was something in the food? Stanley stopped chewing. What if it was poisoned?

"Finish it."

"What's in the food?" he asked.

"Just eat it."

Thinking he'd better obey this mad personage, he finished the plate. The plate was removed, but only for a few seconds before another one landed in his lap. Spaghetti and meatballs.

"Now, eat this."

"I'm stuffed. I really can't eat any more," Stanley said. "It smells great, but I really can't…"

The cold gun was placed to his temple. "Eat."

10

March 2015

I WAS the proudest dad in the entire cafeteria. My twins were both up on the stage holding their recognition awards for hard work. Austin in Math and Abigail in Reading. I knew they had both been struggling in those subjects, and to see them up there so proud for having reached their goals, made my heart overflow with pride. Usually, they mostly got themselves in a lot of trouble at school, and more than once I had been called by the teacher, Mrs. Allen, telling me they weren't behaving well. To see them getting an award, shaking the hand of the principal, almost brought tears to my eyes. Finally, they were doing something right.

I grabbed my camera and took what must have been a thousand photos, while everyone from the class who had received an award was lined up with the teacher. Austin was poking his sister in the side, and then she hit him on the shoulder. Austin squealed and hit her back. Abigail pushed him in return. Meanwhile, the teacher tried hard to smile behind them. I looked at them from above the camera. Austin grabbed Abigail's reward and threw it on the ground. Abigail ran after it and tripped. Now she was crying. The principal looked at Mrs. Allen for help. Mrs. Allen hurriedly got the kids off the stage.

At least it lasted long enough for me to get a picture. It might be a while before they received another, I thought to myself. Their grandparents were going to be so proud.

I was packing the camera away when my phone vibrated in my pocket. I picked it up. It was Shannon. I walked into the hallway, while waving at my kids who were being dragged back to their classroom. I still had water in my ear from this morning's surfing.

"Hi there. I was just thinking about you. I saw Angela in the cafeteria. She seemed happy. I think she already made some friends in her class."

"That's good," Shannon said, distraught. I could tell by the sound of her voice that something was going on.

"What's wrong?"

"I…I got this weird email. I think you need to take a look at it."

I looked at my watch. I had told Ron I would be in later today because of the award ceremony. We had a double stabbing last week that we were finishing the investigation of. A girl and her grandfather had been attacked in their apartment by a homeless guy. The grandfather died from his wounds. The guy was in custody and had admitted to doing it, even though he said he couldn't remember much, since he was completely doped up. But the granddaughter that survived was a very strong witness to the events. It was a pretty easy case, but a lot of paperwork. Sheriff Ron had finally assigned me a new partner, Bethany, or Beth, and we had some good teamwork going on. But I was in no rush. I wasn't in a hurry to get to the office, so I guessed I could take a few minutes to meet up with Shannon. I took any chance I could get to see her.

"Sure. Do you want to meet up for coffee at Juice N' Java?"

"I can't deal with photographers or fans taking pictures with their cellphones right now," she said.

She made it sound very serious. I had no coffee at my place, and I didn't have much time.

"All right," I said. "Let's meet at the bar at the motel in five minutes. My mom makes a pretty mean cup of Joe."

"Sounds like a plan."

We hung up. I was thrilled at the prospect of getting to see Shannon and sprang for my Jeep in the school's parking lot. Three minutes later, I was at my parents' motel.

"Aren't you supposed to be at work?" my mom said. She was cleaning the counters in the bar.

"I'm meeting Shannon here," I said. I threw a glance around the room. It was empty. The bar usually didn't open till noon. "Where is Dad?"

"He's taking a nap," my mom said.

I spotted a table in the corner. "We'll just sit over there," I said. "Do you have any coffee?"

She gave me that *are-you-kidding-me* look that only a mother can do. "What do you mean, do I have coffee? Of course I have coffee."

I chuckled. "Good. Could Shannon and I have a cup each? She uses milk, but no sugar..."

"And you like both in yours."

Shannon had entered the bar and walked up to me. My heart skipped a beat from looking at her. I couldn't believe I still got that feeling when looking at her, even this long after we'd started seeing each other. But I couldn't help myself. Being around her made me feel good.

11

March 2015

"So, what's going on?"

I looked into Shannon's eyes over the steam of my coffee. She sipped hers and looked away. Something was definitely bothering her.

"You said something about an email?"

Shannon inhaled, and then looked at me. "Don't hate me."

"Hate you? How could I ever hate you?" I asked, shocked at the character of her statement. How could she ever think I could hate her? "I love you," I said. Shannon widened her eyes. My heart stopped. It had just burst out of me. I had never told her I loved her before. I didn't even realize I did.

Was it too soon? Was I going to scare her away?

Shannon smiled. Her eyes hit the table and she blushed. I felt a huge relief.

"Well, there is no beating around the bush with you, Detective, huh?" she said, chuckling lightly.

"I'm sorry. I didn't mean for it to come out like that...I..."

She placed her hand on top of mine. "It's okay, Jack." She looked into my eyes. "I think I love you too."

The words completely blew me away. I felt so happy I could scream.

"But that's not why I told you to meet me," she continued with a serious voice. "You might have to rethink everything after you hear what I have to say."

Uh-oh. That sounded really bad.

"You're scaring me a little here, Shannon," I said and sipped my coffee. "What's going on?"

"There is something I've never told anyone. Something I should have told when it happened...but I was just so..." She stopped. Shannon bit her lip. I could tell this was hard for her. It freaked me out a little.

What could be so bad?

"Nothing you can say will make me feel differently," I said. "Whatever it is, we will figure it out...together. Just tell me everything from the beginning."

Shannon sighed. "I got this email today," she said, and showed me her phone. "I think it's from a fan."

"What does it say?"

Shannon read it out loud to me. Her voice was trembling.

"*Dear Shannon King. I am so sorry. I am sorry for what I am about to do. I want you to know how much you inspire me. Your songs make me understand who I really am; they encourage me to follow my dreams. I am sure you had to do bad things too to make it to the top as well. I am just doing what must be done. I hope you understand. Yours truly AM*"

I looked at Shannon. She lifted her eyes from the screen and showed me the email, so I could see for myself.

"But, what does it mean? I'm not sure I understand," I said.

"Me either. I didn't understand it either the first time this person wrote to me, so I ignored it. Biggest mistake of my life. I have regretted it ever since."

"So, it's not the first time this person has written to you?"

Shannon shook her head and sipped some coffee. She ran a hand through her hair. Her face was strained.

"Couldn't it just be some lunatic? You must get a lot of those, don't you?"

"I do. But this one is different."

"How is it different? It doesn't even make sense," I said. "I really don't think it's anything to worry about. Why are you freaking out over this?"

Shannon leaned over the table. "Because the last time I got an email from this person, eight people were shot in a movie theater north of Miami. Four of them died."

I leaned back in my chair. I was confused. "You mean to tell me this email came from the Miami movie theater killer six years ago?"

"I believe it does. I received the exact same email six years ago, right before the shooter killed all those people."

"But, couldn't that just be a coincidence?" I asked.

"No. I'm sure about this, Jack. He's about to do it again." Shannon's voice was trembling again.

"As far as I remember, the man was caught. He killed himself," I said.

"I know. I thought it was over too. But now I receive this? What if that was the wrong guy? What if the killer has been on the loose all this time? I'm telling you, Jack. This email is just like the last time. This is exactly how it went down last time. That's what happened six years ago. He sent me all these emails in the days before it happened, telling me how sorry he was, then one email after it was done, telling me it was him. Asking for my forgiveness. I never heard from him again. Until now."

"And, you're telling me you never told anyone about this?" I asked. "Not even the police?"

Shannon shook her head. "I am not proud of it. But I was just starting out. I was at the beginning of my career and terrified it would be the end of it. I had just gotten my breakthrough. I was a hit. I was afraid it would destroy me. I showed it to my manager at the time. It wasn't Bruce. I had another manager back then. I showed it to him afterwards. When I realized it was serious. At first, I thought it was some nutcase writing me, some sick stalker or something. I had been warned that I would get a lot of those and told to just ignore them. But back then, I read everything, all the fan-mail I got, since I was so proud to be getting any. I got so much junk. I didn't know it was connected to the shootings until it was too late. My manager told me to never tell anyone. It wouldn't help the victims or anything, he said. I was young and stupid and I listened to him. Like I said, I'm not proud of this, but now I feel like I need to tell you."

"Well, I'm glad you finally did," I said.

"You're angry. I knew you would be. I'm sorry. I can't change what I did back then, but I can do something about it now."

"I'm not angry. Like I said, I'm pretty sure the guy is dead."

I knew she hadn't meant to harm anyone. As a detective, it was hard for me to swallow this news. But as a boyfriend and someone who loved Shannon, I chose to be understanding. I put my hand on top of hers and smiled.

"I'm glad you came to me with this," I said. "I'm sure it's nothing, but I'll look into it for you, if that will make you more at ease. Now, tell me. Do you still have those old emails?"

Shannon sighed and shook her head. "I deleted them immediately afterwards. My old manager told me to. There was to be no trace of this, he said. If the press ever hacked into my email or someone got access to it somehow, there could be no trace of this, he said."

"And, of course, you listened to him," I said.

This left us with very little to go by.

12

December 2003

When Elizabeth turned one year old, she still showed no interest in food. She would take the bottle rarely and hadn't started on real food yet. Even though her mother tried to feed her every day, three meals a day, like the pediatrician had told her to. At Elizabeth's first birthday, they threw her a party like they had done for the rest of the girls at that age. Dottie even made a big cake and put one candle in the middle.

She carried it to the table as they sang. Elizabeth clapped her small hands and blew out the candle, and her mother started to cut the cake. They had invited a couple of kids from the playground that they often met when they went there in the afternoons, and then all of her mothers group. All eyes were on the spectacular cake and on Dottie, as she passed the pieces of cake around the table. The kids all dug in, except for Elizabeth. As usual when served food, she merely stared at all the others while they ate without showing any interest whatsoever in her own food.

"Here, let me help you," Dottie said and sunk the fork into the chocolate cake. Her hand was shaking as she brought the fork up to Elizabeth's mouth. She knew in her heart the mouth would remain closed, and so it did. Elizabeth tightened her lips and moved her head away. Dottie felt awful. All of the other moms were looking at her, and she knew what they thought. Elizabeth was so tiny; she knew they all blamed her for not feeding her enough.

"Come on, baby. It's cake. Everyone loves cake. Look at your friends, huh? Just try it, will you?"

But the mouth remained closed. The tiny girl, who was less than half the size of her friends at that age, simply refused to take in solid food. It had started to wear on her parents. Other than with food, Elizabeth was the easiest child Dottie had ever had. She was so sweet, so gentle, and she never cried. But she wasn't developing fast enough. She still hadn't started to crawl, while all of her little friends were constantly all over the place, and their parents after them; Elizabeth simply sat still and watched them. Well, she didn't even sit much, couldn't even sit on her own yet, which worried Dottie a lot. At this age, she should at least be able to sit on her own and roll. Elizabeth could do neither. When sitting in her high chair, they put pillows behind her back to keep her upright. Her body remained this floppy mass that didn't seem to do much. Was she ever going to crawl? Walk? Cry? Eat?

"She doesn't want any," Dottie said, looking up at James, who was standing with his arms crossed.

"Of course she does," James said. "Everybody wants cake. Maybe she just doesn't know what it tastes like. Put some in her mouth and she'll love it."

"Are you sure that's a good idea?"

"I'm positive," James said, but he didn't sound convincing. They had been running to the doctor constantly, asking him what could be wrong with their little girl, and just as constantly they had learned that some kids were just slower developed than others, that there was nothing to worry about, that Elizabeth would catch up eventually; she was just very small and needed more time. She would learn how to eat real food soon enough.

"No grown-ups live only on milk," the doctor said, chuckling. "Just let her take the time she needs."

So they had done so far. But both of them had started to doubt if the doctor was right. James had started to think that they just needed to force Elizabeth into situations where she had to do things she didn't want to. Like put some toy she wanted far away on the floor and tell her to crawl for it, but so far, it hadn't worked. Elizabeth just gave up on getting the toy and found something else to hold in her hand instead. They had even taken away the bottle at one point. Told her there would be no more milk, that now she was supposed to eat real food, but that had only resulted in her simply not eating anything, and after two days, the doctor had told them to bring back the bottle because Elizabeth couldn't bear to lose any more weight. She was too fragile and small.

"Just force the fork into her mouth," James said to Dottie. "Once she tastes the cake, she'll want it." He sounded irritated.

Dottie did as he told her to and forced Elizabeth's mouth open with her fingers, then scooped the cake inside the baby's mouth. She then pulled her fingers out, expecting the baby to start crying, but she didn't. She just looked at her mother with the sweetest little smile, then spat the entire piece of cake out using her tongue. The remains of the chocolate cake ran down her chin and ended up on her shirt.

13

March 2015

Sheriff Ron Harper was on the phone when I knocked on the door to his office.

"Ah, Ryder, come on in," he said, and pointed at a chair. I sat down, holding Shannon's email in my hand. I had printed it out for him to look at. Meanwhile, I had asked Richard, our researcher, to find everything there was about the Miami shootings for me.

"What's up?" Ron asked, when he hung up the phone. "How far are we on the stabbing case?"

"Almost done with that one, sir. But there is something I need you to take a look at. You know Shannon King, right?"

Ron rolled his eyes. "Christ, Jack. Everyone in the country knows about you two. It's on the cover of every damn magazine in Publix."

"Of course." I blushed slightly, thinking about the pictures of me in my board shorts. It was quite intimidating, knowing everyone in the country pretty much had seen the picture. The boys at the office had teased me a lot, placing the magazine on my desk or calling me bad boy whenever they could get away with it. I had told Shannon it didn't bother me, but of course it did a little. I liked to live quietly.

But if that was the price I had to pay to be with her, then I did so willingly. She was worth it.

"Shannon received this email today and she handed it over to me," I said and showed it to him.

Ron put on his glasses and looked at it. Then he looked at me with a shrug. "So, what is this? Some stalker or what? Why is this a police matter?"

I explained everything Shannon had told me at my parents' bar, and told him I thought it was an important matter, that we couldn't ignore it.

"As far as I know, they got the guy," he said. "Case is closed, Jack. We're not touching this. A few emails aren't going to change that."

"Listen to me," I said. "Shannon is freaking out. She is certain this is from the killer. Shannon doesn't remember everything from the first emails, but she said he wrote that her song, "Guns and Smoking Barrels" was his favorite song of hers, and that it made him realize what it was he needed to do. She feels awful and has been blaming herself all these years."

"I know that song," Ron said and started to sing out of tune.

"It was her first number one hit, but she told me she hates it because of this, because of what this bastard wrote to her. She thinks he got the inspiration to do the shooting from hearing her song."

"That's awful," Ron said. "But the case is closed, Jack. I feel like I'm repeating myself here. This is just some lunatic writing his favorite singer creepy letters. Nothing new in that. Case's closed. If they don't open it in Miami, we can't do anything about it."

Ron looked at me for a long time, while leaning back in his leather chair. Ron was a good guy. I had always liked him. But he was also a hardhead sometimes.

He shrugged. "We have plenty on our own plates as it is, Jack. Like I said, if they don't open the case in Miami, then there is nothing much we can do."

I growled at Ron, then walked back to my desk and found a stack of papers from Richard. It was all about the shooting in Miami in

2009. I opened the file and started to go through it. Richard spotted me and came over. He was a tall and skinny guy with a nice smile. Why he never got married was beyond me. He was such a nice guy. Used to play pro-baseball in his younger days. Had been a promising pitcher until an injury drastically changed his entire career. After that, he decided to go into the force like his old man had been. He loved to fish in his spare time. I always told him to start surfing instead. There would be plenty of time to fish when he grew old.

"I got what I could find on the computer," he said. "The case is six years old, so the rest is paperwork and probably down in Miami. I can send for it if you'd like, but it'll take a couple of days."

"I am going to need that," I said. "And try to figure out who worked the case back then."

Richard smiled and put a post-it on my desk with a name and a number on it. "Already done. I've also contacted the IT Department and told them to try and track the email address you gave me as well."

"Excellent."

I looked at the post-it and saw a name I recognized well from my past.

14

March 2015

I CALLED my old friend and colleague at Miami Beach Police, Tim. It was his name on the post-it from Richard, I was pleased to know. I had spent many hours with Tim, watching crack-houses and busting drug dealers in downtown Miami. It was a dangerous job, but I loved getting those bastards off the streets. Apparently, he had worked for the homicide division in Boca Raton at the time of the shooting.

"Jack, old buddy! How the heck are you?"

"I'm good, thanks."

"I heard you moved to Cocoa Beach?"

"Yup. Best place in the world. I get to surf every day. Living on the beach."

"Are you staying at your parents' place?"

"Right next door. Got a condo for me and the kids. Right on the beach."

"Sounds good. Maybe I should swing by some day. Stay for a weekend with the girlfriend."

Tim always had a new girlfriend. He was never known to settle down with the same girl for longer than a few months at a time.

"You should do that."

"I hear you got yourself a new girlfriend too," he said.

"Sure have."

"I can't believe you nailed Shannon King. She's like the sexiest woman alive, man. How did you meet her?"

"She stayed at my parents' motel for a little while. I helped her out with some stuff," I said, trying not to get into too many details. I had to be careful what I told people when dating a celebrity. Not that I thought Tim would ever rat me out, but he might tell someone else, who would sell the info for money. Shannon had warned me how fast things spread.

"I'm glad to hear that, buddy. So, when are you coming back? We need you here. I miss you, man."

I inhaled deeply, then looked at the picture of me and the kids taken on the beach in front of my parents' motel. The happiness in their eyes made my heart melt. "I'm not," I said. "I like it here."

"Really? In small town Cocoa Beach? Man. I feel so abandoned down here. You left me in the middle of a case, man."

"I know. Sorry about that."

"That's alright. I got a new partner and we solved it without you. So, what can I do for you?" Tim asked.

"I've stumbled onto something that might interest you."

"Yeah? Like what?" Tim asked.

"It's regarding the movie theater shooting in 2009."

Tim went quiet. I knew him well enough to sense his smile stiffen. "I'll be...The case is closed."

"I know. I just need to know some details. You caught him, right?" I asked.

"He killed himself in his home. I found him there myself. After he shot those poor people in the theater, he slipped out of the emergency exit where he had come in. We have a picture from a surveillance camera of him when he arrived at the mall and parked his car close to the emergency exit. We tracked the plate to a Laurence Herman, and when we stormed his house, we found him dead. He had shot himself. The case is closed, Jack."

"I know it is. I'm just sniffing around a little. Thought maybe you could help me."

"Not going to happen. I am not touching this case again."

"So, let me ask you this. How sure are you that this guy was the shooter?" I asked, looking down at the case files Richard had printed out for me.

Tim paused. "It was him, Jack. No doubt about it."

I knew him well enough to sense his hesitation. He wasn't sure at all. I had gone through the material again and again, and I couldn't get it to fit. It had probably haunted him for years.

"You know just as well as I do that the autopsy concludes that Laurence Herman died between three and three-thirty in the afternoon. The shooting took place at five thirty-five. The guy was already dead, man."

Tim inhaled sharply. "They could be wrong about the time of death," he said. "Happened before. There's always a margin of error. We have the surveillance pictures. They show Laurence parking his car right outside of the emergency exit and him coming out afterwards and driving off."

I grabbed a copy of the surveillance pictures and looked at them while I spoke to Tim.

"First of all, you can't see the person's face on those pictures. He's wearing a hoodie. Second of all, where did you find the car?"

Tim breathed again. "In a ditch in Ft. Lauderdale. It had been set on fire."

"Exactly," I said. "How is Laurence Herman here supposed to make it back to the house in Boca and kill himself if the car is in Ft. Lauderdale?"

"He probably just drove it up there because he knew it had been seen on surveillance photos and wanted to get rid of it."

"Would he really care about that if he was going to kill himself afterwards?" I asked.

Tim sighed, annoyed. I was getting to him. I could tell. I just hoped I was pushing his buttons enough.

"Jack, Goddammit. How am I supposed to know what goes on in the head of a man like that? He's nuts. Insane. He had just shot eight people, women, men, and children. I don't think he was thinking very clearly at that moment, if you want my opinion. Maybe he didn't intend to kill himself afterwards. Maybe he was overwhelmed by guilt. He had, after all, just killed a lot of people. It's bound to get you thinking. Even the worst mass murderers must feel some kind of regret, don't you think?"

"I'm not sure they all do," I said. The killer's psychology was my field of specialty. "Some feel relief. In a true psychopath, the anger has been building for a long time, and when they finally let it loose, when they finally do it, they feel a sense of great relief. Some are even happy, since it has been building for so long. A malignant narcissist feels no guilt afterwards. He feels the weight on his shoulders lifted. Fifty pounds of emotional weight lifted. He feels like he's the master of his own destiny. He doesn't need anything or anyone. The murder isn't over when the victims die. The murder is over when his anger against them recedes. That's why he keeps killing. He is still killing them even after they're dead."

"Okay, Mister Expert. But it's also true that most mass shooters kill themselves afterwards. Who's to know if it's planned? It's not like we can ask them afterwards, right?"

I wasn't getting through to him. I felt frustrated. What more did he need to know? I had to convince him. My gut told me I simply had to.

"True. But I need you to open the case anyway. I have reason to believe it might be worth it. I have reason to believe the killer is about to strike again."

Tim went quiet, then he exhaled. "No way, Jack. This case was the worst I ever worked on. I loathed it. I love you, buddy, you know I do, but I'm not doing it. Sorry. I simply can't."

15

March 2015

I TRIED MY HARDEST. I told Tim about the emails and about Shannon's involvement, and made him promise to keep it from the press, but nothing helped. Tim was not going to reopen the case. Without him reopening it, there was no way I could get Ron or the rest of the team involved either.

It meant I was on my own with this.

What if they were right? What if it was just some lunatic writing the emails and not the killer? It was certainly a possibility. But, then again, it could be him. It could be the killer of four people from that evening six years ago. I couldn't take the risk of not taking this seriously. I didn't dare to. How would this person, this lunatic, know about the emails in the first place? How would he know what to write? If it wasn't him in the first emails either, how did he know the shooting was about to happen? It made no sense. The fact that Shannon had received the emails hadn't been mentioned anywhere in the media. Shannon and her old manager were the only ones who knew. If this was the killer writing her again, then there was no time to waste. I had to stop him. The movie theater shooting was the most ruthless mass shooting in Florida's history. The killer had shot at entire families, even children, while they were watching the newly released movie *The Princess and the Frog*.

The report said the shooter bought a ticket, entered the theater, and sat in the front row. He was wearing a hoodie in the theater, which the usher noticed, but didn't comment upon. It wasn't that unusual. The AC kept the theater very cold and people wore lots of clothes inside. Other than that, he was wearing jeans. The usher had noticed he had seemed to hide his face in the hoodie when handing him the ticket, but just taken him for being some weirdo. He saw weirdos every day. About twenty minutes into the film, it was believed the shooter left the building through an emergency exit door, which he propped open with a plastic tube.

He allegedly then went to his car, which was parked near the exit door, and retrieved his guns. Thirty-five minutes into the film, at five-thirty-five p.m., he reentered the theater through the exit door.

He then fired a 12-gauge Remington 870 Express Tactical shot-gun, first at the ceiling and then at the audience. He shot first to the back of the room, and then toward people in the aisles. A bullet passed through the wall and hit someone in the adjacent theater. Witnesses said the fire alarm system began sounding soon after the attack began and staff told people in all theaters to evacuate. One witness, a mother with her child, had been in the restroom, and according to her statement she had heard the shooting and screaming on her way back and never reentered the theater. She had lost her husband, while her daughter had been hit by a bullet that ricocheted from the ceiling, but it only hit her in the arm.

I leaned back in my chair with a deep sigh and looked at Beth across from me. My new partner had this aura about her that made people keep their distance from her. I didn't know her story yet, but I was guessing she was one of those officers who was married to the force. She seldom smiled and I often didn't quite know what to say to her. But now, she looked up and our eyes met. Her eyes were actually pretty. Probably the prettiest feature about her. Otherwise, she was small and plump and hadn't been first in line when God handed out female bodies. But I liked her. Even if she kept everyone, including me, at a safe distance.

"So, what's going on with you, Ryder?" she asked. "You haunting ghosts from the past?" She nodded at the pictures and papers on my desk, all telling the story of the mass shooting. I hadn't told her what I was doing yet.

"Looks like it, doesn't it? I don't know what I'm doing, to be honest," I said. I looked at my computer screen and found the web camera from the pier. The waves looked intriguingly good. I needed to get out of there. Clear my head. There was still an hour before the kids came home on the bus.

"Go ahead, Ryder," Beth said. "I'll cover for you here. Out there is a wave with your name on it."

16

March 2015

Stanley couldn't eat any more. His stomach was hurting from all the food he had consumed over the last few days. And it kept coming. He kept getting a plate set in front of him, then a gun to his head with the order to eat. He had thought about trying to fight his guardian and get out, but didn't dare to. What would happen to Elyse if he did?

"Is your stomach hurting? Aw, that's too bad," the voice said, as a stack of pancakes landed in front of him. Stanley had gotten a few hours of sleep before he was awakened and told to eat again. He was so fed up with food.

"Please," he said. "Please, no more."

"Eat," the voice said again.

The smell made him nauseous and he felt like throwing up as he took the first bite. He chewed and felt how the pancakes were growing inside of his mouth. His stomach turned at the prospect of having to contain any more food, and when he had swallowed the first two pancakes, his gag reflex tried to send it all back up. Stanley bent over to the side to throw up, but was forcefully pulled back and his mouth held closed. The vomit came up in his mouth and almost choked him.

"No cheating," the voice said. "Now, swallow it all again."

Stanley felt such pain in his throat and stomach. The thought of having to swallow it all again made him cry.

Please, let me go. Please, don't force me to do this.

"Now, swallow," the voice said. "Or your granddaughter dies."

Stanley whimpered, then closed his eyes and swallowed it with much resistance. He gagged again, but this time it only reached as far as his throat before he managed to press it back down. His gastric system had been enlarged over the last couple of days and he felt it happening again. It was excruciatingly painful.

The grip on his mouth was removed and he gasped for air. His guardian grabbed the fork, then cut out a piece of the pancake, dipped it in syrup, and brought it up towards his mouth.

"Please," he muttered. "I'm so full. I can't take any more in."

But his guardian didn't listen. The fork was forced into his mouth and then he swallowed the piece whole, without chewing it. Stanley coughed and gasped for air, when another forkful landed in his mouth. Stanley tried to chew this time, but soon after, another forkful was pressed in his mouth and he had to swallow the first in order to not choke. It hurt his throat as it went down. Then followed the pain from his stomach, which was expanding in order to make room for more food.

When will this end? Oh, God, please make this stop.

His guardian clapped his cheek and smiled. "There you go. You ate it all. All the pancakes are gone. They were good, right?"

Stanley looked at the crazy personage in front of him, then nodded. He didn't dare not to.

"Excellent," the voice said. "I bet your stomach is hurting now, right?"

Stanley nodded with a deep moan.

"Good," the guardian said. "Now you know what it feels like."

Stanley closed his eyes and breathed heavily. His stomach hurt so badly he could hardly breathe. Stanley had never been a big eater, and his stomach had gotten quite a shock from all the food it suddenly had to contain. He prayed it was all over. He prayed silently that he'd be allowed to go now, that this person that had kept him there and fed him all this food would somehow be done with him and let him and Elyse go.

Please, dear God. Please, let Elyse be unharmed.

His guardian looked at him and smiled. "Now, I do hope you have room left for dessert."

17

March 2015

ALL THE GIRLS changed into bikinis as soon as they got to their room at the motel. Katie watched them as they stood in front of the mirror looking at themselves, putting up their long hair in ponytails, putting on more mascara.

You're going to the beach. You're going in the water. You don't need mascara!

Katie didn't feel like showing her winter-pale body off in any small piece of clothing. She didn't want to apply mascara and fix her hair. She grabbed a book and sat on her bed, where she started reading.

"Look at her," Britney said, as she spotted Katie. "Isn't it cute? A fuzzy little bookworm cuddled up in her corner."

The other girls laughed. Katie was used to that. It had always been this way. Nobody ever saw Katie. Nobody cared enough. Only to mock her. But, one day, she would show them. One day she would be famous. One day she would do something big, make a difference in this world. Once she was famous, they would all want to be her friend. They would all look up to her.

"You think she'll ever turn into a butterfly?" she continued. "Nah, she'll probably prefer to stay underground in the dirt and darkness. Unless..." Britney smiled viciously. "Unless, of course, Greg...oh, sweet *dear* Greg...unless he asks her to come with him into the light. That is why you've come, isn't it? It's because of him."

"Oh, Greg," the others moaned and laughed. "Oh, Greg!"

Britney leaned closer to Katie. "You do know the real reason why he brought you here, don't you?"

Katie's heart stopped. She tried hard to not let these girls get to her, but it was difficult. She didn't belong here with any of them and they all knew it.

"He does this every year, you know," Britney said. "He finds some weirdo who has a crush on him, then he fucks her in the dunes and never speaks to her again. That's his thing. That way, he's sure to get laid over spring break."

Katie didn't look up from her book. Her heart was pounding in her chest. Could it be? Were they right about him?

"Leave me alone," she whispered.

"Just don't be a fool," Britney said, grabbing her beach towel and sunscreen. "You don't belong here and you know it."

The girls followed Britney out the door and slammed it behind them. Katie stared at the book while tears rolled across her cheeks. It had been a mistake to come on this trip. She had known it from the beginning. How could she have been so stupid to believe Greg could actually be interested in her? Now she was stuck here for an entire week. She couldn't afford to go home on her own. She didn't come from some rich family like the rest of the girls on campus did. She attended Princeton on a scholarship. Originally, she was a foster child, who had lived in six different families, constantly moving while growing up, never finding a place to call home. Not until she reached high school, when Phillip and Eve Monroe had taken her in and loved her like she was the child they never had, even though they had tried for many years. All through her childhood, Katie had buried her nose in books, and because of that she always had good grades, and in high school she did so well for herself that she was accepted to

Princeton and able to land a full scholarship. She had always sought comfort in doing well in school, and now she was being rewarded for it. But she had made the mistake of thinking she could be accepted by the other students...that she could be one of them.

Sometimes, it was like they smelled it on her. Smelled the fear on her skin. They knew she didn't belong, even though she didn't tell them. They all knew.

There was a knock on the door and Katie wiped away her tears. Greg peeked inside. Katie's heart started pounding. She'd had a crush on him for what felt like forever. She didn't think people knew, since she had kept it to herself. But, apparently, they did.

"Hi there," he said and entered. He was wearing board shorts and nothing on top. The sight of his torso made Katie blush. He sat on the bed next to her. "Everybody is down at the beach. Aren't you coming? We need an extra man for volleyball."

Greg looked at her with his soft brown eyes. His hair and skin looked like he had been in the sun for weeks rather than cooped up inside of a university, studying. He smiled and put a hand on her arm. "I hope you're not going to sit in here with your nose in a book all week. I was hoping we could have a little fun, the two of us, on this trip."

Katie blushed. She looked at him, scrutinized him. Was he for real? Was he just pretending to be nice to her? She couldn't tell.

Katie closed the book with a slam. It was the first and maybe only time in her life she'd be on spring break in Cocoa Beach. So what if Greg had only brought her there to have sex with her and dump her afterwards. She could enjoy her trip anyway, couldn't she? It was time for her to let her hair down.

"I'll be right out," she said. "Just let me change."

18

March 2015

THE BEACH WAS CRAWLING with college kids. It was always the same at this time of year. Spring breakers came down and drank their brains out. They probably needed it, I thought. There was a lot of pressure on the young people today, a lot of demands regarding what they wanted to do with their lives. A flock of them had just checked in at the motel and I helped them set up the volleyball net before I went surfing.

"Do you give lessons?" a boy named Greg asked me.

"Not usually," I said. "But I might make an exception if some of you want to try it. I have a couple of soft-top boards out the back. I could give you a few tips, but you have to do the hard work."

The three boys looked at each other. Two of them were athletic and would do fine, but I was more concerned about the third one. He was overweight and might have a hard time getting up on the board.

"We'd love to," Greg said. "Right guys?"

They all nodded.

"Okay. Let me get the boards out."

I found two big soft-top boards and carried them to the beach. I gave the boys a basic lesson on how to do a pop-up right, then how to paddle and how to read a wave. Then I took them out in the ocean and pushed them into some little ones. As expected, Greg and his more athletic friend learned quickly, whereas the third boy, Troy, struggled to even lie on the board. I pushed him into a couple of whitewater-waves to make it easier on him, but he never managed to stand up, much to his frustration. Troy had decided to try again when Greg waved at someone on the beach.

"Katie!"

The girl turned and looked in his direction. Cautiously, she waved back. She didn't seem like she was with them. She was nothing like the other girls they had brought, and somehow, she seemed like she wasn't very comfortable in this situation.

"Katie! Come try this. It's fun," Greg yelled from his board. He turned and told Troy to get off his board.

"Give it to Katie. Let her try," he said. There was something in the way he said it that made my skin crawl. He was the one running the show, no doubt about it. He spoke aggressively and commandingly at his friends.

"What are you waiting for? Go ahead."

Troy looked disappointed, then started to paddle in. I was getting a little tired of these kids and longed to go surfing on my own. A set of big chunky waves rolled in from the back. They were calling for me. I saw my buddy Pastor Daniel paddle out not far from me. He waved.

The young girl approached the water cautiously. She looked like she could crawl into a mouse hole. She was way out of her comfort zone. Two other girls were cheering her on, telling her to get out there to Greg. She decided to do as they told her to. Troy gave her his board and wished her good luck, and then I told her to lie on it and then helped her out. She took a bad beating from one wave that washed her right off the board and she ended up in the whitewater being twirled around. The wave took her right back on the beach. When she came up, her hair was in her face and her bikini top had fallen off on one side, so one of her breasts was showing. Greg burst into loud laughter, as the poor girl tried to catch her breath. The girls on the beach giggled and Katie looked up, disoriented, from the tumbling and the steady pounding roar of the ocean. I was still too far out for her to hear me if I yelled.

Don't turn around, please. Don't turn!

But she did. In those disastrous seconds, Katie turned around to face the beach and let everyone see her one uncovered breast. It was brutal. I felt terrible and jumped up on her board and let a wave take me in, then jumped up next to her. I tried to stand in front of her, so they couldn't see it. The two girls were laughing loudly and yelling. Still, poor Katie hadn't realized what was going on. I pointed to her breast.

"Your...your bikini," I said.

She still looked confused, then lowered her eyes and realized what had happened. Her pale face turned very red. I felt so bad for her. Katie fixed her bikini and looked at me again. I could tell how embarrassed she was...how this small incident would mark her for the rest of the trip.

"Maybe they didn't see it," I said. But we both knew I was lying. If it hadn't been too embarrassing, she would have cried. Her eyes fell to the ground.

"I...I'd better go up."

19

November 2005

When Elizabeth was almost three years old, something amazing happened to her. Her mother would never forget this moment that changed her life forever. Dottie was preparing breakfast, making pancakes and scrambled eggs for her family, and she placed the platter of them on the kitchen counter in front of Elizabeth, who was drawing. Since the child had never really shown any interest in food, Dottie didn't expect her to want anything to eat. She grabbed the milk from the fridge and poured the girl a glass like she always did in the morning, since that was the girl's main source of nutrition, but when she turned her head, she saw something truly astounding. The little girl reached out and grabbed a pancake from the stack.

Dottie held her breath.

Could this be? Was Elizabeth finally interested in food? Dottie smiled as she watched her daughter start eating the pancake in her hands. She couldn't believe it. Elizabeth was so tiny from not eating, and it had her mother constantly worrying about her. Dottie herself was a fairly voluptuous woman, all those in the West family were, and they never turned down a meal. Food was everything to them. In the South Georgia town where they lived, elaborate spreads of high-calorie foods were the centerpiece of every social activity. If someone didn't eat, there had to be something wrong with them. And everyone thought something was very wrong with Elizabeth. The neighbors stared at her when they met at church, and even more when they had their usual gathering at the Baptist church afterwards, where all the kids would indulge themselves in sugared doughnuts and cookies. Except for Elizabeth.

Dottie didn't dare to move as she watched her daughter gulp down the pancake...almost without chewing. When it was gone, she approached her and placed the milk in front of her.

"Boy, you've got some appetite this morning," she said, smiling from ear to ear. Dottie wanted to scream in joy, yell to everyone in the house to get down to the kitchen and watch this.

Elizabeth is eating! Elizabeth is finally eating real food!

But, she didn't. She didn't want to get their hopes up too high...or her own, for that matter. This could be a one-time event. It might not happen again. But still, Dottie tried her luck, looking at Elizabeth's sparkling eyes as she eyeballed the stack of pancakes like she wanted to dig in and eat them all.

"Do you want one more?" she asked.

Elizabeth smiled widely. "Yes!" she exclaimed. "They're good, Mommy."

Dottie's hands shook heavily as she reached over and grabbed another pancake and put it on a plate for Elizabeth. She couldn't believe what was happening. She simply couldn't believe it. All this time, James had told her the girl would eventually start eating, and all this time she had feared he was wrong, but now...now...now she had finally come around.

"Would you like to try some syrup on this one?" Dottie asked, her voice trembling. She feared Elizabeth would lose interest and go back to her old not-eating self.

But she didn't. She looked at her mother with the most endearing smile. "Yes!" she exclaimed and gesticulated with her arms. "I am sooo hungry, Mommy. I am so, so, so hungry!"

"Then you better eat some," Dottie said, and poured syrup on the pancake, then cut it up for her daughter. She watched Elizabeth as she ate. Never had she seen such a beautiful sight. Finally, everything would be all right. Finally, she could stop worrying.

20

March 2015

SHANNON COULDN'T CONCENTRATE. Her fingers were drumming on the guitar instead of playing the tune of the song she had been working on for days. The words simply wouldn't come to her. She had planned on finishing it today, so she could go on spring break with Angela when she got home from school. But it was almost time to pick her up and she was nowhere near finished.

It would have to wait.

Shannon sighed and looked down at the beach from the balcony of her rented condo, where she was sitting with her guitar in her lap. She spotted Jack in the water. He was pushing in some kids and screaming in joy when they managed to stand up. Shannon chuckled and shook her head. How on earth could he think about surfing with all that was going on? Shannon couldn't even concentrate on her song. It was unbearable how her past had suddenly caught up with her. The mistake she had made so many years ago when deciding to hide the emails from the police had caught up with her and kicked her in the back. She felt like she was lying on the ground and couldn't get up again. And this time, it was worse. This time, she knew this email was from the killer; she had no doubt about it. So, this time, it would be all her fault if the killer wasn't stopped before it was too late. Jack had told her to relax and not beat herself up about it, but she couldn't. She had kept this bottled up inside of her for too long...this guilt...and it had been eating at her. Now, she would give anything in the world to stop this guy.

But how? How was she supposed to do that? There was nothing in the emails that indicated who this person was. AM didn't tell much, did it? Were they initials? Hardly.

Shannon sighed and closed her eyes. She let the breeze hit her face. It was a very hot day out. She liked these warm days, where the wind was your friend.

Someone was laughing loudly on the beach. Shannon opened her eyes and looked. Jack was talking to one of the kids in the shallows. He pointed at her chest. What was that? Had she lost her swimsuit? It was only on one side, but the entire beach could see her breast, and she didn't seem to notice until Jack told her. Some girls were laughing on the beach. Everyone seemed to be staring at her. Shannon felt terrible for the poor girl. That had to be so humiliating. She remembered how it had been at that age. Nothing worse than a public disgrace. Nothing could ruin your life like that.

It was obvious that Jack was trying to cover her till she got it under control. That was Jack for you, always the hero. Shannon loved that about him. Most men would just have looked, or even turned away and acted like they hadn't seen it. But not Jack. He felt responsible.

Shannon had to admit, she was beginning to like him more and more as time passed. She was very fond of him. But she still had her doubts whether it was too soon for her. She feared he was nothing but a rebound for her...an excuse to move on. He had said he loved her, and she believed she loved him too. But, some days, she was unsure. It was all still so new. He made her feel good. That was all she knew, and all she needed right now. But would he still love her with all the demons she carried around and constantly fought? She knew she wasn't an easy person to love. Jack deserved someone much better than her.

As she thought about it, her phone started to ring. She picked it up. It was Joe—again.

"You gotta stop calling me," she said as she answered it. Her first thought was to ignore the call, but he had called at least six times today, and she had a feeling he wasn't going to stop until she picked up.

"Please, Shannon," Joe said. "Just talk to me. I miss you so much. You and Angela. The house is so big and empty without you in it. I'm not sure I can take it. You've gotta come home, Shannon. You've got to."

Shannon closed her eyes and touched the bridge of her nose. When was he going to understand this? "I'm not coming home. I'm never coming back. You have to realize that, Joe."

"But, what about us? Remember how it used to be? How much we used to love each other? Don't tell me you don't love me anymore, because I don't believe it."

Shannon sighed. She spotted Jack on the beach again. He was running towards the water with his own board under his arm. Life with Jack was so easy. Life here in Cocoa Beach had been so easy for her the past month. But, Joe was right. They had a lot of history together.

"I'm the only one who really knows you, Shannon," he said. "Think of all we've been through together. Are you just going to bail on that? Just like that? Throw it all away? We have a daughter together. I helped you build your career. Without me, you would be nothing, and you know it. Angela is mine too. If you don't come back, I'm going to take her away from you. I hope you realize that. I will be forced to reveal everything, Shannon. Don't force me to tell them all your secrets."

"You wouldn't!"

"Of course I would. Not only the judge will know. The entire world will. I'll have a press conference of my own. Tell them the entire story. I'm sure they'll looove that, aren't you?"

Joe laughed. Shannon snorted in anger.

"Go to hell."

Then she hung up.

21

March 2015

STANLEY WAS CRYING. It had been many years since he last cried. Stanley didn't believe a real man should cry. He had told his son many times and let him know it wouldn't be accepted. Crying was a weakness.

Nevertheless, Stanley was wailing and howling now. Tears were streaming across his cheeks as his guardian forced food into his mouth. In between swallowing, he pleaded for it to stop.

"Please. Please. I'll do anything."

"If you want that beautiful granddaughter of yours to live, you'll open your mouth and eat," the guardian said.

"I can't. I can't. No more food. Please."

His guardian shook their head with a *tsk*. In one hand was the gun, in the other, the spoon. The dreaded spoon, where potatoes in thick gravy leaned on some undefined chunk of meat. Stanley couldn't stand the sight or the smell. His stomach was so full it was painful to breathe. He was beginning to wonder what this person really wanted from him. To kill him with food?

"Don't give me that. Now, be a good boy. Open up."

Stanley gagged. Food overflowed into his mouth and made him

feel sick. His guardian reacted by pushing the potatoes and meat into his mouth and forcing him to swallow it all. Stanley would have bent over in pain if he had been able to move. But he couldn't. It hurt too badly.

Please, God. Help me out of this mess.

The sessions where he was fed were getting longer and longer. This time it had been going on for several hours. Meal after meal was brought into the small room, and spoon after spoon was brought to his mouth. Stanley was so tired and wanted so badly to sleep, but his guardian didn't seem to want to take a break from this strange game. He barely had time to think about escape or how to save his granddaughter from the hands of this crazy person.

He had tried to grab the guardian's wrists once to force the spoon away, but his guardian had let him know that wasn't acceptable behavior by walking out of the room, then coming back with a fire poker that was soon after poked through Stanley's right shin. The pain had made Stanley scream at the top of his lungs. And, then again—even worse this time—when it was pulled out again.

"Don't ever do that again! Do you hear me?" the guardian yelled even louder.

Stanley wasn't going to. He had to think of Elyse. If only he did what this mad person told him to, then maybe he would eventually be able to save her. There were many decisions he had made in his life that he wasn't proud of. So many times he had done what he would later regret. It haunted him daily. But, this time, he was going to make the right decision. And that was to make sure nothing bad happened to Elyse. He would never be able to live with himself if it did.

"Open up, Stanley," his guardian said, and forced yet another spoonful of potatoes into his mouth. He had to swallow in order to not choke. Stanley cried as the wave of pain struck through him. He couldn't stand being in his body anymore. So much pain, so much aching. This time, he was certain he heard his stomach enlarging. He was sure it sounded like a balloon being blown up. Or maybe that was just how it felt.

Stanley moaned and closed his eyes. He tried to dream himself away, to think of something that would make him happy, anything that could take him away from this awful place, even Disney World would be better than this. Ah, yes. Disney World with Elyse seemed like Heaven compared to this. He groaned in sadness, feeling sorry for himself.

Was this nightmare ever going to end?

22

March 2015

NEXT MORNING, I woke up with all of my muscles sore from surfing the day before. The waves had been excellent and I had enjoyed myself, even though I couldn't stop thinking about the email. Now, I was awake in my bed, while the waves crashed the beach outside my window. I stared at the ceiling, wondering what to do. Shannon was sleeping next to me, and I enjoyed listening to her deep breaths.

We had eaten dinner at my parents' place the night before, and the kids played so well together. My mom told us to go have some fun without the kids for a change. Even Emily decided to stay at the motel, where my dad promised to teach them all to play pool. I had taken Shannon to Friday Fest downtown. I loved Friday Fest, where they locked down all of downtown for traffic, and there was music and people were everywhere. We had a wonderful evening and ended up letting all the kids sleep at the motel, since it was the weekend and spring break on top of it.

"Good morning, tiger," Shannon said and opened her eyes.

I looked at her, feeling so proud to be with her. She was gorgeous, even after a night out and just waking up. It was unbelievable. My head was spinning. I felt like I was getting in trouble. There was no way out now. I was all in with her.

I leaned over and kissed her. She closed her eyes. "Good morning, gorgeous," I said. "Thank you so much for a great night last night."

"It was quite enjoyable, wasn't it?"

"Sure was."

I tasted her lips once more and forgot everything about the world around us for just a few seconds, then slipped under the covers and pulled her close to me. We made love while the sun rose over the Atlantic Ocean outside my windows. It was beautiful and so intense. I never wanted to let go of her again.

We fell back asleep again and woke up at nine. "What do you say to coffee in bed?" I whispered. "You can stay right here all day. You don't ever have to move again."

Shannon laughed. "If only that was true." She turned and looked into my eyes. "You know very well I have that gig at Runaway Country. I couldn't say no to them when they called. I mean, it's right here."

Runaway Country was a music festival featuring country musicians from all over. It was all the big names, and naturally, the amazing Shannon King had to be one of them. It was a huge event around here and attracted thousands of people.

"I wish you had, though," I said and kissed her again.

"What? You don't want me on stage?" Shannon asked. "You don't want thousands of people adoring the woman you love? What a big surprise, Detective Ryder."

I chuckled. She was right. I never thought much of celebrities and the lifestyle they led. It seemed to me it hurt more people than it helped. I knew Shannon's story of drug abuse and how the pressure of being a celebrity had a part in it. It wasn't a healthy lifestyle and it complicated things. I wasn't the jealous type, but I had thought about how I would feel if she took off on a tour that lasted several months. I knew the temptations and offers were many. She could easily find someone much more handsome and interesting than me. Would I be able to keep her?

I didn't want to think about it. My phone vibrated on the table next to the bed. I groaned, stretched my arm out, and grabbed it. It was Ron. I sighed and rubbed my forehead.

"I gotta take this."

"On a Saturday?"

"If Ron calls on a Saturday, I better take it. That means it's serious. Ron appreciates his weekends more than anyone at the office. Believe me."

"Ryder," I said, with the phone to my ear. I got up and walked to the kitchen to put on a pot of coffee. Shannon whistled behind me as she watched my naked body. I smiled and shook my behind for her. She laughed.

"Ryder, Goddammit. I can't believe I'm saying this, but you need to come in today."

That didn't sound good. "What's going on, Ron?"

"We have a body."

23

March 2015

"WHAT DO WE HAVE?"

Ron was waiting for me in the parking lot when I drove up. The place was called The Grapefruit Trail, located on a strip of woods on the south shore of the Tillman Canal in Palm Bay on the mainland. It was a place where cyclists rode their mountain bikes on the hilly trails through the woods.

"A cyclist found something early this morning. He stopped to... well, to take a leak when he spotted something on the ground. He thought it looked strange and called us. We have to walk there."

I followed Ron through the woods for about five minutes and was quickly surrounded by deep dense forest. It was a strange place, with many trails great for biking and hiking. It was also a place that was excellent for hiding a body, I thought.

"It's right in here."

The scene was already packed with crime scene technicians. It was blocked off, and two officers from Palm Bay Police blocked the entrance. We showed them our badges and were let inside. People roamed everywhere among the bushes. The vegetation was heavy.

"Watch where you step," Ron said.

In a place like this, you had to watch for snakes. The area where the body had been found was almost impassable, but as we came closer, I could tell it was almost like a small clearing. Perfect for taking a leak without anyone seeing you, and perfect for hiding something you didn't want to be found.

The remains of what was once a forty-something aged man had been pulled out of the soil. He was still wearing clothes, but by the decomposition, I guessed he had been dead for quite awhile.

"We found his wallet in his pants," Ron said, and showed me a small plastic bag with an old leather wallet and a driver's license in it with the name Daniel Millman. Date of birth told me he was forty-seven years old. At least, he would have been.

"Has the family been notified?" I asked.

Ron smirked.

"Oh, come on," I said. "You want me to do it?"

"Take Beth with you. She can be the compassionate one."

"I have a feeling you don't know Beth very well," I said.

Ron chuckled. Then he shook his head. "So what do you make of it?"

"I don't know," I said, kneeling next to the body. "He's been in the ground for quite some time."

"How long would you guess?"

I shrugged. "You can see how the animals have been eating off him here and here. The body was in the ground, but I'm guessing a fox or something might have tried to dig it out, then the rest of the animals could get to it. Dead things decompose fast here in Florida, but we have to remember, he was in the ground, where the temperature is lower, until the animals dug him out. You can see here and here on the ground where it has been disturbed by digging, and you can tell that his face was scratched when the animals tried to get him out. I'd say maybe three-four months?"

Ron nodded. I could tell the sight of the body moved him. He tried to never show it, but he was a softie. I remembered when I first discovered it. Right after I had moved here and started working at the

Sheriff's Office in Rockledge, Ron's dog, the cutest labra-doodle, got sick and had to go through surgery and stay away overnight. Ron had tears in his eyes all day, and even though he tried to hide it, we could all see it. He was devastated and missed the dog like crazy. Ron was a family man. I liked that about him. Three kids and four grandchildren were his accomplishments and pride in life.

"So, what happened to Daniel Millman?" he asked with a sniff.

"There don't seem to be any visual signs of trauma," I said. "No bullet holes, no bleeding. It's hard to tell if he was strangled when the body is decomposed like this, so we'll have to wait till the ME finishes to determine if that's the case."

Ron cleared his throat. "So, are you going to call Beth or should I?"

24

March 2015

I PICKED up Beth at her home in Satellite Beach. She lived in a small house just a few blocks from the beach. In the yard played three kids in a jumpy-jump house, spraying each other with water from a hose. I smiled when I parked the car. I watched as Beth came out, kissed the kids, then sprang for the car. Boy, had I misjudged her.

"Mommy will be home in a few hours," she yelled, as she jumped inside with her plump body into the passenger seat. "You behave, you hear?"

The kids hardly noticed. They were having too much fun. "I got the neighbor to watch them while we're gone," she said as I drove off. "I just hope they don't burn the house down."

I chuckled.

"What?"

"Nothing. I just didn't know you had children."

I continued towards Lansing Island in Indian Harbor Beach, where our victim lived when he was still alive.

"Well, I do," she said with her usual harsh tone, letting me know I wasn't getting any closer to her than this.

"Husband?"

"What's with the questions all of a sudden?"

"Sorry. I just wanted to get to know my partner. That's all." I took a turn and hit the entrance to the island.

Lansing Island was a gated island, where I had been told Bruce Willis owned a house. I didn't know if it was true; there were a lot of rumors about it, as there always were with places only few people were allowed to enter. The island was located in the river and had the most spectacular houses of anywhere around here. I drove up to the gate and a uniformed man came out. I showed him my badge.

"We're here to see Mrs. Millman."

"Is she expecting you?" he asked.

I shook my head. "No."

The guard nodded with a sigh. He understood. "I'll let you in. She's in 219."

He went inside his small guard house, pressed the button, and the gate opened. I drove by and waved to the guard. I drove past many gorgeous houses and could hardly believe anyone lived like this. It was as far from my world as it could possibly be. Not that I would ever trade for anything.

"219, it's here," Beth said.

I looked out the window and spotted a house of about ten-thousand square feet. Maybe even more. It was huge. The gate wasn't closed, so we drove right through. I parked in the enormous driveway, then walked up towards the front door, closely followed by Beth. I found a doorbell and rang it. I took in a deep breath as I heard footsteps approaching behind it. It opened. A woman in her early thirties looked at us, surprised. The look in her eyes made her seem sad. I wondered if she already knew.

"Mrs. Millman?"

"Yes?"

I showed her my badge. "I'm detective Ryder. This is my partner. We're from the Sheriff's office. Can we come in?"

"Of course." The woman stepped aside.

We walked inside the foyer with its marble floors. Mrs. Millman closed the door behind us. She showed us the way into the library, which had the most spectacular views over the river.

"Do you want anything?" she asked. "Coffee?" I detected nervousness in her voice. Her eyes were avoiding ours.

"No, thank you. We're good."

"Do sit down." She pointed at the set of leather chairs and we sat down. She put her hands in her lap. It seemed like she had to pull herself together to focus. I was wondering if she was on something. She didn't smell like alcohol, but something was off.

"I'm afraid we have some bad news," I said.

She nodded, like she was expecting this.

"Your husband...we found his body this morning."

Mrs. Millman didn't seem to react at all. She kept nodding. Beth leaned forward. "Mrs. Millman, do you understand what we're telling you?"

"Yes. Yes. You found Daniel." Mrs. Millman's hands were constantly moving, rubbing against each other in a nervous way.

Beth and I exchanged looks.

"Mrs. Millman. Your husband's body was found in the woods. Buried in the ground. We don't know what caused his death yet, but he seemed to have been in the ground for quite some time. When did he go missing?"

Mrs. Millman shook her head. "November. I reported him missing to Indian Harbor police."

"I am sorry to say this, Mrs. Millman, but you don't seem very surprised that your husband is dead," I said.

She looked at me. She corrected her hair with small fast movements. I couldn't determine if she was in shock or in some kind of denial, or if she already knew her husband was dead.

"Mrs. Millman. Your husband is dead," I repeated. It wasn't uncommon that we had to repeat this kind of information several times before the relatives fully understood what we were telling them. It could be a lot to take in at once. Mrs. Millman was rubbing her hands together while her eyes hit the floor. I detected sadness in her, but couldn't figure out if it was from the information I had just given her or if it was something else.

"I know," she said. "I heard you. It's just...well...He's been gone for a long time now. I wasn't expecting to see him again."

It was like she wanted to tell us something, like we saw the real Mrs. Millman for just a second before she decided to pull back behind the façade protecting her.

"It is, of course, terrible that he's dead," she continued, as emotionless as if she had told us about what she had for breakfast. Her voice sounded blurred.

"We're treating the case as a homicide," I said.

Mrs. Millman looked at me. "Homicide?" she asked.

"Yes. We believed he was killed. We need to know some information about him."

"Like what?"

"Like, what does your husband do?"

"He owns Millman Technologies," she said. "Founded it himself twelve years ago. They make components for the rockets at the Space Center and for Boeing airplanes."

I wrote it on my notepad. I had heard about Millman Technologies. It was one of the biggest and fastest growing companies on the Space Coast.

"So, you reported your husband missing in November, you say. Where was he last seen?"

"Driving home from the office in Cape Canaveral on November eighth," she said. "It was a Saturday. Daniel was supposed to come home for Christopher's sixth birthday party, but he never made it home. His secretary told us he left at five fifteen, and someone saw his car on the A1A driving by the statue of Kelly Slater when entering Downtown Cocoa Beach. It was one of our friends who recognized the car, but no one has seen him since. They found the car in a ditch in Melbourne. No trace of Daniel. I have to admit, I thought he had run off with some twenty year-old."

"And I take it Christopher is your son?" I saw a painting of all three of them over the fireplace.

"Yes. He's in boarding school in Palm Beach Gardens. He comes home every weekend."

"Boarding school in Kindergarten, huh? That is early."

"It's the best school around. Can't compromise with education."

"As I said, we have reason to believe your husband was killed, ma'am," I said. "Do you know if your husband had any enemies? Anyone who would want him dead?"

Mrs. Millman looked indifferent. "You mean, besides me?" Then she chuckled.

"You wanted your husband dead?" I asked.

Mrs. Millman hardly reacted to my question. "Of course I didn't," she answered sharply.

"How was your relationship?" I asked.

"Dead, like him," she answered emotionless. "Has been for years."

I nodded as I wrote it down. I couldn't quite figure out what was going on here. Maybe their marriage had just been so bad that she had stopped caring?

Beth asked for the restroom, then disappeared for a few minutes. I stared at my notes on my pad. Mrs. Millman looked at me.

"Can I get you anything, Officer?"

"Detective," I said. "And, no thank you. I'm still good. Is there anyone you would like us to call for you, ma'am?"

She looked at me like she didn't understand what I said. "Why would that be, Detective?"

"Well, in times of loss, it's often a good idea to…"

"I'm alright," she said.

Beth returned and I got up. I handed Mrs. Millman my card. "Call me if you think of anything that we might need to know."

"Of course, Officer."

"And, don't leave town."

We left the house and got into my Jeep. I started the engine when

Beth looked at me. She showed me something in her hand. A small orange bottle of pills.

"Benzos," she said. "It was tucked in between the towels. And this was just in one of the guest bathrooms."

"That explains a lot," I said, and drove out of the driveway.

"The woman probably has them stashed all over the house. Nothing makes you stop caring about things like a benzo. They don't necessarily make you happy, or necessarily make you sad. They just stop your thinking. I once had a depression-induced panic attack and took a benzo. It literally manifested as a vision of a white elephant running through my mind, clearing the negative thoughts and feelings of ultimate doom out. I went to sleep feeling a bit shaken, but not stirred."

It explained why Mrs. Millman hardly reacted when I told her that her husband had been killed and her repeated questions. But it still didn't explain what had happened to Daniel Millman. I had a feeling it wasn't the last time I'd question Mrs. Millman.

25

March 2015

SHANNON STILL FELT happy from spending the night with Jack. She was standing backstage at Runaway Country in Wickham Park in Melbourne, smiling to herself, while Blake Shelton was on. She was going on right after him. She had her stage clothes on, the diamond-covered boots and hat, and she was holding her microphone in her hand, the one she never walked on stage without. It had followed her for years and was covered in diamonds. It was a little much, but that was what a real star had, her manager had told her when buying it for her. It was the first time she'd be going on stage since she left Joe, and she was feeling pretty good about herself for the first time in years. She sensed she was on the right track. Leaving him was the right thing to do.

Wasn't it?

She thought about Angela. The girl missed her dad a lot, especially since Joe went back to Nashville. He was, after, all her father. Shannon hated to do this to her child...to keep her away from her father, but what else could she do? Joe was out of control right now and threatening her with all kinds of things one moment, then pleading with her desperately to come back the next. It was hard.

Shannon still had feelings for him. She knew she did, and standing here backstage, where she used to be with Joe for all those years, she missed him. Just a little bit. She didn't miss the yelling and the blaming afterwards or the beating, but she missed what they had before all that started. Before he became jealous of her success. Maybe if she stopped this? Maybe if she dropped her career? Maybe then they could be a real family?

No. It was wrong. Shannon knew it very well. Jack was so right for her. Cocoa Beach was the right place to be. She had never felt better. Angela was happier here too, even though she missed her father.

Blake Shelton finished his last tune and people clapped. The females in the audience screamed. He was good. Shannon had met him on many occasions and liked him. Joe had, naturally, been mad every time she had spoken with him, and that never ended well.

Shannon chuckled and smiled to herself. So many memories she had from her life as a musician. Good and bad. But it all came down to this...it was her dream, her passion. This was what she loved.

She only wished that Jack could be there to see her.

Blake came out and looked at her with a wide smile.

"They're all yours, baby," he said and gave her a kiss on the cheek. "I warmed them up for you."

Shannon smiled while getting ready. The announcer took the microphone. People were already chanting her name.

Shannon King, Shannon King, Shannon King.

Shannon closed her eyes and took in a deep breath. She loved this part. The entrance, the anticipation, the screaming, the fans. Oh, how she loved her fans. They were the reason she could live doing what she loved. It was amazing.

"Please welcome Shannon King!"

Shannon walked onto the stage, holding her microphone in her hand with her guitar around her shoulder. The fans screamed. Shannon stared into the ocean of faces.

"Hello Runaway Country!" she yelled. "How are you out there? Are y'all ready for some music?"

The crowd screamed and Shannon hit the first note of her first song. She sang three songs, then the new one that she had just finished last night, just her and her guitar. The crowd went wild. Shannon enjoyed their applause, thanked them, and went back stage. As she did, she spotted Jack. He was clapping while walking towards her. Shannon smiled and threw herself around his neck.

"You made it!"

"You killed it out there," he said and kissed her. "I'm so proud of you."

"I did, didn't I? I don't think I have ever been better."

They walked back to her dressing trailer and closed the door. Jack poured them some complimentary iced tea and they sat down, Shannon with a deep satisfied sigh.

"It's good to see you smiling again," Jack said. "I'm glad I made it just in time for your set."

"So, what's going on? Did they find a body?" Shannon asked.

"Yes. We don't know much yet. But, let's not talk about that. That's boring depressing stuff."

Shannon smiled and picked up her phone to make a tweet about her set, when she noticed she had received an email. Her heart stopped.

"What's wrong?" Jack asked. "You're completely pale, Shannon."

"It's from him," she said, sensing the panic growing inside her. "It's that guy again."

26

March 2015

You were good on stage today, Shannon. You nailed it. Better than any of the other many times I have seen you in concert. I'm guessing this Jack Ryder that we read about in the magazines really does you good. I'm happy for you. It's always good when it works out, isn't it? Unfortunately, it doesn't always work like that, does it? I'm afraid not. That is why I have to do what I must do. Again, you have my apologies. I am so terribly sorry for what I have to do. I hope for your forgiveness.

With love,

AM

Shannon looked at me as I read the email. She was biting her lips. I finished it and gave her the phone back.

"I need you to forward it to my email address. I'll have Richard send it to the IT guys, who will try and track the email address once again. Last time, nothing came of it, he said. The IP address led us to some computer in India. But we'll give it another try. This is another address."

"Do you think he's here?" she asked. "He wrote that I was good on stage. Do you think he was in the crowd?"

"It's definitely a possibility," I said. "He said that he goes to many of your concerts." I paused and looked at Shannon. I wasn't quite sure what to do next. If this person was in the crowd out there, could I find him? I had no idea what he looked like. Even if I blocked all the exits I didn't know what I was looking for. It would only ruin the entire festival and make me very unpopular with Ron. Runaway Country was a huge event around here. I couldn't destroy it without really strong grounds, and so far, an email wasn't quite enough.

"You stay here," I said. "Lock the door when I'm out."

"Where are you going?"

"I have to go look around for a little while. Maybe talk to the officers at the exits, tell them to look for anyone suspicious. Ask them if they've noticed anything. I'll be back for you afterwards."

Shannon nodded and did as I had told her to. I left her trailer, then walked into the festival grounds among the thousands of happy guests with beers in their hands. I walked to the entrance and found Officer Rogers from Melbourne Police.

"Ryder," he said with a nod. "I hear she did good today. I could only hear it from here, but it sounded good."

"Yes. She did really well."

He told me everything had been very calm up until now.

"It's still only the second day of the festival," he said. "There's always tomorrow."

That was one part that worried me. The shooter could strike anytime today or tomorrow. Runaway Country would be the perfect place for this shooter to make his move, if he wanted to repeat what he had done back in '09. There were lots of people gathered in one place, lots he could kill in just a few seconds. But what made me wonder was...how he was planning on escaping? A large fence surrounded the place. Police and security guards were everywhere.

I left Officer Roger and found Officer Taylor inside on the festival grounds close to the Main Stage. Another singer had taken the stage. I talked to Taylor for a little while, but he hadn't seen anything either.

"What exactly are you looking for?" he asked.

I shook my head, while trying to look at every face in the crowd to see if I could spot anything out of the ordinary. Any look in someone's eyes telling me he wasn't there for the music. Any nervous tic that could reveal him.

"That's the damned thing," I said. "I'm not sure I know."

27

March 2015

THE KILLER WAS WATCHING the show. The singer on the stage was good, but not as good as Shannon King. Shannon was the killer's absolute favorite singer. Everything about her songs just made sense somehow. They were inspirational.

Through the crowd, the killer spotted Jack Ryder, the detective who was known as Shannon King's new boyfriend. He was talking to an officer on duty. The killer smiled. Jack Ryder looked worried.

Guess you got my email.

The killer knew it complicated things that Shannon had started seeing this detective, but the killer wasn't concerned. The killer had prepared this well. Better than last time around. Back in the movie theater, things hadn't turned out exactly like expected, like planned. It had kept the killer from doing anything like this again for all these years. The killer couldn't risk everything going wrong like last time. But that was six years ago. This time, the killer had more experience. This time, everything would be perfect.

I'm so sorry for all this.

The killer imagined lifting the gun and shooting into the crowd.

The killer still remembered the feeling from last time. The feeling of complete power. The power of life and death.

So exhilarating. Yet so devastating.

The sensation of the weapon going off, the fear in those faces, the screams, the eyes staring in terror at this mad person with their finger on the trigger. A chill ran across the killer's spine. It was a shame it had to happen again. The killer hated having to do this again, hated to have to feel it again, to see how the victim's chest would explode when it met the bullet from the killer's weapon. It had haunted the killer ever since. It had been all the killer had been able to think of for the last six years. Day and night.

The singer on the main stage stopped and thanked her audience. The killer clapped along with everyone else. Another singer took the stage. People cheered. It was getting dark now. The killer stepped out of the crowd and walked towards a stand.

"A Corona, please."

A woman in a tank top handed the beer over the counter. The killer paid with a ten-dollar bill, asked the woman to keep the change as a tip, save up for college so she didn't have to keep working in places like this, and took the beer.

The killer sipped the beer while glancing at the crowd of happy people. Some were dancing while holding their beers up in the air. Most were singing out loud and recording on their phones. A couple was kissing not far from where the killer stood. None of them knew what was about to happen. None even suspected it coming. The killer felt a deep sense of sadness. They were going to be so surprised. Baffled even. Scared. The killer hated to do this to all these happy people. But it had to be done. There was no one who could prevent this from happening. Not even that detective.

The killer looked at Jack Ryder again. A look of desperation was painted all over his face.

I'm so sorry for this. Sorry for causing you all this distress. But you must understand, there is nothing I can do about it. I am nothing but a means to an end. What I do serves a higher purpose. One you might never understand. And I'm not asking you to. I'm not asking for anyone to understand this.

Detective Jack Ryder was on the move now. He walked behind the crowd and approached the killer. Their eyes met and locked for just a second. The killer's heart started racing.

Has he spotted me? Does he know who I am?

"Could I get a bottle of water, please?" he asked the woman with the ten-dollar bill stuck in her bra. He smiled at the killer with a nod. The killer smiled back.

I'm so sorry, Detective. I'm so terribly sorry.

Part Two

NO NEED TO BE COY

28

March 2015

STANLEY WAS IN PAIN. His entire body was hurting so badly from overeating for days now. Finally, his guardian left the room and he had a break for a few minutes to go to the bathroom. The door to the hallway was locked. He heard his guardian turn the key. All Stanley wanted was to run to the bathroom and throw up.

He could hardly get out of the bed. His leg hurt too badly, and he had to roll from the bed to the floor and hit the carpet with a thud. Stanley whimpered, then dragged himself by his arms towards the bathroom. The pain was excruciating. He felt like he had gained fifty pounds over the last two days he had been locked up in this room. Barely a moment had passed without him being fed. It was torture. All he had been allowed to do was to go to the bathroom whenever he needed to, but constantly under his guardian's supervision. Finally, they had run out of food, and his guardian had left to get more.

Stanley pulled himself to the toilet, panting and gasping for air. He opened the lid and pulled himself up towards the toilet. He hardly had to put his finger down his throat before food started to pour out of him. Stanley had always hated to throw up more than most things in this world, but now it felt like such a relief. The pressure on his stomach was being relieved slowly as the food sprayed out of him and into the toilet bowl. How on earth could it even contain all this food? He was stumped that he could have this much inside of him. How was it possible?

When Stanley was done, he flushed in a hurry and dragged his body to the sink, where he managed to open the faucet and splash water on his face with one hand, while the other held his body up. He felt so worn out. Completely exhausted. He started to wonder about getting out of this place of hell, but he felt so weary he could hardly think. What was this place anyway? By the look of the decorations, it was a nice house. The curtains were heavy and the carpet was deep and looked expensive. The bed was nice too. King-sized and the sheets made from silk. The room had no other furniture other than a dresser, which he had already looked in the first time he was left alone in there, but found all of the drawers empty. On the walls were paintings of the beach and fish, one of a sea turtle. The air seemed fresh, and he wondered if he was close to the ocean. He hadn't heard any waves, though, but the windows were hurricane-proof, and he knew from his own house that they blocked out all sounds...even from a roaring road. Stanley knew he didn't have much time before his guardian would be back. He had tried to look out the window, but hurricane shutters were closed from the outside, so he couldn't see anything. He did, however, have a feeling that he was on the second floor and the room was facing east, since he could see the light coming through the small holes in the shutters at sunrise and it was gone by midday.

Stanley splashed more water on his face and washed out his mouth, wondering how he had gotten himself into this mess and how he was going to get out of it. What was the idea behind all of this? Why was he being forced to eat all this food? He looked down at his hurting leg, where the fire poker had gone through the pants and the skin. Blood had soaked his pants. The bleeding had stopped. He just hoped it wouldn't get infected. Stanley let his body sink to the cold bathroom floor, where he rested for a few seconds just to get his strength back. He pulled himself up to a sitting position and planted his back against the wall with a sigh. Then, he folded his hands and did something he hadn't done in many years, not since…Not since the time he had started blaming God for making his son what he was. But now wasn't a time to hold a grudge against his Creator. Now was the time to make amends.

Stanley closed his eyes and said a quiet prayer.

"Dear God. I need your help. What do I do? Oh, God, what am I to do? If I try to escape, Elyse might get hurt. If I stay, I am afraid I might die. What do I do? Help me, God," he said, crying.

As he sat there on the floor with his eyes closed not expecting to hear anything from the God he had turned his back on many years ago, he heard an answer in the form of a small knock from the other side of the wall. Stanley doubted it was from God, but it was something. It was hope.

Stanley gasped. He listened to hear it again, and seconds later, it was repeated. A small knock again. Stanley pulled himself to the wall, and then put his ear towards it. There it was again. And again. Three short, three long, then three short again. S-O-S. Stanley knocked back. S-O-S.

"Is there someone in there?" he heard a voice say.

"Yes," he said with tears in his eyes. "Yes, I'm in here. I'm Stanley. Who are you?"

"I'm Roy. Help me. I am being held captive and force-fed for hours non-stop!"

Stanley felt how the blood left his head. He couldn't believe this. He wasn't the only one here. He wasn't the only one being held captive. There were more.

29

March 2015

I STAYED all night at the festival, until the doors closed at one in the morning. Luckily, nothing happened. There were a lot of frustrating hours, where I kept seeing ghosts everywhere. With every face I looked at, I wondered if that could be the killer. Every loud noise made me jump, thinking this was it. He had struck. It was exhausting.

When the music finally stopped, I couldn't wait to get the people out of there. Soon, the area was emptied completely and I dared to breathe normally again. My two fellow officers went home, and as soon as I had said goodbye to them, I jumped in my Jeep and drove back to my condo. Shannon had decided to go home earlier and was already in her condo when I got back. The kids stayed for one more night at their grandparents' and I knew Angela was with them. I stopped outside of Shannon's door, thinking there was no reason for us to sleep separately when the kids weren't even home. It was funny, but I really missed her when we were away from each other. Even if it was just for a few hours. But, at the same time, I was terrified of smothering her, of scaring her away by coming off too needy and clingy. I knew that was how my ex-wife Arianna had felt when we first met, because I insisted on us being together constantly. I smothered her, she said. She needed her space every now and then. But that was just the way I was. I didn't need any space. Once I found a woman I liked, I didn't see any reason not to be together if it was possible. I didn't know Shannon well enough to know if she felt the same way. Not yet, at least.

I bit my lip, wondering if I should just go up to my own condo. Shannon had a big day tomorrow, with her last concert at the festival. Maybe she needed her sleep. I had to remember who she was. Meeting me and moving here was a big step for her, and she still had her career to consider. She also still had a husband, even though she had filed for a divorce. Joe was resisting it and refusing to sign the papers, which only made everything more complicated.

I sighed and let my hand fall back down. When I was about to turn away from the door and walk towards the stairs, the door opened. Shannon looked at me with a smile.

"Were you seriously going to leave?"

I chuckled and shrugged. "I...I guess."

"I've been watching you through the peephole for the last few minutes. I could hear you on the stairs and you stopping outside my door. To be frank, it freaked me out a little, since I can't stop thinking about that shooter, but then I saw it was just you." She pushed me lovingly. "Don't ever do that to me again. You hear?"

I smiled and pulled her close to me. I leaned down and kissed her soft lips. After a day like this, this was exactly what I needed. "I promise," I whispered.

She pulled my shirt. "Now, come in."

I didn't get much sleep all night, even though I was with her. I kept wondering about Daniel Millman and the shooter's email. I was so relieved that nothing had happened at the festival and started wondering if this person could just be some idiot pulling our legs. Was he just messing around trying to scare us? Or was the threat real? So far, it hadn't turned out to be. The case of the body of Daniel Millman haunted me as well. Something was really off with that wife and that odd place he had been found. It just seemed so wrong. I was still waiting for Yamilla to finish the autopsy and hoping that would provide me with some answers, since the wife couldn't. This coming week, I would have to interview their neighbors at Lansing Island and their friends. It was never easy when it was wealthy people, who, for the most part, thought they were somehow elevated above the law, or at least above suspicion of any kind. They rarely wanted to contribute to any investigation, since they were often too busy for that kind of distraction.

"Go to sleep," Shannon finally whispered, half asleep, and put her arm on my chest. "You're keeping me awake and I have a big day tomorrow. Sunday is the main event of the festival. It's the biggest day with the most people. I have to give them my best."

30

March 2015

Sunday morning, I went to check on the kids, since I had hardly seen them in two days. Shannon was getting ready in her apartment while I walked across the beach to the motel. All of our kids were playing beach volleyball with my parents on the sand by the back deck. They were laughing and screaming with joy. Even Emily seemed to be enjoying herself, I was pleased to see. She had a lot of exams right after spring break, and I knew she was worried about them. It was good to see her enjoy herself a little as well. Children's lives had gotten so serious. It was so different from when I grew up. The demands on them were getting too heavy, it seemed. I felt sad that they hardly got to be kids anymore and just goof around like I did.

"Daaad!" Austin yelled and ran towards me.

"Hey, you can't just leave in the middle of the game," Abigail yelled after him.

Austin threw himself in my arms. I grabbed him, lifted him up, and kissed him. "Hi there, buddy. Having fun?"

"You've gotta come play with us, Dad. Can you pleeease?" he asked.

I could feel he had missed me. So, I nodded. "Just a few rounds, then. I have to be at the festival at one when it opens. Shannon is singing again today."

"Can we come, Dad?" Abigail asked.

My veins froze at the very thought. I wasn't very fond of the thought of them being at the festival, when we didn't know if this shooter might show up or not. "That's probably not a very good idea," I said.

"Aw!" Abigail whined. "I really wanted to hear Shannon sing."

I looked at my mother for help. "I have to work, Abigail. Maybe your grandmother has something fun you can do today?"

My mother smiled. "Sure. How about we take a trip to the zoo?"

Austin and Angela cheered. "Yaay!"

But Abigail didn't. "I don't want to go to the zoo. I've been to the zoo before. I have never been to a country festival before. I have never seen Shannon sing. I want to hear Shannon sing."

I looked into her eyes, then played the grown-up card. "The festival is not for children, Abigail. There's beer and there will be drunk people present. I don't want you there with all that. You're too young. I'll ask Shannon if she will sing for you some other time, all right?"

Abigail growled. "That's not the same and you know it, Dad."

"I do. Maybe another time, all right?"

My mom put an arm around Abigail's shoulder. "If you're real nice, then maybe we can go on the zip line? How would you like that?" she asked, knowing very well that Abigail had been pleading me to take her on the zip line above the zoo for ages. I mouthed a thank you to my mother as we returned to the game. I played some rounds and had a lot of fun with my kids, then ate some breakfast that my mother served me on the deck, while the kids decided to go swimming with my dad. I watched the waves and felt horrible that I had to be away all day, since it was a perfect day for surfing. March was always one of the best months. The swell was a reasonable size and often glassy in the morning, as it was today. It was completely wind-still and just plain beautiful. It did look promising for all week, though, and that was great for the kids who were going to surf camp starting Monday.

"So, is there any particular reason why you didn't want the kids present at the festival?" my mother asked.

I shrugged. "We don't know yet. But I have a hunch that it is best they stay home."

"I can tell by your worried face that it is serious. Has it anything to do with that body that was found yesterday at the trails in Palm Bay? It was on all the stations last night. The creator of Millman Technologies? He's a big name around here."

I shook my head. "That's a completely different case. We still don't know much yet."

"Well, it's good you're being careful and protective of your kids," she said and picked up my empty plate. "Just be careful with yourself and Shannon too. Promise me that?"

I smiled reassuringly. The last thing I wanted was for her to worry. "I promise, Mom. There's no need for concern. Nothing will happen to either of us."

31

June 2006

DOTTIE WAS WORRIED AGAIN. Ever since Elizabeth had started eating, she hadn't stopped again. At first, it was a thrill and an answer to Dottie's prayers, but watching her now, eating her breakfast seven months and fifteen pounds later, Dottie started to wonder when Elizabeth would take a break. She seemed to be hungry constantly. And if Dottie told her she had to wait till food was on the table, she would respond by throwing a hysterical fit so big Dottie saw no other way than to accommodate her wishes. At first, it seemed like the right thing to do, since she needed the food, but the child had almost doubled her weight in a little more than six months. Before that, she hadn't weighed more than eighteen pounds, the same as an average nine month-old baby, and for a long time it had seemed like she wasn't growing at all, but now she was getting bigger by the day. And it wasn't because she was getting taller.

"I want more," she said, with her mouth still full.

Dottie looked at the kitchen counter. It was filled with empty boxes and bags. Just this morning, Elizabeth had eaten a big bowl of Cheerios with milk, two pieces of toasted bread with Nutella, three breakfast bars, and eight waffles. Dottie felt exhausted. She couldn't keep up with the little girl's demands. It was suddenly like she was bottomless, like she couldn't get full. Where did she put it? How could she hold so much food?

"Maybe I can cut up some fruit for you?" Dottie asked.

Elizabeth looked at her mother, and then let out a deep scream. "I don't like fruit. I want more waffles!"

"I...I'm afraid I don't have anymore," Dottie said, showing Elizabeth the empty package.

Elizabeth burst into tears. "But, Mommy...I'm so hungry! I'm so hungry. I'm so hungry!!"

Elizabeth grabbed her plate and threw it on the floor, where it shattered into pieces.

"Elizabeth!" her mother exclaimed.

Dottie felt confused. She had never seen her usually calm daughter act like this. Was it really the same girl? The same tiny girl who never cried as a baby, who slept through the night and was always content? How could she suddenly act like this? What had happened?

"No!" Dottie said. "You're not having any more food right now. You've had enough," she said.

It was James who had told her she needed to stop the girl; she needed to start saying no. They had discussed it on that same morning before James went off to work. Elizabeth's constant eating was wearing on Dottie and she wanted to share her concern with her husband.

"Just tell her no," he said. "She's at a difficult age, where she needs you to set boundaries for her."

He made it sound so easy. It wasn't. Not when it came to Elizabeth. With all the other girls, Dottie had no problem telling them no or telling them to grab a piece of fruit instead of a doughnut when they came home from school. But, when she did the same to Elizabeth, the child whet into a frenzy, a mania, a tantrum that could go on for hours afterwards. Just like she was doing now.

Elizabeth screamed and started reaching for things that she

immediately threw on the floor. She growled and groaned and yelled at Dottie, while screaming for food like she hadn't had any for weeks. In her eyes, Dottie saw a desperation she didn't understand. It was like she was actually hungry. Like she thought she would actually die if she didn't get more to eat. Elizabeth screamed, grabbed a fork, and started to poke herself with it.

"I'm so hungryyyyy!!!"

Frantically, Dottie grabbed the fork and took it from Elizabeth, who stared into her mother's eyes while screaming:

"I want food! Please, Mom. Please!"

Dottie gasped when she saw the desperation in her child. What kind of a mother wouldn't want to feed her child? She felt like crying, then rushed for the freezer, pulling out another pack of waffles.

"Gimme. Gimme!" Elizabeth screamed, and reached out for the frozen package.

Dottie looked puzzled at her daughter, while tears streamed across her cheeks.

"GIMME!!!" her daughter screamed so loud her face turned red.

Dottie handed the frozen waffles to her daughter and watched with anxiety how her three year-old ripped the packaging, and like a wild animal, started eating the frozen waffles, almost swallowing them whole without chewing. When she was done, she licked her fingers, then looked at her mother.

"More. Mommy. MORE!"

32

March 2015

I DROVE Shannon to the festival in Melbourne. She seemed to be feeling better than the day before, when she had received the email. I was too. I was getting more and more convinced that this might just be some phony idiot trying to be smart with her. Maybe even get her to pull out of the festival and not perform. I wasn't going to let that happen. I wasn't going to let a fool like that destroy her performance today. For all I knew, that was all he wanted. To make her scared. That was how terrorists like him worked, wasn't it? Filling us with fear so we would change our ways and not live our lives like we wanted to. Well, it wasn't going to work on Shannon or me. We weren't going to live our lives in fear. There were always crazy people out there, and it was always a risk going on stage. Life was a risk. It wasn't going to change the way we lived. And, no matter what, I wasn't going to make her nervous by talking about it. I was determined to protect her, should anything happen, and had brought my gun and badge.

"I'm looking forward to seeing you up there again," I said, as we were let into the festival grounds. I parked in the designated spot reserved for Shannon King. It kind of made me feel important. I had to admit, I was a little proud of having Shannon as my girlfriend. She was such a big star.

She sighed. "I don't know if I can do this, Jack. This thing. It's getting to me. I thought it wasn't, but I can feel myself getting nervous. This email. I keep thinking about it. What if he shows up again today? What does he want from me? Maybe if I didn't go on stage…"

I looked at her. "Don't go there. Listen to me, Shannon. Don't let a guy like that ruin everything for you. You're smarter than that. There are always reasons to be afraid. Even driving here by car could easily have killed you."

"You're not that bad a driver," she said with a smile.

"I'm serious, Shannon. Life is dangerous. There are so many crazy people out there. You can't live your life without running into at least some of them. Just don't let the fear rule your life. You'll end up miserable. This is your passion. This is you. Standing on a stage. Singing your songs for your fans. This is what you love to do. No one should tell you not to. No one should scare you from doing what you love. Think about all the things I see in my line of work. If I didn't have hope, if I didn't believe that what I did made a difference, that there was still goodness in this world, in people, I wouldn't be able to live. I wouldn't be able to do my job. I can't let it get to me. Neither can you. You've got to get this email out of your mind. This is exactly what this guy wants. Now, shake it."

Shannon looked at me and then chuckled. She kissed me and stroked my cheek. "You're so sweet, Jack. Especially when you say things like *shake it*."

"No, I'm not," I said. "I'm a bad-ass cop and you know it. Now get out there and sing."

Shannon chuckled again and opened the door. "As you wish, Detective."

We walked to her trailer, where she was going to change into her stage outfit. I told her I was going to make a couple of rounds and talk to the officers on duty. Make sure everything was running smoothly.

Shannon wasn't on until three o'clock. We still had two hours. It gave me plenty of time. Shannon kissed me, standing on the first step of her trailer, holding her guitar in her hand.

"Just make sure you make it back before I go on. I need to know you have my back."

"I will."

33

March 2015

SHANNON LOOKED at Jack as he walked away. She liked watching him. He didn't know it himself, but he was so handsome. Girls walking by him stopped and looked when he passed them. He never noticed. Or maybe he didn't care.

Shannon smiled to herself and walked inside of her trailer. She put down the guitar and found the outfit she had picked out for this performance. This was one of her favorite moments. The time when she got herself ready. The anticipation, the butterflies in her stomach, the thrill of it all was always biggest from this moment up until the seconds when she went onto the stage.

Shannon looked at herself in the mirror, then stripped down before she put on her outfit. This wasn't an entire concert, but just four of her most popular numbers, so there wasn't going to be any changing in between songs. She had to choose something that would go with both up-tempo songs and the one ballad she had chosen for this set. She had found this gorgeous dress...just right for the occasion. It wasn't too much or too sparkly, since it was an afternoon performance. Shannon put it on and put on some make-up. That was the part she didn't enjoy too much. Stage make-up was so heavy, but with the light up there, she was going to need it. She was starting to get lines by her eyes and mouth and the light was merciless.

When she was done, she put on her black jacket and favorite hat. She grabbed her guitar and began strumming it, when there was a knock at the door to her trailer. Shannon walked to it and opened the door.

Outside stood Joe.

"What the hell are you doing here?" Shannon asked.

He looked confused. "Well, you invited me."

Shannon shook her head. "No, I didn't. How did you get in here anyway? This is only for performers and their families."

"Well, I am still your husband."

Shannon closed her eyes with a sigh. Of course, he had sweet-talked the guards. Joe could sweet-talk anyone.

"What do you want, Joe?"

"You're the one who asked me to come," he said.

Shannon frowned. "No, I didn't."

Joe pulled out a ticket for the festival. "You sent me this. A ticket just for today. Backstage passes and everything. It came in the mail yesterday. I have to say, I was quite surprised. In a good way. Figured you'd finally come to your senses."

Shannon grabbed the ticket and looked at it. "I never sent you this. Why would you think that?"

"Who else would send me a ticket to a country festival where you're performing?" he asked with a smirk.

"I don't know, Joe. But certainly not me. We're in the middle of a divorce, remember?"

"Well I kind of hoped we would discuss that, since you sent for me and all. I figured you were willing to finally talk about this, to come back to the ol' man. Back where you belong."

Shannon sighed again. "I'm not coming back, Joe. You know it and so do I. It's over. I'm done."

Joe grabbed her arm and held it tight. It hurt. "You're not going anywhere. You hear me? I'm not giving you that divorce and you're not getting Angela. Or else…"

"Or else what, Joe?" Shannon asked, trying to get her arm free from his grip. She tried to see if she could spot a security guard anywhere, but they were too far away, guarding the VIP entrance. The noise from the stage was too loud for them to hear her if she screamed.

"Or else I'll tell your little secret to the entire world."

"You won't do that," Shannon said. "It'll hurt you as much as it'll hurt me. You'll never dare."

"Oh, you better believe I will. I don't mind going down, as long as I take you with me. If I reveal this secret, you know just as well as me that this will all be over. No more screaming fans, no more record label, no more millions."

Shannon's heart raced in her chest. She had no idea what to do or say. He was right. If Joe revealed this secret, it would all be over.

"And, don't try anything," he said. "I've put all the evidence in a safety deposit box, along with a letter explaining everything, and gave the key to my lawyer with the instructions to open it in case something happens to me. He will then reveal everything to the press. So, don't send that boyfriend of yours after me."

"Those are your methods, not mine," Shannon said. She felt like crying. Joe was hurting her arm, and now she was slowly realizing she was never going to get rid of him. He was going to force her to be with him, wasn't he?

"Hey, you let go of her this instant!"

The voice was Jack's. He was running towards them. Joe turned his head and spotted him as well. Shannon smiled.

"Ah, the knight in shining armor, huh?" Joe looked at Shannon. "Enjoy him as much as you can. Tomorrow, you and Angela move back to Nashville with me, or else you know exactly what will happen."

"Let go of her now!"

Joe let go of Shannon's arm and pulled away. "She's all yours," he said with a smirk. "For now."

34

March 2015

"DID HE HURT YOU?"

I stared at Shannon. Her hands were shaking. She was about to cry. I grabbed her in my arms.

"Did he hurt you, Shannon?" I repeated.

She shook her head. "No."

"What the hell is he doing here anyway? I need to talk to those security guards. They're supposed to protect you."

"He had a ticket. Backstage passes. He has a right to be here," Shannon stuttered.

I helped her get back into the trailer, then gave her a bottle of fresh water.

"Here, sweetie. Calm down. My God, you're shaking. God, I hate that guy. I should have punched him right there when I had the chance."

Shannon looked at me, then leaned her head on my shoulder. "No, you shouldn't, Jack. You're a good guy. Don't stoop to his level."

"I'll tell you this much, I really wanted to. Boy, I wanted to. The way he had his hand on you, holding you. I could tell it hurt. Let me have a look, did he leave a bruise, 'cause if he did, you can press charges. We should report this anyway. It would help your case when you fight for Angela. No judge will let a wife beater get the kid."

I felt Shannon's hand on my arm. I looked into her eyes. God, she had beautiful eyes. I felt so protective of her.

"Don't, Jack," she said. "Not now. Let's talk about something else."

I looked into her eyes. Something had changed. Something was different. These weren't the happy warm eyes I was used to. These had a deep sadness to them, a secretive sadness. I didn't understand what was going on, but something was.

"What did he say to you? He said something, didn't he?" I asked, knowing very well I should leave it alone.

"Not now, Jack. I have a show in ten minutes. I can't discuss…"

"Why not? I don't understand."

There was a knock on the door. Shannon jumped.

"Ten minutes," the voice said.

Shannon put a hand to her chest.

"Look at what he is doing to you. You're shaking again. Jumping from someone just knocking on your door. Let me report him for what he did to you today. You can just talk to me. I'll take your statement, so you don't have to face some other officer. That way, you'll get to keep Angela. He can't hurt you anymore."

Shannon's eyes hit the floor.

"There's something you're not telling me," I said.

"Let's talk about it after the set," she said and kissed me. "I need to be backstage now."

I nodded, feeling slightly hurt. I didn't like that she was hiding something from me. It felt so uncomfortable. What could be so bad she felt like she couldn't tell me? She told me about the emails, and I believed I handled that quite well. She knew I would listen and understand, didn't she?

I walked with her backstage and held her hand while she waited for her name to be announced. Then, she leaned over and kissed me and whispered:

"I love you more than you'll ever know," before the crowd demanded her, yelling and screaming her name.

I watched her as she took the stage with the same presence and professionalism as she always did. The audience would never know she was hurting. Like she had done for years, she hid it behind a smile and the performance of a lifetime.

"A rare beauty, isn't she?" a voice said behind me.

I turned and faced Joe. My blood was boiling. I wanted to wipe that smirk off his face.

"Enjoy her while you can," he said, touching his goatee. "She's coming home with me tonight."

My heart stopped. "No, she's not," I said. "She's never going back. At least not to you."

"We'll see about that," he said and disappeared.

What the hell did he mean by that? Was that what Shannon hadn't told me? Had she decided to go back to him? I couldn't believe it. I stared at Shannon as she performed, while I felt like small school-child who had just had his lunch money stolen.

I refused to believe it. I simply refused.

35

March 2015

Barbara Robertson was at the concert of her lifetime. She had always wanted to see Shannon King live on stage, and now she finally had her chance. It was something she knew she would never forget.

Barbara clapped and screamed Shannon's name when she came on stage. She had managed to elbow herself all the way up to the front, where she could see Shannon King up close and with no tall guy in front of her blocking her view. Shannon King yelled something and they all yelled back, before she hit the note of the first song on her guitar and the crowd went wild.

No Heart of Mine blasted out from the stage and Barbara screamed, in awe of her favorite singer. She started to sing along, her best friend since they were children, Lindsey, right next to her, trying to dance, even though the space was tight. They were sweating like crazy, salty droplets were running into their eyes and left a stinging sensation. Barbara felt how her hair was getting soaked and slapping onto her forehead. Lindsey laughed and sang along with the crowd.

"*No Heart of Mine shall ever be, ever be, ever be yours to break again!*"

It was Barbara's favorite song. She knew the lyrics by heart from listening to it over and over again. It had meant so much to her when Sam broke up with her after they finished high school because he "felt like they had grown apart." She didn't understand why he insisted on saying that instead of admitting to her what she already knew, that he had slept with Tracy after prom night, even though he was still going out with Barbara. It was a tough breakup and Barbara had listened to Shannon King's songs over and over again to get through it. It had helped her immensely.

"What a great crowd," Shannon King said when she finished the song. She was sweating too. Barbara was so fortunate to be close enough to notice it. She looked at the woman on stage, who over the last year had become her hero, her idol. Barbara read everything they wrote about her in the magazines and knew that she had left her husband recently and that she was now dating some police guy, who, by the way, was really handsome in all the pictures, but who also had a lot of children. Barbara thought it seemed like a good choice for Shannon, even though the magazines wrote these stories about her destroying her family with her love affair and her cheating on her husband and him being the victim and all. Barbara didn't believe it. And, even if she did, she thought Shannon King was allowed to be with whomever she chose to be with. She was a powerful woman. Barbara had decided to be one too.

"You can either be pitiful or powerful; you can't be both," her mother always told her, quoting Joyce Meyer, her favorite TV preacher.

She liked that saying.

"Y'all ready for some more?" Shannon King yelled out.

"Yeeeeeaaaahh!" the crowd roared back.

"All right, y'all," she said. "I think I might have a little something for ya. A little song called *Break my Heart Again and I'll Put Two Bullets in Yours.*"

The crowd screamed with excitement. Shannon King smiled and started playing, and the band followed along. Barbara screamed with joy. That was one of her favorites too. Lindsey had already started dancing with her beer in her hand. She grabbed Barbara and swung her around. Barbara accidentally bumped into the guy standing next to her. She spilled some beer on his western shirt. He looked at her from under his cowboy hat.

"Watch yourself," he growled.

"Sorry," she giggled, then returned to face Lindsey, who had closed her eyes and was dancing while singing along.

Barbara looked up at her idol on stage, as Shannon approached the crowd and started touching the hands of her fans. Barbara pressed her body towards the fence and reached out her hand as far as she could, as Shannon King approached her and touched it, their eyes locked for just one second, and Barbara screamed in excitement.

"Oh, my God, she touched me!"

Shannon continued down the line of people, not disappointing one single fan, while singing *"If you hurt me, if you break my heart again, I'll put two bullets in yours, and you'll have no more hearts to break,"* when suddenly, a terrifying sound cracked through the air. Barbara went cold all over, recognizing the sound from a drive-by shooting she once witnessed staying at a friend's house. It was the sound of someone shooting into the crowd. The man in the cowboy hat next to her fell to the ground with a loud thud.

After that, there was nothing but panic.

36

March 2015

"Cover your heads! Get down!"

I was screaming at the top of my lungs, while holding my gun tightly between my hands. Gunfire sounded through the air. It was coming from the other side of the stage. People were screaming. I ran out there and yelled to Shannon to get off the stage. People had started to panic and were trampling on one another.

It was the scene of a living nightmare.

"Help people in the front get onto the stage," I yelled at the security guards. The panic had made the crowd move back and forth in waves, and was crushing the people in front.

"Help people get out of here!"

The guards started pulling people free. Some had fallen and were being trampled on. They risked getting killed. The gunfire had ceased, and I jumped down to help get people out. A girl was screaming from underneath people's feet. I managed to get a hand in and pull her out. She had blood on her face and arms. She looked at me with terror in her eyes.

"Run backstage!" I yelled, while trying to pull another girl out.

"There was a guy," the girl said, as I reached for her friend and she grabbed my hand. "He was shot. The guy next to me got shot."

She was in shock. She was staring at her bloody hands.

"Get inside!" I yelled at her, while pulling out her friend who had been badly trampled upon. Her face was already bruised. I grabbed my phone and called for ambulances and backup, then went back to pulling people free.

The sound of gunfire blasted through the air once again. My heart stopped. It sounded like it came from backstage. People screamed in panic and moved for the exits.

"Shannon," I whispered, jumped up onto the stage, and ran with my gun in hand behind the curtain. Terrified faces and people screaming told me I was right. There had been shooting backstage as well.

"Seek cover!" I yelled at all the faces. "Get down!"

I walked with my gun in hand through the corridor created for the musicians to wait before they went onstage. A woman was screaming not far from me.

It was Shannon. I'd recognize that voice anywhere.

"Shannon!" I yelled and ran to her. I found her on the floor, kneeling next to a body on the ground. I lowered the gun. I was speechless.

It was Joe.

He was lying on the wooden floor, bleeding from the two gunshot wounds right in his heart. Shannon cried and looked up at me.

"He's dead, Jack. Oh, my God. Joe has been shot!"

I couldn't believe it. I grabbed Shannon by the shoulder. "Did you see anything? Did you see who shot him?"

"I was hiding like you told me to. Right behind the stage, when I heard the shot. I thought the shooter had entered this area and I was trying to get away when I saw him. I did see someone in a dark blue hoodie run out of here, but I don't know if it was the shooter or not. I can't believe it, Jack. Joe didn't deserve this."

She looked at me with desperation. I knew she had once loved the guy, just like I had once loved Arianna before she broke my heart.

"Who did this?" Shannon asked, holding a hand to cover her mouth. "Who would do such a terrible thing?"

"I don't know. But we don't know if he's done yet. We need to get you out of here," I said. "You and all the rest of the people. It's not safe here."

37

March 2015

THE PLACE WAS SOON CRAWLING with police and paramedics and I helped everyone get out from backstage. The scene outside on the festival grounds was like a warzone. People were walking around in a haze, their eyes wide and frantic, crying, looking for each other, asking everyone if they had seen their friends. Some were hurt and getting help from the paramedics. I held on to Shannon as I escorted her out. A paramedic asked her if she needed attention, but she told him she wasn't hurt. We told him about Joe in the backstage area, and he ran to get a stretcher and some more paramedics to help. Shannon was questioned by one of my colleagues for a little while and told him her story before I escorted her to my car.

"Is everyone alright?" she asked me.

Her eyes were flickering in panic and sadness. Just like me, she simply couldn't grasp what had taken place.

"Who...? Why...?" Then she started to cry.

I held her in my arms and told her it was all over now.

"I think I need to take you home," I said.

She sniffled and nodded. I helped her get inside the car, then called Ron, who was by the entrance directing his crew, who were questioning the witnesses, then helping them get home.

"I'm taking Shannon home, then I'll be back," I said.

"Don't take too long. We need all the hands we can get," he said.

I hung up, then started the car and drove off. We drove through crowds of people simply standing in the parking lot, or in the street, talking and crying, asking the same question we all were.

Why?

A news chopper was already circling the scene, and reporters were trying to get through the entrance that had been blocked by the police as soon as they arrived. I hoped it had been before the shooter had managed to get out. I wanted this bastard, and I wanted him to fry for a lifetime.

"I changed my mind," Shannon said, as we hit A1A towards South Cocoa Beach. None of us had spoken a single word since we left the park. I had turned the radio off, since they were all talking about it. On our way, every other car we met was a police car. The entire force was on their way there.

"About what?" I asked.

"I don't want to go back to the condo and be all alone. I know you have to do your duty and help out at the scene, so I think I want to go to your parents' place."

"That's a great idea," I said. "My mom can take good care of you."

"I keep seeing those images, Jack," she said, when I parked the car in front of the motel. "There was a guy. He was right in front of me. I was shaking hands with the audience, like I always do during this song. I was looking at him and giving him a high-five, right when the shots were fired. I looked into his eyes, Jack. I was staring directly into his eyes when he died."

I kissed her and looked into her eyes. I had no words left; nothing I could say would make her feel better. I chose to stay silent and simply kiss her and hold her tight. I was glad to leave her in the hands of my mother.

The kids were playing on the beach, so they didn't notice us coming back. My mother had already heard about the shooting on the news from the TV constantly running in the bar of the motel.

"Oh, my God, I'm so glad you're okay," she exclaimed when we walked inside. She gave me a small slap across the face. "I called you a thousand times. You pick up when a worried momma calls, you hear me? You almost gave me a heart attack, seeing those things on the news and knowing you were both there. I'm an old woman, you know."

"Yes, ma'am," I said, and let her kiss me like she used to when I was a child, holding my face with both her hands. I guessed she needed it.

Then she kissed Shannon.

"Oh, my sweet thing. It must have been terrible for you. They said it happened during your performance?"

Shannon nodded. She bit her lip. I could tell she was holding back her tears.

"I have to get back," I said.

"You go and catch this bastard," my mom said, grabbing Shannon's hands in hers. "I'll do what I do best." She put her arm around Shannon's shoulder. "Come with me, dear. I'll make us all some hot chocolate."

It was with a heavy heart that I left them, since all I really wanted right now was to be with my family. But duty called. At least it felt good to know all my loved ones were in safe hands.

38

March 2015

"Okay, people. Now that we're all here, let's go through what we have and know." Ron was holding a bagel in one hand and a coffee in the other. It was Monday, before noon, the day after what the media called the Shannon King-inspired shooting at Runaway Country. I had hardly slept all night, since we had been at the scene cleaning up, figuring out what had really taken place.

"Jack. You go first."

"Alright," I said. "We know multiple shots were fired into the crowd at Shannon King's concert yesterday. As we have told the press, two were killed, seventeen hurt by the panic that erupted; one is still in critical condition. Both victims were male. Phillip Hagerty, forty-two, was a captain at Cocoa Beach Fire Department. He leaves behind a wife and two children, a boy and a girl. Second victim was Joe Harrison, thirty-nine, leaves behind a wife and a daughter. His wife was, as many of you know, since it has been all over the media last night and this morning, the singer Shannon King."

There was a silence in the room, and I knew what they were all thinking. The media was relentless when it came to this kind of stuff and had already speculated about whether Shannon had him killed or had even killed him herself. I couldn't believe the insensitivity. They were, after all, in a custody battle, the newspapers had been told by some of Joe's friends. They made him out to be a saint and Shannon to be the bad guy, which made my blood boil. Shannon had made me promise to never tell the real truth. It never helped anyway, she told me. The press believed what they wanted to.

"Both victims were shot twice, directly into their hearts," I continued.

"Someone knows how to shoot," Beth said.

"Yes. Much unlike in the mass-shooting in the cinema in Boca Raton, where it seemed to be very uncontrolled," I continued. "Which is strange, since I had a feeling they were connected, since the shooter sent emails to Shannon King before and after last time, as he did this time."

"Did she receive an email yesterday too?" Ron asked.

I nodded and pulled the printout from my folder. "Yes." I read it out loud for everyone in the room:

"'Dear Shannon, I'm so sorry for what I have done, but I believe you must know by now, I only did what was necessary. Joe deserved to die and we both know it. I did you a favor.' And then, like all the other emails, it is signed AM."

"What the hell is AM?" asked Duncan, another member of our homicide unit. Next to him sat his partner, Ann.

Richard, our researcher and computer expert, leaned over the desk. "As you might guess, it could be a lot of things. It might be the person's initials, but that's hardly realistic. Since the sender of the email goes to great lengths to hide the IP address, we hardly think he would be so stupid as to actually use his real initials. What first comes to mind is naturally AM versus PM. In that context AM stands for *ante meridiem*, which means before noon. But since the shooting in both cases were done in the afternoon, that's not an angle I'm looking into anymore. It could also possibly be Artic Monkeys, the band who called their fifth album simply AM and is called AM by their fans. We do know this killer loves music, so maybe that's an angle..."

"Anything else?" I asked, thinking it sounded all very far-fetched.

"Will.i.am?" he said and shrugged.

"Keep looking into it," I said. "And keep trying to track the email."

"I am," Richard said. "So far, I have been led to India, through Indonesia, to Japan, and now I'm in Africa. Whoever is doing this knows how to cover their tracks in cyberspace. I'm also keeping an eye on social media. I've put a tracker out so I'll be alerted as soon as anyone posts about the shootings in the coming days. There might be witnesses we haven't talked to yet or people with knowledge they haven't told the police."

"Good. What else have we got?" asked Ron, as he finished his bagel.

"According to the techs, the shooter was located somewhere in the stage area when he fired the first two shots into the crowd, the same two shots that hit Phillip Hagerty in the heart and killed him instantly. By the angle, they believe he was actually on the stage when it happened. We'll conduct interviews of the band members later today, but the initial questioning told us they didn't see anyone on the stage with them. Neither did the singer Shannon King," I said. "He must have crept up from behind."

"So, the shooter had a backstage pass?" Beth said. "And, after shooting into the crowd, he ran backstage and killed Shannon King's husband?" Beth paused and looked at me. "Soon to be ex-husband, sorry."

"Exactly right," I said. "How hard are those passes to get ahold of?"

Beth answered. "As far as I know, you can get access to the entire backstage area, if you have enough money."

"Anything else?" Ron asked, as the silence lay upon us in the room again.

"We have multiple videos from the shooting taken with phones," Duncan said. "Ann and I have been going through them. They don't show the shooter's face, though, since he's wearing a hoodie and it's too far away. But you can see a figure up on the stage on two of them, and then the sound of the gun going off twice. The rest is just screaming and panic."

"Okay. Bummer," Ron said.

As the meeting continued, I couldn't stop thinking about Shannon and how hard this had to be for her. She was going to tell Angela about her father's death this morning when my kids were at surf camp and she had her to herself. She knew the girl would see it on TV or hear about it from someone at some point, so she might as well get it done right away, even though she herself was still shaken pretty badly. It was an understatement to say I was worried about her. She was about to face a whole new media-storm of entirely new proportions. She didn't need that. Her fragile mind certainly didn't need that at all.

39

March 2015

"WHAT'S THIS?"

Stanley had managed to pull himself back into bed from the bathroom, when his guardian entered with another tray of food. The guardian stuck their nose in the air and sniffed.

"What is that I smell?"

Stanley shrugged and shook his head. "I don't smell anything."

"VOMIT!" the guardian screamed. "VOMIT. FILTHY DISGUSTING VOMIT!"

Stanley's heart was racing. It had felt so good to relieve himself, and he had hoped to be able to hide it. His shin was throbbing from the effort of getting back to bed in time. He was afraid it was getting infected.

"Did you THROW UP?" the guardian yelled and almost dropped the tray of food in dismay.

Stanley cleared his throat. He could feel how his newfound hope was filling him with new energy. He had talked to someone on the other side of that wall. He wasn't alone.

"I...I had to," he said, fearing his guardian's reaction. Last time he had ended up with a fire poker in his leg.

The guardian stormed to the bathroom and opened the toilet lid. "Did you waste all that good food?"

"I...I'm sorry. I couldn't contain any more. It was just too much."

"You didn't like the food?"

"It wasn't that I didn't like it, but it was just too much," he said. "You forced it inside of me."

"So, it was a little too much, now was it?"

Stanley could tell his guardian was mocking him. It was impossible to talk reason to this mad person.

"Listen. I just really want to get my granddaughter and get back home," he said with a deep sigh. "I don't know what this is all about. But, don't you think it's about time to stop? My leg feels wrong. I think I need to get to a hospital."

The guardian made a grimace. "Oh, you think you need to go to the hospital, do ya? Well, that's a completely different matter, then." The last word was followed by hollow laughter.

Stanley looked at the crazy person in front of him. How did someone become like this? How was this person free to walk around, obviously in need of help, endangering other people? How had no one stopped this person? How many like him had been abducted and kept in this house? What was the idea behind it all?

The guardian leaned over. "You think maybe little Timmy might have felt the same way when you beat him with that fire poker for showing up in your living room wearing his mother's dress and shoes, huh? You know what I'm talking about. Don't look so innocent. I'm talking about the time when you beat him senseless and he couldn't walk for days. Yes, now you're getting it. That's right."

Stanley stared at his guardian with wide-open eyes. His first response was—like it had always been in his life—anger. His blood was boiling. How did this...this character know about his son?

"What the hell...?"

His guardian let out some more loud laughter. Stanley imagined what it would feel like to kill this person, to simply place his hands around that broad neck and press till there were no more sounds coming out.

But, before he could react, the fire poker was brought out once again, swung high into the air, and poked through the thigh of his good leg.

"Now, EAT!" his guardian yelled, while snorting and panting in what Stanley could only assume was excitement. The poker was still in his leg when the food was shoveled into his mouth, drowning out his screaming.

40

March 2015

"I HAVE SOMETHING."

Richard came to my desk and sat down. So far, it had been a bad day. I had interviewed all the band members, but none of them had seen the shooter. They had all been facing the crowd, and when panic broke out, they remembered nothing but chaos. I had tried to recreate the concert by drawing on the whiteboard, and with the help from a crime scene technician, had come to the conclusion that the shooter had to have been walking out on stage during the song, on the left side, behind the bass player from Shannon's band. Mark, the bass player told me he had been playing along when he heard the shots coming from behind him. As soon as he saw the person in the crowd get shot, he had thrown himself to the ground, holding the bass over his head. He hadn't dared to turn and look. He had screamed at everyone to get down. When I asked him if he had any idea where the shooter had come on stage, he had said that he was right behind him. It added up well with what the crime scene techs told me, and with the fact that the shooter afterwards sneaked out the back and shot Joe on the way out. The theory was that he was just shooting his way through the crowd, but I kept wondering why no more than two people were killed. It was odd, since the shooter had the possibility of killing a lot more. Maybe we had just lucked out. The fact was, the shooter had gotten out somehow right afterwards, and before we had managed to lock down the area. How or where he had found his way out, we still didn't know. That was as far as we had gotten all day. I needed something to open up this case. I was nowhere near close to catching this guy.

"A witness tells me she saw the killer," Richard said. "She posted in Wake-Up Cocoa Beach, a Facebook group for locals in Cocoa Beach."

"I know the group," I said.

"Alright. Here she is. I printed out her Facebook page. Her name is Barbara Robertson. She wrote in the group that she was up in the front when the shots were fired and that she was standing right next to Phillip Hagerty when he was shot. As a comment to someone else's post, she writes that she is lucky to still be alive."

"Barbara Robertson? Have we questioned her before?" I asked, thinking of the thousands of statements we had right after the incident that I had no idea how to sort through. I had asked Beth to go through them, but didn't think she was even halfway.

"I tried to find her statement in the pile, but her name didn't come up. I'm thinking she might have been one of those that got out of there before we started getting statements, when we still believed the killer was on the loose."

I nodded. We had no idea how many had left while we were trying to get people to safety. My guess was it was at least a couple hundred. I couldn't blame them. At that point, it was all about getting out of there. There had been forty thousand people present. There was no way we could have interviewed all of them. It was all a mess.

"Good work," I said. "Could you please contact her and have her come in for an interview? Any news on tracking that email?"

Richard shook his head as he got up from my desk. "Not yet. But I'll keep on trying."

"You do that."

When he left, I grabbed my phone and called Shannon. Her voice was thick with sadness as she answered.

"Hey. How're you holding up?" I asked. My stomach was hurting from worrying about her.

"Okay, I guess."

"Did you talk to Angela yet?"

"Not yet. It's been quite the morning. The press is camping outside the building and yelling at us from the beach. Bruce is taking care of the calls, but they are relentless. I closed the shutters while Angela and I watched a movie and ate popcorn, just enjoying each other. I've been trying to build up the courage to tell her. I'm about to do it now," she said. "I'll get it done. Just need to...Just need to get it done. Like a Band-Aid, right? She is just so happy right now. She's playing with a cardboard box. She cut holes for her eyes and uses it to dress up like a robot. How am I supposed to break her heart like this? I can't do it, Jack. I simply can't!"

Shannon's voice cracked.

"You have to. She has to hear it from you, remember?" I said, and pushed back my tears, thinking about how hard it had been for me to tell my kids about what had happened to their mother. I couldn't bear the devastation in their eyes while they asked if *she never was coming back, then*? It was agonizing.

"You have to do it, Shannon. Even if it hurts so bad you wonder if life will ever be good again. You have to do it."

41

March 2015

You have to do it.

Jack's words lingered in Shannon's mind as she put the phone down.

"Look at me, Mom. I'm a robot. Beep-beep-booop," Angela said, as she waddled towards her mother dressed in the cardboard box. She had drawn little buttons on the outside of it and made holes for her arms and legs. She was so adorable, Shannon started crying.

"What's wrong, Mommy?"

Shannon sniffled and wiped her nose. "Nothing, nothing sweetie. Mommy's just a little upset."

Angela looked at her mother and tilted her head. Oh, how badly Shannon craved a drink right now. Anything would do.

"Is it those people down on the beach yelling at you that are bothering you? 'Cause if it is, I'll tell them to leave my mommy alone! I hate those people."

Shannon bit her lip. She sat down on the couch and asked Angela to come sit with her. "No, sweetie," she said. "Those people aren't why Mommy is sad. But, they do have something to do with it. See, baby girl, something happened and they want to ask Mommy about it."

Angela frowned. "What do they want to know?"

"They want to know how I'm feeling, how you're feeling, since this thing happened."

"What thing?"

Shannon grabbed Angela's hand in hers. She put it between both of hers and closed her eyes. She pictured the bottle of vodka that she had bought when grocery shopping a few days ago. It was a slip up; she knew it. She had hidden it under the sink in the bathroom, wrapped in a towel, and promised herself to not touch it. Now, all she wanted to do was to run in there and grab it. It was all she could think of.

"What thing, Mommy?" Angela said.

Shannon looked into her daughter's eyes. She stroked her cheek gently, wondering if her life would ever be like a normal little girl's, if she would grow up to be a normal girl or if they had completely ruined her chances of that.

"What thing, Mommy?" she was getting impatient now.

"I..." a tear rolled across Shannon's cheek.

"Mommy. You're crying," Angela said. "Why are you crying?"

"Yesterday, something really bad happened," Shannon said.

"Like what?"

"Someone shot some people at one of Mommy's concerts." As she spoke, Shannon relieved the nightmare in her mind. The sound of the gun going off, the screaming, the panic. She felt sick to her stomach. It was all her fault, wasn't it? She could have stopped it. She knew something would happen. The email had told her, and still it happened. People had been killed.

Joe had been killed.

"Are you sick, Mommy? You're all pale," Angela said. "Are you going to throw up?"

Throwing up was the worst thing anyone could do in Angela's

eyes. "Maddox threw up in class on Friday. Maybe you caught what she had. It's probably going around."

Shannon shook her head. "No, Mommy's not sick. I'm just really, really sad because of what happened yesterday."

"Did he shoot many people? Did Jack get shot?" she asked with a small gasp.

"No. No. Not Jack. But someone else did. Someone we love very much," Shannon said.

This is it. I'm going to tell her. There is no way back now. God, I could use a drink. Just one.

"Who, Mommy?" she asked with anxiety in her voice.

"Daddy, sweetie. Daddy was shot. He had come to see Mommy, and then..."

Angela let out a small shriek. Shannon grabbed her and held her in her arms. "It's going to be alright," she whispered.

"...Did he...?"

"Yes, sweetie. Daddy died." When the words left her mouth, Shannon felt like she had to throw up. It hurt so badly. She had no idea how much Angela understood of death, but she had once had a cat that died, that they had buried in the yard. But it was so long ago and she had been so young.

"Daddy is not coming back?"

"Remember Milo?" Shannon asked, referring to the cat.

Tears sprang into Angela's eyes. "It's like Milo? He's in heaven waiting for me together with Milo?"

"Yes. They will be waiting for you up there, looking down at you every day, checking to see if you're alright."

"But I'm not going to see him again? I'm not going to visit soon like you told me I would? He's not coming down here anymore?"

Her voice was shrill when she spoke.

"No, honey. It's just the two of us now. And we have to promise each other to be strong. You hear me? We need to take care of each other, now that Daddy is no longer here. You promise to help me with that?"

Angela held back her tears with a sniffle. She nodded while wiping her nose on her sleeve. "Pinky promise."

Shannon swallowed hard and tried to push away her tears. Angela bit her lip, then stroked her mother's cheek gently. "It'll be fine, Mommy," she said, her voice breaking. "We'll take care of each other. Like we always have."

Shannon sighed and closed her eyes. She kissed her daughter's hand, then got up from the couch.

"Do you want to watch another movie?" Angela asked.

Shannon nodded. "I would really enjoy that."

"I saw that *Maleficent* is On Demand now," Angela said. "Could we watch that, please?"

"Of course. Any movie you'd like," Shannon said.

Angela turned on the TV. Shannon could tell she was being brave for her mother's sake. She was holding her tears back. It hurt like crazy to watch. Shannon's stomach was turning. She felt sick.

"Do you think there are movies in Heaven, Mom? Do you think Dad can watch *Maleficent*? I know he wanted to watch it with me."

Shannon swallowed hard to stop herself from crying. "I'm sure he can," she said with a quivering voice. "I'm sure he can watch any movie he'd like."

Angela scrolled through the movies and found *Maleficent*.

"You go ahead and start," Shannon said. "Mommy just needs to go to the bathroom first."

42

March 2015

"You're the man that saved my life."

Barbara Robertson looked at me before we sat down in Ron's office, which I had borrowed for the interview. The atmosphere in his office was a lot calmer and more comfortable than most places at the station.

"I knew it as soon as I saw your eyes. I knew I had seen you before," she said, grabbing a chair.

I remembered it too. She was the first one I pulled out from the crowd. She and her friend were about to get crushed. Her face was still bruised and she had her arm in a sling.

"You pulled me out and up on the stage. I was about to get trampled. You reached in and pulled me out. Then you pulled Lindsey out as well. She was in bad shape, so I helped her get to our car. I drove the both of us to the hospital afterwards. She's still there. She got a concussion from being kicked in the face when we fell to the ground and people around us panicked and tried to get away. It was awful."

"It was," I said, trying hard to block the memory.

"Well, anyway, thanks for saving my life," she said. "You saved both me and my best friend."

"My pleasure." I cleared my throat. "But the real reason why I called you in today is that it has come to my attention that you were standing right next to Phillip Hagerty when the shots were fired."

Barbara nodded. The expression in her young eyes was gloomy, almost remorseful, like she was blaming herself.

"I...I couldn't believe the bullet hit him and not me. I can't help but feel like I was being protected or something. Maybe I was just really lucky. I heard more than one gunshot. It could easily have struck me instead. I...I feel a little guilty. Why did this guy have to die while I was allowed to live?"

"Survivor's guilt," I said. "It's a very common phenomenon when someone has survived a traumatic event. It's a mental condition that occurs when people perceive themselves to have done wrong by surviving a traumatic event when others did not. It is very common in soldiers surviving combat and after natural disasters."

"Survivor's guilt, huh?" Barbara asked. "Well, that sounds like it. I've felt bad all day. Kind of haven't slept since it happened. I keep hearing the shots, you know?"

"Also very normal," I said and found my wallet. I handed her the card of a psychologist I knew who helped soldiers through PTSD. " She helps private people as well," I told her, as she took the card. "You and your friend should call her. Tell her I sent you. She'll give you a discount."

Barbara nodded and looked at the card. She was very young...in her early twenties. I hated that she had to go through this, and I hated having to rip into the wounds again and again, but I had to get some answers.

"So, tell me," I asked. "You were right next to Phillip Hagerty. Where was the killer?"

Barbara looked at me. I saw anxiety rooted deep in her eyes as she relived the moment in her memories. "He was right in front of us," she said. "On the stage."

"To the left side of the stage from where you were?"

"Yes. I didn't see him as he stepped out, 'cause I was dancing with Lindsey. Then I reached up to touch Shannon King's hand when she walked across the stage, so I didn't look at anything but her. She'd just high-fived the guy next to me, the one that got shot, when I heard the sound. I looked at Shannon; her face was completely frozen and she threw herself to the ground. That was when I saw him. He was standing way back, pointing the gun towards me. It looked like he was shooting at me when he fired the next shot, but it hit the same guy again. I don't know why he hit the same guy twice, but he did, and then the guy fell to the ground. I looked down and screamed, then looked up again, and the shooter was gone."

I noted everything Barbara said, while thinking we had to be dealing with an excellent marksman, since he had hit the same person in the heart twice without hitting Shannon or anyone else in the crowd. Was that a coincidence? Had he maybe really been aiming for Shannon? It seemed so initially, but something told me he wasn't. The email, among other factors, told me he wasn't interested in hurting Shannon. He loved her way too much for that. But why Phillip Hagerty? Was it a coincidence? It seemed less and less likely. In my mind, it was starting to look more like murder. Why else would you shoot the victim twice? Both Joe and Phillip Hagerty had been shot twice in the heart. Something didn't add up.

"Did you see anything...did you get a look at his face?" I asked, thinking we could get a drawing made if she remembered anything.

"He was wearing a green hoodie. I couldn't even see his eyes."

"A green hoodie?" I said and wrote it down. "Was there anything on it? Like words or a picture?"

She shook her head. "There was something written in white, but I can't remember what it was. "Oh, no, wait, that's not true. Now I remember. It said: Angel Girl."

"Angel Girl?"

"Yes. Like the song. Like one of Shannon King's songs. It's the title. *Angel Girl* is the story of a little girl that has to take care of herself. She packs her own lunch, and picks out her own clothes for school. Even though she has bruises, no one dares to think she may be abused until it's too late. It's a very sad song. One of my favorites. Well, all of Shannon's songs are my favorites, but this one is truly special."

"So, the killer was wearing a green hoodie with the title of one of Shannon's songs?" I asked, wondering how much fun the media was going to have with this. It would be obvious to anyone that this killer was heavily inspired by Shannon's songs. It was going to devastate her.

"Yes," Barbara said.

"And you're sure of this?"

"Completely."

I wrote it all down. It wasn't much, since Shannon sold a lot of merchandise all over the country to many of her fans, but it was something.

"Anything else? What kind of pants was he wearing?"

"Jeans."

I noted it. "Good. Anything else you noticed?"

"I saw him leave."

I froze and dropped the pen from my hand. "What did you say?"

"It was the scariest moment of my life, after the first one where he almost shot me. But when I helped Lindsey get to the parking lot and we had just gotten into the car and driven off, we were passed by a big black truck. It accelerated fast past us, but, as it did, I looked through the window and saw that same green hoodie sitting in there. I completely panicked and almost ran us off the road. I didn't touch the gas pedal again until it was out of my sight. I was certain he would be waiting for me somewhere, ready to shoot at me again."

"So, you saw the truck?" I asked. Why on earth had this girl not come forward before?

"Yes. I was terrified he would find me," she said, like she had read my mind. "That's why I didn't report it before. I know I should have.

When that Richard guy contacted me and told me to come in, I didn't know what to do. I almost ran away instead."

"You made the right decision," I said. "Can you tell me anything about the truck besides the fact that it was black?"

"The license plate ended with YRJ and it had a large red bumper sticker on the back," she said.

I wrote the information down with great eagerness. She had seen the plate; she knew the last three letters. That was a big breakthrough.

I looked up at Barbara. "What did the sticker say?"

"Shit happens."

43

December 2008

By the time Elizabeth turned six, she weighed close to 200 pounds and had diabetes, pulmonary hypertension, asthma, and sleep apnea. Her weight gain was so fast she would wear something twice, then outgrow it. At birthday parties, Dottie caught her stealing cupcakes. When the ice cream truck drove by on their street, it would result in the most outrageous tantrum from Elizabeth, as she screamed to get out of the fenced yard. Once, Dottie even caught her eating the dog's food from the bowl, just shoveling it into her mouth and swallowing it without chewing. Dottie had contacted a nutritionist and tried to limit portion sizes and kept rigidly scheduled mealtimes. She took Elizabeth and her older sister, Anna, walking at a local track for exercise, and she got Elizabeth physical therapy. But she couldn't seem to halt Elizabeth's rapid weight gain. And, more than ever, she couldn't escape her neighbors' constant staring and her relatives blaming her for her daughter's size. Even her husband James made his comments.

"You need to control her," he would say. "It's your job as her mother. She needs to learn self-discipline."

But it was easier said than done. Dottie did what she could to keep Elizabeth out of the kitchen and out of the food and kept the entire kitchen on lock-down. Literally. She had a padlock on the refrigerator, no food in any of the cabinets, and the pantry door was always locked. One day, Dottie had made a pot roast and had turned her back on Elizabeth for a few seconds, and when she turned back, Elizabeth had eaten the pot roast and was choking on it. Dottie grabbed her from behind and managed to get it out, but from that moment on, she knew she had to keep a constant eye on her daughter. Elizabeth didn't chew her food, she swallowed it. On top of that, she constantly acted like she was starving, like she was constantly craving food. It was all she talked about...when they were to eat the next time, how much she would have. It seemed to be constantly on her mind.

"I'm hungry, Mommy," she said this morning on her birthday, like every morning when she opened her eyes.

Dottie smiled and kissed her daughter's forehead. "We're going out for breakfast," she said and smiled. "It is, after all, your birthday."

That made Elizabeth smile. She loved going out to eat. Dottie didn't, but it was, after all, the girl's birthday. She deserved it, didn't she? Dottie was an optimist. All her life, food had meant joy and, in times of trouble, comfort. Denying her daughter a treat when it was her birthday felt like denying her the celebration. She feared that she was failing Elizabeth if she wasn't allowed just a little fun. Yet, she was terrified at the way things were heading. With the way her daughter was breathing, she would probably die before next Christmas.

They went to Ihop for pancakes. Elizabeth was panting heavily from walking from the car to the front door. Dottie helped her out and, walking backward and holding both of her hands, led her up the curb. To move forward without falling, Elizabeth rocked from side to side, inching her feet ahead a little at a time. Dottie felt her husband's eyes on them and lifted hers to meet his. She shivered from what she saw...the disgust in his eyes when he stared at his outrageous daughter. It was written all over his face.

He blamed Dottie too.

"Pancakes!" Elizabeth yelled, as they sat down in a booth. Her sisters hid their faces behind the menus when a group of girls their age walked by. It broke Dottie's heart.

"So, you want pancakes?" Dottie asked with a sniffle.

"Yes! Pancakes!" Elizabeth exclaimed. "I'm sooo hungry, Mommy."

The pancakes arrived and the family ate in silence. James kept looking at his watch, like he had somewhere else to be. Dottie got the feeling he would rather be anywhere else than where he was right now. Elizabeth leaned in over her plate with her arms surrounding it, like she was afraid someone would take it away from her. Her older sister Tiffany laughed.

"She's hoarding it," she said.

"No, she's not," Dottie said. "Don't talk like that to your sister."

"Oh, come on," James said. "She's right. It's like she thinks we're going to steal her food...as if she really needs any more."

The revulsion gleamed in his eyes. He wasn't even trying to hide it. He was sitting on the edge of his seat, like he was ready to leave any moment. Dottie wondered how it had come to this. How they had all drifted apart like this. Had she been too busy attending to Elizabeth's needs to notice?

"Okay then," James said. "Let me have an end piece of your pancake, then."

Elizabeth let out a desperate cry. "No!"

"Come on," Dottie said. "Let Daddy have a little piece. You have an entire stack of pancakes. He doesn't have any."

"NO!" she screamed. "If he has a piece, there won't be enough to fill me up! You're not going to touch my food!"

The girl screamed so loud everyone in the diner turned to look. Dottie felt how she blushed. Was she embarrassed of her own daughter?

Elizabeth couldn't stop screaming. "I'm so hungry! I'm starving!"

"That's it," James said and got up. He threw a few bills on the table. "I'm out of here."

"You can't just leave," Dottie said. "It's Elizabeth's birthday."

"I'm done," James said. "I can't take this anymore. Every time we go somewhere with her, she screams like that. It's even at the house. I've told you this for years. You pamper her. You've completely spoiled her. I don't know how many times I've told you to stop feeding her."

"But...but...I've done everything I could, James. You know that. I put locks on the refrigerator and everything. I think something is wrong with her. I really do. I think she really believes she is starving and she is desperate for food. That's why she tries to break the lock to get into the refrigerator. That's why she attacked the fridge with that hammer the other day. Because she genuinely believes she is in desperate need of food. Every minute of her waking day is filled with this intense hunger. I think we need to get her help."

James looked at Dottie and snorted. "Nonsense. It's all just nonsense. You feed her too much, that's it. If she can't understand that, then she needs to be disciplined. No one was ever harmed by a good spanking. That's how my parents taught me what was right and wrong."

"I'm not going to hit her. What are you saying, James? I'm telling you. It's not her fault. She can't help herself."

James shook his head. His eyes glistened in contempt. Dottie had never seen such resentment in her husband's eyes.

"Of course she can. Just like everyone else. She has no self-control. Look at her. She's a whale."

"How can you say such a thing?!" Dottie yelled and got up.

James threw out his arms. "You know what? I give up," he said.

Then, he turned on his heel and left. Back in the restaurant, Elizabeth had attacked Dottie's plate and started shoveling down her food using her fingers, while crying for more.

"I am hungry, Mommy. I'm so HUNGRY!"

44

March 2015

WE SENT out a search for a black truck, a Ford with YRJ on the license plate and the bumper sticker saying "Shit happens" to all the TV stations, newspapers, and even radio and had them ask people to look for it. We even posted about it on Twitter and Facebook, in various local groups. Two days later, we had a breakthrough.

Richard came to my desk in the morning when I had just gotten in and had my first cup of coffee. He leapt towards me and I knew something had happened.

"We caught a break, Ryder," he said. "Finally. We found the truck."

"I'll be...Where?"

"Parked outside a house on Indian Creek Drive in Cocoa Beach. A local patrol spotted it. It had a sticker like described and the license plate ends with YRJ."

I strapped on my Glock and asked Beth to come with me before I rushed out. On the way, I called Weasel, the Head of the Cocoa Beach Police Department, and asked her to send all the men she had to the address.

"We think the truck belongs to the shooter at Runaway Country," I said.

"Already done," she said with her raspy voice. "Joel, Jim, and Marty are almost there. George was the man on patrol. He's waiting for all of you there."

"Who does the house belong to where the truck is parked?"

"A Jennifer and Travis Goodman. That's all I know so far."

"Does the truck belong to them?"

"Yes," Weasel said.

Ten minutes later, I drove through the roadblock into a quiet residential street. George, the officer who had spotted the vehicle during his patrol, pointed towards a truck parked in the driveway of a house from the sixties. It was placed on a canal and had a boat in the driveway next to it.

I walked closer and looked at the sticker on the back and the plate. It all seemed right. "Anyone tried to contact the owner?" I asked, looking at the house.

"They're not home," George said.

"You know them?" I asked.

"Sure. Travis used to be captain at the fire station next to us. We saw him all the time."

"So, he knew Phillip Hagerty?" I asked.

"Sure. They were colleagues. Until Travis was kicked off the force."

"What happened?" I asked.

"Ah, it's an old story," George said.

"Tell it anyway."

"Well, apparently, Travis wore some T-shirts at work that offended some people."

I frowned. "T-shirts? What kind of T-shirts?"

"Racist ones. Some of the shirts included slogans like *MADD—Minorities Against Dumbing Down*, stuff like that. Apparently, it created a hostile environment, according to their supervisor."

149

"And I'm guessing Travis wasn't too fond of giving his job to Phillip Hagerty?" I asked.

George shrugged. "Probably not. Especially since it was Phillip who reported him for wearing the shirts."

"Let's take a look at this thing," Beth said, as she came up to me. She grabbed her gun and started approaching the car, sliding up its left side. The windows were all closed. It was hard to see from where I was standing, but it looked empty.

"We need to get ahold of this Travis guy before he leaves town," I said and grabbed the phone to call Weasel to ask her to bring him in. It was her town. She knew where the unemployed hid during the day.

While I was dialing the number, Beth grabbed the handle of the car door. I knew somehow, instinctively, at that second I should have stopped her, but it was too late. I looked up just as the truck exploded in an inferno of fire.

45

March 2015

THE KILLER WAS WATCHING the scene.

Kabooom!

The bomb went off.

"I'm so sorry," the killer whispered.

The killer put down the binoculars, feeling sorry for what had to be done. The radio played Shannon King's newest album. The killer listened to the lyrics and sang along. The killer felt like sending her another email. The killer needed Shannon to know...needed Shannon to know how sorry the killer was for what had to be done. Shannon hadn't expressed gratitude for the killer ridding her of that bastard, Joe. She had been awfully quiet, even though the media wrote about her constantly, some even claiming she had her husband murdered. That wasn't quite the point to it all. The killer wished they knew the entire truth. If only they knew how he used to beat Shannon up, how he used to mistreat his own family. The pig didn't deserve any better. Once the killer had realized what was going on behind those doors, the killer just knew it was time for action. Shannon couldn't do this all by herself. The guy wasn't going to stop.

It had to be done!

The killer drove off towards the A1A and ended up on Minuteman Causeway. Sirens blared in the distance and several police cars passed the killer's car on the way to the scene. A fire truck emerged from the brand new fire station next to city hall. The killer could still see the pillar of smoke in the rearview mirror.

"Such an awful mess," the killer mumbled and stopped at Simpler Times Market to pick up some groceries. "So sad it has to be this way. But, what's done is done. It had to be this way. It simply had to."

The killer paid for the steak and beers, then left the store. In the distance, the pillar of smoke had disappeared. At least they had managed to put out the fire.

"I'm so sorry," the killer whispered again, then drove off.

The killer stopped the car in front of the house and put it in park. The killer's sister opened the door. "Did you get everything?"

The killer nodded and put the bags down in the kitchen. "First Publix, then Simpler Times."

The sister smiled. "Good. Simpler Times is the best, don't you think? Everything is organic."

The killer never cared much about such things. A steak was a steak, wasn't it? The killer grabbed a beer and opened it.

"Really?" the sister said. "At ten-thirty in the morning?"

The killer lifted it. "Cheers."

The sister rolled her eyes. "You're impossible. Well, at least you got the groceries right."

"Anything for you, sis."

"We do make a good team, the two of us, don't you think?" the sister asked.

"I do."

"I have to say, I'm really happy to have you here," she said. "At first I thought it was a terrible idea, you know, based on how we used to fight as kids, but it has been quite nice to have you around, I must admit."

The killer lifted the beer in the air again. The buzz was already taking off and drowning out the guilt. Life was bearable again. At least for now.

46

March 2015

"BEEEETH!!"

I didn't believe my eyes. I simply refused to believe it had happened. When the explosion sounded, Beth was thrown backwards into the air and landed in a bush. I ran to her. Her face was covered in blood, her eyes closed. I felt her pulse, while screaming for someone to call for an ambulance. All I could think of while performing CPR on her was the three children playing in her front yard.

"You're not leaving them, Beth," I yelled and prayed in desperation, while pressing her chest down and blowing air into her lungs. "Stay here. Oh, Jesus. Those kids need her. Let her stay, please, please, please."

The ambulance arrived and took her away. Her pulse was weak, but she wasn't dead yet. There was still hope. Luckily, she was the only one who was hurt by the explosion. It hadn't been a very big bomb.

Just enough to kill one person.

It was the killer who had placed it there. I just knew it was. The same guy who had shot Phillip Hagerty and Joe Harrison at the country festival. The same guy who had killed four people in Miami six years ago. Unlike the majority of mass murderers in history, he hadn't committed suicide; it wasn't a planned suicide where he took other lives with him on the way. This was murder. This guy was a serial and serials didn't stop until you made them.

While firefighters came and put out the fire, I grabbed my phone from the ground where it had landed when the explosion sounded, and called Weasel. She already knew what had happened.

"I need to find Travis Goodman, pronto," I said.

"I talked to Jennifer this morning. She works at City Hall as a secretary. Travis moved out a couple of weeks ago, according to her. He lives with his sister in Cape Canaveral. Apparently, it was too much for them that he lost his job."

"Give me the address and I'll take the scumbag in on my own."

"Don't go alone, Jack," she said. "You're upset about Beth, I know, but he could be dangerous. Let me meet you there."

I met Weasel outside the beautiful house overlooking the river in Cape Canaveral. We walked up the driveway and rang the doorbell. A heavily overweight man in his mid-thirties opened the door.

"Weasel?" he asked.

"Travis. We need to talk. Can we come in?" Weasel asked. "This is Jack Ryder from the Sheriff's Office."

"Sure."

Travis moved aside and we walked in. The TV was on in the living room, the coffee table overflowing with chips and empty beer bottles. Weasel looked at it with a sniffle.

"Are you drinking beer before noon now?" she asked.

"What's it to you?" he snarled.

I tried hard to hold back my anger, but it was hard. "Let's cut the BS, shall we? Let's stop playing pretend for a little, can we?"

Travis looked at me. He was wearing one of his racist shirts. It made my skin crawl. I thought about Emily and wanted to rip it off him.

"My partner is on the way to the hospital because of your little homemade bomb," I said. "She has three children. They will be orphaned if she dies. Are you happy about that?"

I felt Weasel's hand on my shoulder to calm me down. Travis stared at me. "What are you talking about?"

"Your truck. You own a black Ford, right? On the back it says, *Shit Happens?*"

"Yeah, but..."

"No buts...we're taking you in."

47

March 2015

"SHE'S ALIVE, BUT IN A COMA," the doctor says. "Her skin is badly burned. If she wakes up, she'll need transplantation."

If she wakes up.

Ron was standing in the middle of our room at the station as he told us the news about Beth. It was the end of the day and I had let Travis roast in detention for most of the day. He had resisted his arrest and Weasel and I had to bring him in by force. Now, he was yelling and screaming in his cell, stating he wasn't saying another word without a lawyer. I didn't care. I was upset. Not just because of his shirt, but about everything. I had made sure Beth's kids were able to stay with the neighbor. Luckily, they were. Travis could get himself a lawyer if he wanted to. We had a pretty strong case against him. The truck that blew up was his, it was parked in front of his house, he had a grudge against Phillip Hagerty, and he was a stinking racist. He fit the profile of the psychopath we were looking for. I just needed more evidence.

While going through what I had, my phone rang. It was Yamilla.

"Ryder, I have finally finished the autopsy on Daniel Millman. With all that has been going on, I haven't had the time until now."

"Daniel Millman. I had almost forgot about him," I said, thinking about the trail in the woods where we had found his body. It hadn't been a pretty sight. "So, how did he die?" I sipped my coffee and spat it out when I heard the answer.

"His stomach exploded," Yamilla said.

"What?"

"You heard me. It exploded."

I put my cup down and didn't even bother to dry up what I had spilled. "But how is that possible?"

"I don't know. But it is. It's not the first time it has happened."

"But how?"

"It takes a huge amount of food and liquid. The stomach is capable of extending to quite a massive capacity, but even that has limits. It ruptured. The human stomach can hold up to three liters, and it risks rupture at the five liter point, just for reference. When you eat to the point that you think you might vomit, you're probably at the one to one and a half liter level."

"So, you're telling me that he ate more than five liters of food?"

"It hardly sounds possible, right? I mean, think of it. When you know you're so full you're about to throw up, you have to power through that sensation and up your food intake to the level that will cause your stomach to rupture. At some point during this feast, your gag reflex will kick in. Now, it does happen that some people have such unusual eating habits that their bodies' reflexes no longer respond as they normally would. If the reflexes have been ignored for a long time, the person would no longer vomit at the appropriate time. And then, when the stomach gets to this extremely distended point, the stomach muscles are too stretched out to be strong enough to vomit the food out. That's one scenario."

"What's the other?" I asked.

"The food was forced into him over an extended period of time, causing his body to learn how to ignore its reflexes and let the stomach to expand till it burst. There are signs on his body indicating that might be the case here."

"What signs?" I asked. This had to be one of the strangest cases in my time as a homicide detective.

"Signs of trauma in and around his mouth," Yamilla said.

"Around his mouth? Hm. Given the fact that Daniel Millman was never overweight in any of the previous pictures of him that I've seen, it all seems quite dubious," I said.

"It sure does," Yamilla said. "Now, I have looked into it a little bit and found another case that has similar traits."

"Really?"

"Yes, in 2009, six years ago, the body of a man was found floating in a canal in Boca Raton, north of Miami. His stomach was also ruptured. The ME concluded back then that he had simply overeaten and fallen into the canal, but when I looked into the autopsy report, I noticed the same trauma to the mouth as Daniel Millman had."

"Sounds like we should take a closer look at that," I said.

"I'll send over the details for you to look at. The victim's name was James West."

48

March 2015

Katie wasn't feeling well. Ever since the incident in the water, she had stayed away from everyone else as much as possible. She hardly left the room at the motel and didn't talk to any of the girls. All she wanted was for this break to be over so they could go back home. The girls kept laughing and giggling at her. After she had come out of the water on the day it happened, she had been so embarrassed, she had picked her things up, then ran to the room to get dressed. The girls had come in afterwards, while she was still in the shower, and she had heard them talking about her, thinking she couldn't hear them.

"I kind of feel bad for her," Irene said.

"It's her own fault, if you ask me," Britney said. "Her breasts are way too big for her to wear such a small bikini. It was bound to happen."

"Did you see how everyone was looking?" Leanne asked. "It was soooo embarrassing. I'm so glad it wasn't me."

"You would never be so stupid as to go out and try to surf in a bikini," Britney said. "She only did it because Greg told her to. She thinks he likes her. So stupid."

"Don't you think he might like her?" Irene asked. "I mean, he did invite her here, and he seems interested in her."

Britney scoffed. "Nah. Not Greg. Remember Dianna that he brought last year? Same story."

"I'm not sure it's the same," Leanne continued.

Katie could tell that Britney was annoyed with her. She could tell by the tone of her voice.

"Come on. It's exactly the same. Don't you see it?"

"I think it's different with Katie. He seems to really like her. If he hadn't been so far out in the water, I think he would have been the one to help her, not that surfer dude from the motel."

Katie had stepped out of the shower and stood behind the door, listening, while the water was still running to make them believe she couldn't hear them. She couldn't help smiling at what Leanne had said. Could it be? Could it really be that Greg liked her? It wasn't just an illusion? It wasn't just in her head? She put a towel around her body.

"He just feels sorry for her because she's so pathetic," Britney said. "I mean, how else can you feel for her? She is really sad. I can't see how they could ever be together. Greg is in a completely different league than her."

"You're jealous," Irene said.

Britney snorted again. "As if. I can get any boy I want. I could get Greg without even trying."

Katie pushed the door open. The girls all turned and looked at her. "You stay away from Greg," she said with a courage she had no idea she had. "He's mine."

Britney looked at Katie with a frown. Then she chuckled. "Yours? He'll never be yours. He'll use you for sex and then throw you away like a used towel."

Leanne stepped forward: "Just because it happened to you, doesn't mean he'll do the same to Katie."

Britney threw her a glare. "That was told to you in confidence."

Katie felt her heart race. So, that was what this was all about? Greg had used Britney once, then thrown her away. It made sense.

"Well, I'm going for him," Katie said and looked with confidence at the girls. Britney cupped her mouth and laughed. Leanne and Irene looked at her with compassion. Leanne made a grimace while they all stared at her legs.

"You might want to wipe that blood off your legs first," Britney said with loud laughter.

Katie looked down. Three drops of blood had run down the inside of her thighs and was approaching her knees.

"Guess there isn't going to be any sex for you and Greg this week, after all," Britney said and laughed again.

Katie blushed, then ran back into the bathroom and closed the door, while panting. She put her back up against the door, then slid to the ground while crying.

Why did she have to come on this trip? Why?

49

March 2015

I'm okay. I'm okay. I'm still alive and no one knows!

Shannon felt sick to her stomach as she walked around her condo. She and Angela hadn't been outside the door since Joe had died. They had stayed inside for several days, simply watching movies and talking. Jack had stopped by and brought them groceries, and she had told him she needed time, that Angela needed time. It was, after all, the truth. Angela was watching some cartoon when Shannon finally saw the chance to get into the bathroom and relieve the pain a little.

She found the bottle wrapped up in a towel under the sink and took off the top. Her hands were shaking heavily as she brought it to her mouth. It felt so good when those drops hit her tongue.

She knew it was a slippery slope, but so far, she had managed. No one had known that she had a few sips of vodka every day. It made her calmer and relaxed and a better mother, she believed. Jack hadn't seen it on her or smelled it when he stopped by, and she had made sure to keep his visits short, since she didn't want him to suspect anything. The pain would go away soon, and then she would stop again. It was no problem; it was just the way she would deal with this.

It was what she needed right now.

Shannon gulped down the vodka, then removed the bottle from her lips. She closed her eyes and let the drink do its job inside of her. Her hands soon became steadier, her thinking calmer. She could now focus on just one thing at a time and not have her mind race with the millions of thoughts flickering through her mind.

It's your fault those people died. It's all your fault. Now Angela is fatherless because of you. You should never have taken the stage. Maybe if you hadn't sung that song, maybe if you hadn't touched that guy's hand, maybe...

There were a lot of maybes in her thoughts these days. She couldn't stop them on her own. She kept wondering about that guy that was shot right in front of her, right when she touched him. What if she had touched someone else? Would that person have been killed instead? Was it an accident that he was killed? Was the shooter aiming for her instead? And what about Joe? Why did he have to die?

Shannon grabbed the bottle and took another large sip. She was beginning to feel the alcohol, the delicious warmth it left inside of her body, then the serenity. Finally, her thoughts were numbed enough to quiet down. Finally, she felt at peace. At least for a little while.

She took another sip to make sure she could stay this way before she put the top back on and hid the bottle under the sink wrapped in its towel. She washed out her mouth and brushed her teeth to make sure Angela didn't smell anything, then opened the door.

Angela looked up from the couch. "What took you so long, Mommy?"

Shannon felt the buzz and the earth spun for just a second under her feet. She grabbed the door to not fall.

"Mommy! Are you alright?" Angela shrieked.

"Mommy's fine. Don't worry. Just a little tired, that's all. I'll just lay down for a little while."

Shannon found the couch and put her head down on the soft pillow. She drifted away into a happy dream and soon didn't hear the

TV, not even when Angela accidentally zapped onto a news channel and saw her mother's face plastered all over under the headline:

BREAKING NEWS: COUNTRY SUPER-STAR SHANNON KING STOLE LYRICS TO HER FIRST ALBUM AND KILLED THE ORIGINAL CREATOR, HER EX-HUSBAND REVEALS IN LETTER AFTER HIS DEATH

50

March 2015

I COULDN'T BELIEVE what I was looking at on the screen of my computer. A news-ticker had brought me to CNN's main page, where the story of Shannon was plastered all over the screen in blinking yellow and breaking news signs. According to the news channel, Joe had left a letter with his lawyer telling a story of how Shannon had stolen the lyrics to her first album, *Struck by Love*, the megahit that made her the star she was today, and then allegedly killed the person who originally wrote it. According to the letter, the person's body had been buried in a location that the police in Nashville were now examining.

Now, the news channel was speculating on the theory that maybe Shannon was also behind the killing of her husband, that she hired someone to kill him, since they were facing a custody battle. They had interviewed a friend of Joe's, who was also a police officer, to tell the story of how saint-like Joe was and how he wanted to be there for his child, but Shannon was trying to keep him away from his own daughter and how devastated he was.

"This is bull..." I said and leaned back with a deep sigh. "I don't believe this guy!"

Richard looked at me from across the room. I didn't care what anyone else thought. I grabbed my phone and called Shannon. She didn't pick up. Her phone was turned off and went straight to the answering machine. Of course it was, with all that was going on. She had been in hiding from the world, and especially the press, for days as it was.

It was almost four in the afternoon and I was supposed to pick up Abigail and Austin at surf-camp at four o'clock. So, I decided to call it a day. I drove the Jeep to the camp, which was only a few blocks south of where we lived. I tried hard to not show the kids how I felt and smiled as I grabbed their surfboards and threw them in the back.

"What's wrong, Dad?" Abigail said as soon as she saw me.

I could never hide anything from her.

"Nothing's wrong. I'm happy to see you. Did you have fun today?"

"No," Austin said.

It made me sad. I really wanted him to enjoy surfing as much as I did, but somehow, it didn't seem like he could really get into it.

"I had a lot of fun," Abigail said. "I caught the biggest wave ever. Open-faced, Dad. It was so much fun. I paddled out in the back on my own too. Reached my goal of catching seven waves on my own. No more being pushed into waves for me."

"Wow, that's two more than yesterday," I said impressed.

Catching your own waves and paddling out on your own was a huge step, they were the hardest parts of surfing when starting out.

Abigail got in the car. Austin followed. I looked at him. "I tie-dyed a pillowcase," Austin said. The surf-camp was surfing in the morning and art in the afternoon. "I made a heart."

"That's great too, buddy. But, didn't you surf?" I asked.

Austin sniffled as an answer.

"He did," Abigail answered for him. "But only on the inside."

"That's good," I said. "There is nothing wrong with surfing whitewater."

"No, but he got tumbled really bad," Abigail said. "He cried."

"I got the board in my face!" Austin almost yelled at his sister.

"Hey, let's not fight here. At least you tried," I said and started the car. I felt bad for Austin. He was always beat by his sister, no matter what they did. It wasn't fair.

"I'm gonna drive you to Grandma's and Grandpa's; I have to go see Shannon."

"Yay," Abigail said. "Can I go surfing?"

"If someone watches you."

"I'll get Grandpa to look after me. He loves to watch me surf."

"Sounds good," I said, and drove the four blocks to my parents' place, where I dropped them off.

I tried to call Shannon again as I drove up to our condominium, while cameras flashed and reporters knocked on the windows of the car. I tried to call Emily, but she didn't pick up either. I had no idea what she had done all day. It was spring break for her as well, and I had a feeling she hadn't done anything all day, except sleep in and then play on the computer. I knew she hadn't been at my parents' to eat all day, so I figured she had eaten at the condo if she had eaten at all. She had been so into healthy eating lately, I got a feeling she'd hardly touched anything. I didn't like it.

I left a message on her machine telling her I loved her and I would be at the condo after dinner, and that I hoped she would join us for dinner at the motel. I felt like I had hardly seen her all week, except for in the evenings when we watched *The Tonight Show with Jimmy Fallon* together before bedtime. It had kind of become our thing.

51

March 2015

It was a drag getting through the horde of reporters camping in front of our condominium, but somehow I succeeded in elbowing through and avoiding answering questions like:

"Did Shannon King kill Robert Hill?"

"Is your girlfriend a murderer, Detective?"

"Did she kill her ex-husband Joe Harrison too?"

"How can you, as a detective, date a murderer?"

It was Angela who opened the door when I rang the doorbell. She looked sad. "Mommy's all over the news," she said when she saw me.

The TV was on in the living room and Shannon's face was plastered all over it. I walked in and shut it off. "Don't watch that garbage," I said. "And don't believe a word they say, you hear me?"

Angela nodded. I turned and spotted Shannon on the couch. She was heavily asleep.

"She's been sleeping all morning," Angela said.

Looking at her left me with a bad feeling. I felt her forehead; she wasn't warm. I leaned over and smelled her breath. Just as I suspected. It stank of alcohol.

"Goddammit, Shannon," I whispered. "Not in front of your daughter."

"Is Mommy alright?" Angela asked. I could hear the anxiety in her tone of voice. The girl was terrified. She had just lost her father. She had enough on her plate, I thought. I grabbed Angela in my arms and held her.

"Mommy will be fine. She just needs some rest. How about I take you to my parents' place? Abigail and Austin are there. Maybe you can play together? Would you like that? You could go in the motel's pool if you like."

Angela lit up. "Are you kidding? I would love it! But, what about the reporters? Mommy said we had to stay in the condo and close the shutters so the reporters wouldn't see us."

I kissed her cheek. "You let me worry about them," I said, as I grabbed my phone and made a quick call.

"Will you take care of Mommy while I'm gone?" Angela asked when I had hung up.

I glanced at Shannon. She was sleeping heavily still. Probably wouldn't wake up for a few hours.

"Sure thing."

I helped Angela pack a backpack with her swimsuit, goggles, a towel, and her favorite pool toy. I wrote a note for Shannon, in case she woke up while I was gone, then grabbed Angela's hand and we walked to the elevator.

"No," I said, when Angela went to press the button. "I know another way."

I opened the door to the fire escape and we walked down the stairs till we made it to the basement. Every condo had a garage in the basement. I opened mine and saw the impression on Angela's face.

"Wooooww!"

"I know," I said and walked closer to the old red Ducati Street-fighter. I'd had it for many years and spent many hours fixing it up. Until Arianna left us, that was. After that, I had other more important things to attend to. I felt a pinch in my heart as I looked at the old lady. Arianna and I had ridden her together. It had been our thing. She had loved it, loved the feeling of the wind in her hair.

God, I miss you, Arianna.

I missed her and resented her at the same time. It was confusing. I missed what we used to have, but I was so incredibly angry with her for cheating on me and leaving me the way she did.

I pulled the bike out of the garage, then found a helmet for Angela. It was a little too big, but we weren't going very far, so I figured it would do. Her small hands held onto my back really tight.

"Okay, sweetie. Hold on now. Once they spot us, they're going to try and follow us to see where you're going, so I need to lose them, okay? Hold on to me really tight."

"Okay," Angela said.

"Here goes nothing."

I started the engine with a roar, then opened the gate, and the Ducati sprang out of the garage. The entire media corps was focused on something by the front door and didn't notice us at first.

"Look!" Angela yelled through the sound of the engine. "It's Emily!"

I nodded as I swung the bike into the street, and before the reporters realized it was us, we passed the scene. I was the one who had called Emily, and luckily she had picked up this time. I had told her to go down and talk to the reporters. Stall them. Create a diversion. They knew she was my daughter. I knew they would throw themselves at anyone who was vaguely a part of it all, and I would rather it was Emily than Angela, who would only be hurt by their questions. It worked. By the time I had passed all of them, they hadn't even found their car keys yet. Not one of them managed to follow us. I owed Emily big time for this. But it was worth it.

52

March 2015

I DROPPED off Angela at my mom and dad's and told them she couldn't be seen by any reporters, and that she should stay away from the beach area, where they might be lurking. My mom promised to take good care of her, and Abigail and Austin immediately grabbed her and pulled her inside the motel to be a part of some game they had started. Angela laughed as she ran off with my kids. It calmed me down. The poor girl needed a break.

I drove through the garage into my building and parked the bike, then ran up the stairs, opened the door to the front entrance, and pulled Emily inside, out of the claws of the press.

"Thank you!" she moaned. "Those people are awful! How does Shannon put up with them?"

"I'm not sure she does," I said.

"Is it true?" Emily asked, as we took the elevator up to Shannon's floor.

"Is what true?"

"Did she kill some guy and steal his songs to make a career?"

I sighed. The elevator stopped. "I don't know," I said. "I don't think so. It doesn't sound like her. I haven't been able to ask her yet. But I can hardly imagine she could do anything like this."

"Probably that Joe guy was behind it," Emily said. "Figures. Even though he's dead, she still has to deal with him and all his shit."

"Watch the language, young lady," I said, thinking she was so right. Joe was still hurting her, even if it was from beyond the grave.

"Just shows you that you gotta be picky when you chose your man," Emily said. "Can't let yourself be blinded by love or great looks."

I chuckled and kissed her as I left the elevator. "See you at dinner at the motel?" I asked as the doors were about to close.

"Sure," she answered.

I stared at the door as it shut and my smart daughter left for our floor. I had done many things wrong while bringing her up, but it couldn't all have been bad. She was one clever girl.

I walked to Shannon's condo and let myself in. She was still asleep on the couch. I walked inside and kneeled next to her. I kissed her forehead and stroked her thick hair. She was such a beautiful woman. Her features so delicate, her hair long and thick. Why had life decided to be so hard on her?

"How long have you been drinking? Is that why you've been so busy getting me to leave lately when I stopped by? You were afraid I'd find you out, weren't you? You know you can't handle it, dammit Shannon. You know."

I decided I wasn't just going to sit and wait for her to wake up. I walked into the kitchen and started searching. I wanted to remove the bottles of alcohol so she wouldn't fall in again. I went through all the cabinets in the kitchen, in her bedroom, the living room, and finally the bathroom. I found a bottle of vodka wrapped in a towel underneath the sink. My heart dropped. It was almost empty. A tear escaped my eye and I was filled with such an anger I could hardly contain it. I took the bottle into the kitchen and threw it in the garbage can so hard it broke. Then I took the garbage out. When I returned, Shannon was awake. She was sitting up on the couch, her hair all messy on one side of her head. Her eyes were small. She looked terribly pale.

"Jack?"

I closed the door.

"Jack..." she moaned. She forced a smile. "What are you doing here? Where is Angela?"

"I took her to my parents," I said.

I sat next to her on the couch and grabbed her hand in mine. I forced her to look into my eyes.

"We need to talk."

53

March 2015

"I NEVER KILLED ANYONE. I swear to God, Jack. I never killed anyone. You have to believe me."

I looked at Shannon. Her eyes had grown wild when I told her what had happened, how the media was all over the story of her apparently killing this Robert Hill and stealing his songs. I told her I needed to know the truth, no matter how hard it was to bear.

"I want to, Shannon. I really, really want to. You need to tell me what happened first. I need to know. I deserve to know."

Shannon tried to avoid looking at me. I could tell she was miserable. All I wanted was the truth from her. Then, we could take it from there.

"It was so long ago," Shannon said. She pulled her legs up on the couch and put her chin on her knees. She suddenly seemed so small, so frail. She was talking slowly and I could tell she was still under the influence of the alcohol. I wondered how far out she had gotten the last couple of days. Was it just a relapse, a setback that she could recover from? Or had she gotten in too deep, so deep she would need professional help?

"Robert Hill was a good friend of mine," she said. "We wrote songs together. We performed together frequently at bars and clubs around Nashville. He didn't enjoy the stage as much as I did, so he mainly hid behind his guitar, while I got to sing the songs. He loved when I sang his songs."

"Did he write the songs for your first album?" I asked.

Shannon looked at me quickly, then at the ground.

"He did, didn't he?" I asked.

"That part is true," Shannon said. "But he wrote them for me. I didn't realize it until it was too late, but he was madly in love with me. I was with Joe. Joe could tell and tried to warn me, but I cut him off and told him he saw ghosts everywhere. I didn't see it, not until it was too late. He wrote the album for me, he told me. He came to the small cottage where we used to live one night and handed me the songs. He told me they were for me. He had been working on them for years, he said. Ever since he met me. He had written them for me to sing. No one else would do them justice, he said. He told me he didn't want his name on them, told me they were mine to keep. I didn't under-stand until I read the songs. They were a declaration of love to me. At first, I thought I could never sing them, but they were so good. I showed them to Joe, and he told me they were too good to not use. I had to produce an album with them. He knew someone who could help me. But he never liked the idea that it was Robert who had written the songs. He hated him because he was so into me. After Robert gave me the songs, Joe told me to not see Robert again. That it was bad for our relationship...that he was coming between us. In some way, it was true. I was feeling different about Robert since I had found out how he felt about me. But, as soon as I started to avoid Robert, things turned bad. He started following me everywhere I went."

"He was stalking you?" I asked.

Shannon nodded. She bit her lip. "He was everywhere, Jack. If I performed, he was in the audience. If I went to a restaurant, he would stand outside the window and watch me or sit at a table not far away. It was like, the more I avoided him, the more obsessed he got. One day, when Joe and I came home from a performance, a little drunk, since we had celebrated that I had landed my first record deal, he was sitting in our living room. He was angry and had a gun in his hand. I asked him what was wrong and he told me he wanted what was his. I thought he meant the album, the songs, and told him I could try and get him credited for it, but he didn't care about that. He wanted me. He was there because he wanted me. He pointed the gun at Joe. It was so scary, Jack. I was sure he was going to kill him. All his anger was directed at Joe. He was the one who had kept me away from him, he said. I screamed and cried and tried to get him to back down and leave Joe alone, but he wouldn't. His hands were shaking in anger as he spoke. I was terrified, Jack. I was so afraid."

I put my hand on hers. She was in deep distress. "No wonder," I said. "So, what happened?"

"I...We had our instruments at the house. I...I...I had to stop him. He wanted to shoot Joe. I grabbed a microphone stand and slammed it into his back. He fell to the ground and Joe grabbed the stand out of my hand, then slammed it into his back again. He kept going, Jack. He wouldn't stop. He kept hitting Robert, again and again, while yelling and screaming. When he hit the back of his head, it sounded like a watermelon landing on the ground. It split his head open. I told him to stop. I yelled and yelled, but he wouldn't. Joe was so angry. I couldn't stop him."

"So, Joe killed him," I said. "You just knocked him out."

Shannon looked at me and shook her head. "It was a terrible thing we did. It has haunted me ever since. Afterwards, we didn't know what to do. We couldn't call the police; no one would believe us. I had just signed a record deal, the chance of a lifetime. What should I have done? I would lose everything." Shannon paused. A couple of tears escaped her eye. "So, we buried him. In the backyard of the house. The next day, we told the landlord we wanted to move and started looking for a new place. We left the next day and never looked back. We never talked about it again. Not until Joe brought it up a few days ago. He told me he would reveal the secret if I didn't come back to him."

"That's why he was so certain you were going to come back to him," I said. "He told me while you were on stage."

Shannon chuckled lightly then sniffled. "That sounds like him. He told me that day that he had left a letter with his lawyer with the instruction to reveal it all to the press if something happened to him. It was his insurance."

"And it worked. It's all over the media," I said. "In the letter, he claims you were the one who killed Robert Hill. Now, we have to figure out how to avoid having you go to jail for this. It's his word against yours."

54

March 2015

Spring break was almost over when something wonderful happened to Katie. After dragging herself through days of going to the beach with the girls, trying to hide in the room and avoid the others, especially the boys after the incident surfing, she was sitting on her bed on Friday morning, two days before they would go back to school. Katie was counting the minutes and digging her nose into her book to escape reality. She was alone in the motel room when she received a text. She picked up the phone and saw that it was from Greg. Her heart pounded when she opened it.

THERE'S A FULL MOON TONIGHT AT SUNSET. THEY SAY IT'S GOING TO BE BLOOD-RED. DO YOU WANT TO MEET UP AND WATCH IT RISE TOGETHER?

Katie stared at her screen. A smile spread across her face. Could it be? Could it really be? She had avoided Greg ever since the incident in the water, thinking he was probably repulsed by her, and he had left her alone, so Katie had kind of figured he wasn't interested in her anymore. She still liked him and had observed him from afar every day at the beach, while sitting on her towel and reading, but he hadn't spoken to her, so she had almost given up.

He does like me. He wants to meet with me.

Katie texted him back that "Sure, she would love to, what time and where?" He answered right away.

7:30 IN THE DUNES. THERE IS A SMALL BENCH ON THE LEFT OF THE MOTEL. WE CAN BE ALONE THERE.

Katie's heart was racing in her chest.

Oh, my God. He really wants to be alone with me. Oh, my God. He wants to really be with me. Like, really be with me.

Katie took in a deep breath, remembering what Britney had told her earlier on the trip. That Greg brought girls to have sex with them, then tossed them aside afterwards. She had to be careful to not let that happen to her. She still had her period, so that was an excellent excuse for not sleeping with him. She wanted more from him. She wanted them to get to know each other first. She wondered why he hadn't tried to make a move before now. If he was so eager to have sex with her, he could have had her for the entire trip. Had he waited so it wouldn't be awkward afterwards? Or maybe he did really like her for who she was and had taken his time to find the courage to ask. Now that time was running out, he knew he had to act fast before they went back home.

Yes, that was probably it. That had to be it. After all, he had invited her to play volleyball and to go surfing with him. He did want to be with her. The fact that he had left her alone all this time was probably just because she had avoided him; she was the one who hadn't seemed like she wanted to be with him or any of the others.

Katie put her book down, then texted him back.

SURE. SEE YOU THERE.

She wondered if she should add "Looking forward to being alone with you," but decided not to. She didn't want to come off as too eager. If he was the player they said he was, she had to play her cards right. She had to be hard to get. That was the only thing guys like him respected. They liked the chase.

Well, so did she, and she would soon have him in her net. That would show those girls.

Katie got up from the bed, walked to her suitcase, and found the dress she had picked out for the trip. The dress she had bought with the sole intention of wearing it if she ever got the chance to be alone with Greg.

Now was that time. She could hardly wait.

Katie took a shower, then got dressed and looked at herself in the mirror. The other girls had told her they were going to The Lobster Shanty to eat dinner, so they wouldn't be back any time soon. There was an event at the port where girls drank free all night that they would hit afterwards. Katie wouldn't see them until tomorrow.

At least they wouldn't somehow ruin it for Katie. She had decided to skip dinner because she wasn't hungry and felt so nervous about meeting Greg. She put on some make up to make her look really pretty, then sat on the bed and waited. At exactly seven twenty-nine, she got up, corrected her dress, then sighed and looked at her reflection.

"This is it, Katie," she said to herself. "Don't blow it."

She put on lip gloss one last time, then corrected her hair and pulled down the dress again. It was very short and she wasn't too fond of her legs. But, as she pulled it down, her breasts showed too much flesh, so she pulled the dress back up.

There. This was as good as it got.

Katie looked at her watch again and walked out. She had planned on being a couple of minutes late, to make sure he didn't think she was too eager; desperate women were repulsive to men.

Katie closed the door to the room behind her, then walked towards the beach, hoping her tampon would keep her safe for long enough so she didn't have to suddenly run back to the room. She smiled when she felt the evening breeze hit her face. It felt so nice. The ocean was in front of her now and the sun almost set over the Intracoastal on the other side. The moon would rise above the ocean. The light was gorgeous. The moon was already peeking above the horizon. It was big and very red. It looked just like a sunrise. It was spectacular. Katie couldn't wait to enjoy it in the arms of Greg. She walked along the beach to the left, where the bench was placed in front of the big white condominium that was neighbor to the motel.

Katie spotted Greg sitting on the bench as she approached the place they had agreed to meet. He was looking at the moon. Katie waved, but he didn't see her. She walked closer, then waved again, but he still didn't wave back. He didn't seem to see her. She took off her shoes to better be able to walk across the sand and held them in her hand. It felt so nice between her toes. She loved the sand here. It was soft and you could walk with your bare toes in it without ever stepping on a rock or a shell. Katie looked at the moon quickly once again and sighed at the beauty of the scenery. Sandy beach as far as the eye could see, perfect temperature, the moon and the light, and... him. Katie turned her head and looked at Greg again. That was when she realized why he hadn't waved back at her, why he hadn't seen her.

Katie stopped. Everything inside of her froze to ice. It wasn't because he was busy staring at the moon. It wasn't because he didn't notice her. It was because his eyes were closed. He was sitting on the bench with his eyes shut, and Katie realized in that second, as she took the last step towards him, and parts of him were no longer covered by the sand dunes. Now she could see what was going on, and it made everything inside of her turn.

On her knees in front of Greg was Britney, sitting with her back turned to Katie. She had her head bent over his crotch, his pants wide open. Greg was moaning. Britney's head was moving faster and faster. Greg moaned louder and louder until he suddenly arched his body and led out a loud groan.

That was when Britney turned her head and looked directly at Katie. Their eyes locked and Britney licked her lips. Katie bent over and threw up in the sand.

Part Three

GET YOURSELF FREE

55

March 2015

STANLEY HAD LOST count of the days. He guessed he had been in the room for maybe a little more than a week. Maybe it was more, he didn't know. But he hadn't lost hope yet. Both his legs were badly hurt and one was infected and gave him a fever with hallucinations that followed. And then there was the food. He had been forced to eat more food than he had ever imagined he could contain, and his stomach hurt so badly it was almost impossible for him to move.

He kept thinking about Elyse and wondering if she was alright. She was his one thing in life that mattered, his one true pure thing, his second chance.

Things had been bad with Timmy when he was a child. Stanley didn't like to be reminded of it. Stanley hadn't known what to do, what else to do when the boy kept acting so strangely, than to try and beat it out of him. Only, it hadn't helped. Timmy had stayed the same way. He had kept putting on Mommy's dresses and walking in her high heels. He had also brought home a boy as his *partner* when he came back from college to visit at Thanksgiving. Later, he had told his parents that he was going to go through a change and that he would be a woman soon. It was all far too strange for Stanley, and he had told him to never come back again. He simply couldn't cope with it.

Today, he regretted it all. He regretted having beaten the boy so badly he could hardly walk, in pure frustration over the fact that the boy wasn't like others. It was wrong. Stanley knew that. You shouldn't beat a kid. But he hadn't known what else to do. He hadn't known what this was or how to respond to it.

Now, it was too late. Timmy was now Tiana and lived somewhere in California. Stanley hadn't heard from him since the day he told him to leave and never come back. It was Stanley's own fault, and Melanie never hesitated in telling him so. She went to visit their son—or daughter—every now and then, and never told Stanley anything when she returned except *it was a good trip. No delays.*

Stanley had tried to make amends by being a better grandfather than he was a father, but it hadn't changed the fact that he missed his son like crazy, and so badly wanted to get back into his life. Or her life. Or whatever it was. Stanley was confused. It was all so strange and complicated, and he had no idea how to do it. So, for years, he simply hadn't. He hadn't done anything about it. He had pretended it never happened, pretended his son was still his son, only living far away now. At least, that's what he told the neighbors.

"Oh yeah, Timmy is good. Doing great. A lawyer now. Hoping to make partner next year."

The stories got better and better every time. The picture he had created of his perfect son became more and more polished as the years passed.

"Yes, he has two children now. The youngest is adorable. Cute as they get. Yes, it is too bad they live so far away and hardly ever have time to visit. It is a shame. But, what can you do? They got to live their own lives, you know?"

Over and over again he would say things like that and Melanie would shake her head, but she would never correct him or tell on him. She would never embarrass him publicly. It was her way of loving him. He was grateful for that.

Stanley sobbed in his bed, knowing that in a few minutes the crazy person holding him hostage would be back with enough food to feed a small African village for days. He wasn't sure he could take more. It was all so...so miserable.

It was while feeling sorry for himself that Stanley suddenly realized that maybe there was a God after all. Maybe he did hear him when he had cried out his pain and misery in the few moments he had been left alone during the day.

His guardian had forgotten to lock the door. A gust of wind, or maybe it was the air from the AC as it started, now made it open just a little bit, just enough to let the smell of freedom slip inside.

56

January 2009

JAMES HAD LEFT THEM. When they returned home from the diner that morning on Elizabeth's birthday, on Christmas Eve, he had packed his things and left them a note telling them he was gone and he wasn't coming back. Dottie was devastated. She cried for days in despair, not knowing what to do next. How was she supposed to support four children and especially one that ate more than the rest of them put together? How?

She asked James that when she called him a few days later, after she had finally gotten ahold of herself just enough to be able to speak to him.

"How are we supposed to get by?"

"I'll send you money."

"What about us? What about the kids?"

"I don't know."

"Come home, James. We'll talk. We'll figure it out. Make some changes. Please, just come home."

"I've met someone else."

The words hit her like arrows to her chest. "Someone else... but...James?"

"We're moving in together. There's nothing you can do about it, Dottie. I'm done. It's over."

"You can't just leave me?"

"I just did."

Then, he had hung up and left Dottie to sob in self-pity for weeks afterwards. He had kept his word and sent her money every week, but it was barely enough to keep Elizabeth satisfied. The rest of them had to eat too. Dottie knew she had to get a job. She found one as a waitress at Denny's and that kept them going for a little while. But it meant a lot of changes for the family, and especially for Elizabeth, who had to go to aftercare at the school, and she didn't take any of the changes well. It was hard enough for her in school, where she was constantly teased about her size, and where she couldn't eat until she was allowed to. But to have to stay at the school's aftercare for three more hours every day was crushing for her. Every day, when Dottie brought her home after a long day at work, she would scream and cry, and the only way Dottie knew to calm her down was to give her food. So, she started bringing home leftovers from the diner, and as long as Elizabeth got those, she kept quiet. It didn't help with her rapid weight gain, but Dottie didn't quite see any other way. She simply couldn't deal with it on top of everything else.

At Elizabeth's annual check-up in January, her doctor looked at Dottie with a deep sigh.

"I know she has gained a lot again, Doctor," Dottie said. "I just can't control it. I've tried everything. I don't know what to do. James tells me to discipline her more, to help her get better self-control, but I don't know how to. I guess I have given up."

The doctor leaned back in his chair and looked at Dottie. "I have come upon something that you might find interesting," he said, much to Dottie's surprise. She was certain she was in for another of his scoldings, which she usually got when visiting with Elizabeth.

"You what?" she asked.

"I think I might know what is wrong with Elizabeth. I read an article about it recently and it just hit me. This is what is happening to Elizabeth West, I said to myself. This is what's wrong with her."

"So, what is it?" Dottie asked, her heart racing. Was there an explanation for her daughter's condition? Was Dottie really not the one responsible for this?

"It's called Prader-Willi Syndrome," he said and leaned forward. "It's a rare genetic disorder in which seven genes on chromosome 15 are deleted or unexpressed on the paternal chromosome."

"I don't think I follow you, Doctor."

"She was born with it," he said. "It's a rare chromosomal abnormality. It causes low muscle tone and impairs signaling between the brain and the stomach. There is no sensation of satiety that tells them to stop eating or alerts their body to throw up when they have eaten too much. Elizabeth feels like she is starving constantly because her brain tells her she is. Patients describe the hunger as a physical pain. To make matters worse, it also causes an especially slow metabolism, predisposing Elizabeth to morbid obesity. Most die from obesity-related diseases later on in life, many from choking because they swallow their food too fast. She does not know when to stop eating. You'll have to keep an eye on her constantly. Food can be a death sentence for patients like her."

57

March 2015

Travis Goodman wasn't talking. Even after days in jail, he wouldn't say anything. He simply refused to speak a word to any of us. Told us we were all after him, that no matter what he said, he would only harm himself. He knew that much. He wasn't that stupid. Then he started raging on about some conspiracy theory that he had read online about how the police were being run by the blacks and how they had infiltrated the government and put Obama in post. Then he went on to tell me about The Third Reich, about some Nazi leader who was believed to be dead, but allegedly had never died, and was building his empire underground and he knew about how the blacks were planning on taking over the U.S. as a revenge for their slavery.

I stopped listening after a few minutes and knew I would never get anything useful out of him. He couldn't afford a lawyer, so the court appointed one to him. The judge was on our side. He didn't make bail. The guy was suspected of having put an officer in coma and shot into the crowd at the country festival. There was no judge who would let him out, which was good for me. I had time to build his case.

But it wasn't easy. All we had was the truck. His truck that had been blown up in front of his home. His wife, Jennifer, claimed Travis took the truck with him when he moved out of the house. Travis said it had been stolen from his sister's house. There were no reports on the vehicle being stolen anywhere.

Beth was still in a coma, and the doctors feared she would remain that way. They still couldn't tell us if she would get better or not. I feared the worst. I was so mad at this situation. It reminded me of the time with my old partner in Miami, Lisa, who had been killed in the line of duty when I should have protected her. I had taken in her daughter Emily and loved her like my own. I wasn't going to stand and watch while three other children were made orphans. The least I could do was to get justice. I had never found the shooter down in Miami and it haunted me like crazy. This wasn't going to end that way. I was determined to find evidence to put this guy away for the rest of his life. And then some.

The weekend came and Shannon still stayed in her condo, behind closed shutters, while the media speculated about her involvement in the disappearance of Robert Hill. I think she had managed to stay sober. I had removed all alcohol from the condo, and since I was the one shopping for her, she couldn't get ahold of any more. I felt like a prison guard, but if that was the way it had to be to make her well again, then so be it.

The police in Nashville hadn't found the body of Robert Hill yet, to her luck, and so far no charges had been made. We were still holding our breath. On Saturday, she told them everything. I had convinced her it was the only way to get through this properly. They were using radars on the backyard of the house, and if they had buried a body there, it was going to be found sooner or later. I asked them to send a guy down, and he took her entire statement. I told her to use the word self-defense as often as possible, and so she did. With her lawyer at her side, she told him she didn't know where the body was buried, since Joe had taken care of it. But it was somewhere in the backyard. As she spoke to the detective from Nashville PD, I suddenly thought of something.

"Where is the gun?" I asked.

"What gun?"

"You said Robert had a gun. He was threatening you with it when you hit him with the microphone stand. Where is the gun now?"

Shannon shrugged. "I don't know. Joe must have gotten rid of it somehow. I never saw it again."

"Maybe he buried it with the body?" I asked.

"That's definitely a possibility," she said.

The Nashville detective nodded, satisfied. "If that is what happened, then that certainly speaks for your case. We find the gun and it has Robert Hill's fingerprints on it, then we know you're telling the truth, Mrs. King."

All we had to do was to find the smoking gun.

58

March 2015

"Early bird gets the worm," was Allan MacGill's favorite saying. And, unlike everyone else in his family, he lived by it. Especially on Sunday mornings when he didn't have to go to work, but could spend the day fishing from the jetty in Cape Canaveral. It was his favorite time of the week. When everyone else in his family went to church at ten, he could be found leaning against the railing at the end of the pier with his fishing line in the water, enjoying God's true church...His creations.

Allan grabbed his bucket and fishing pole from the back of his truck and started walking from the parking lot to the jetty. It was quite a walk, but he enjoyed every moment of it. The freshness in the air before sunrise was indescribable. It had to be experienced.

Allan greeted the other early fishers who were setting up their poles at the jetty, then found a spot by the railing where he could put up his. He took in a deep breath and enjoyed the quiet. In a few hours, it would be spoiled by the many boats coming out of Cape Canaveral Port. Worst were the cruise ships at the end of the day. All those people standing on the deck waving at the people on the pier... the big awful ships with all their waterslides and smell of grease and fried food they brought with them. Boy, how he loathed those. They all left on Sunday afternoon and scared away all the fish. He would usually try and leave before that.

Last Sunday, Allan had lucked out. It had been his best fishing day ever. He had hauled in a bonnet-head...a big bonnet-head shark, at least two feet long. It had been quite the crowd-puller. He had brought it home and cut the meat out and prepared it as steaks on the grill, then invited the neighbors over for a feast and use of bragging rights. It had been perfect. They had all loved it. Allan knew he probably wouldn't be able to do it again, but he was hoping for something as spectacular today as well. He had only one week left on the Space Coast before they went back to Boston, where they lived the rest of the year. Usually, they stayed in Florida for three months of the year. The three best months of Allan's year. He wished they could stay all year around, but his wife, Angie, wouldn't hear of it.

"I get grumpy when it's hot," she always argued. "And you don't want me grumpy, do you?"

She was right about that. He certainly didn't want her to be grumpier than she already was. No reason for that.

So, Allan had to settle for three months out of the year. And he loved every minute of it. He was already looking forward to January next year. Allan lifted the pole and swung the line through the air and into the canal. He was hoping to see a few dolphins as they swam by, like he usually did here at sunrise.

The sun was peeking over the horizon now and Allan closed his eyes and enjoyed the rays of sun hitting his face. He wasn't looking forward to going back up north to the cold again. Life up there simply wasn't as pleasant as it was down here. This was Allan's small slice of paradise. At least it had been, until this day when his fishing line suddenly tightened and Allan sprang for it to reel in whatever he had caught.

Maybe it's another bonnet-head. It sure is heavy! Maybe it's even bigger than the last time?

As Allan tried to pull the fish in, he became aware of his own weakness and started worrying he might lose his catch. He called for the other fishermen to help. Soon, there were three big heavy men reeling the fish in.

"This is huge!" one of them said with a groan.

Allan smiled, thinking it would be the perfect way to end the season...with the biggest catch of his life. Allan couldn't stop smiling until they pulled again and something came into sight above the wooden railing.

It almost sounded like it was planned, like it had been rehearsed, when all three fishermen gasped in unison at the sight of the long blonde hair.

59

March 2015

I GOT the call when I was sitting on the deck of my parents' motel eating breakfast. Shannon still didn't want to leave the condo, so it was just me and the kids. Well, except for Emily, who wanted to sleep in, and, as usual, wasn't hungry. Shannon's sister Kristi had told me she was coming over today to spend time with Shannon and Angela. She had helped out a lot, keeping an eye on Shannon for me when I had to work or couldn't be with her for some other reason.

"Did not," Austin said.

"You did too," Abigail said.

"No, I didn't," Austin said.

"Daaad. Austin's lying," Abigail said.

I sighed with a smile and sipped my coffee. I looked at my beautiful twins. No one could hate each other and no one could love each other as much as those two. Now Austin pulled Abigail's ponytail and she let out a wail.

"Hey, you two," my mom said as she brought out more waffles. She looked at me. "You're just going to let them act like this?"

I chuckled. "They'll figure it out," I said, finishing my coffee.

My mom scoffed. "You're too weak, Jack. You need to be harder on them."

I looked at her. No one spoiled those kids more than she did. She was the last person to say anything. Yet she still was on my case constantly about how I brought them up. I guess she was just worried, since they didn't have a mother, and in her opinion, a mother was by far the most important person in a child's life. I hoped to prove her wrong. I had to believe that a dad could do this alone.

My phone was ringing in my pocket and I got up to take it, kissed my mom on the cheek, and went inside.

"Ryder."

"Ron here. Sorry to disturb you on a Sunday, but we just pulled a corpse out of the canal in Cape Canaveral."

I looked at my family sitting on the deck in the sunlight. I had hoped to spend the day with them for once. The twins had been on my case lately for not being home enough. Even though they loved their grandparents, they still needed to spend time with their dad. At least, that's how Abigail explained it to me. I missed them too. I missed hanging out with them and with my parents as well. I wasn't going to have them around forever. Chances were it was a suicide, a jumper from one of the cruise ships, or a drunkard who fell in last night. It didn't sound like it was my field. Still, I had to be there. Any suspicious death was my area. Sunday or no Sunday.

"I'll be right there," I said.

I hung up and looked at my beautiful family. Abigail stuck her tongue out at her brother. Austin made an ugly face at her in return. I chuckled when Abigail's eyes met mine. I approached them.

"Not again?" she said, reading my face.

"I'm sorry," I said. "Duty calls. You know how it is. It's my job..."

"To catch the bad guys, yes, I know," she said with an angry frown. She crossed her arms in front of her chest. "You promised you'd take me surfing. I wanted to show you how much I have learned at camp."

I sighed. "I know, sweetie. Believe me, I would much rather be out in the water surfing with you than going to Cape Canaveral, but I have to."

"And what about Austin?" she said, pointing at her brother. "You promised you would go fishing with him. You know how much he loves to fish."

I looked at Austin, who avoided my eyes. He never was one to complain. Abigail did that for him.

"I'm sorry, buddy," I said. "Maybe grandpa can help you set the poles up? He's an excellent fisherman, you know."

"I know," Austin said. He forced a smile, trying hard to not let me know how sad he was. I could see it on his face he was disappointed. Sunday was our day together as a family.

"He never spends any time alone with you, Dad," Abigail said. "He needs a father figure. You're his role model."

I looked at my six year-old daughter. Where did she learn stuff like that?

"It's okay," Austin said and patted me on my arm.

"Just go, Jack," my mom said. "We'll take care of it."

I felt awful leaving them all like this. I had promised to fix the sink in one of the rooms at the motel and to paint the upstairs deck as well. There simply weren't enough hours in the day to make everybody happy.

60

March 2015

"So, what do we have?" I asked Ron, as I parked the Jeep at the jetty and walked with him towards the scene. The area had been blocked and a huge crowd of spectators had gathered behind the police tape. It was Sunday, usually the busiest day for the park and the jetty. There was a camping area right out to the canals and a big playground with a picnic area where people grilled and spent their Sunday afternoon with their families.

"A girl. Early twenties. She was pulled out of the water by three fishermen this morning. It looks like she drowned."

We walked under the tape and onto the jetty. I nodded to a couple of technicians that I knew from earlier crime scenes.

"So, why am I here? Sounds like an accident or suicide?"

We approached the body, which was still lying on the jetty where it had been pulled out of the water. Her skin was as pale as her blonde hair. Yamilla Díez was sitting bent over her.

"You're here, Ryder," she answered, "because she was heavily beaten before she fell or was thrown in the water, where she drowned."

I froze when I saw the face of the girl.

"We don't know who she is yet," Ron said. "She didn't have any identification on her body."

"But I do," I said. "I know her."

"You do?"

"She's one of the girls staying at my parents' motel. They're a flock of spring breakers. I gave some of them surf lessons."

I felt sick to my stomach looking at the young girl. I remembered her from the beach when the girl Katie had lost her bikini top. She was one of the girls who had laughed.

"Talk to me about the beating," I said with interest. I kneeled next to the body, while Yamilla went through what she had found so far for me. "She has taken some blows to the body and the right cheek here has a subcutaneous bleed as well in the musculature. You see, here and here there's bleeding under the skin that occurs from broken blood vessels. She also took some blows to the chin and nose. The bruise on the chin looks like she was hit with something hard."

"So, what you're saying is, she was beaten, then thrown into the water?" I asked.

"That's what I believe, yes. Might have been a fight. Maybe the other person took some beating as well, but looking at her fists and knuckles, I hardly believe this girl managed to defend herself much."

I looked down the canal. "If she was thrown in the water, then the current must have brought her down here before the fisherman got his hook in her."

Ron stood beside me. "You're thinking she was attacked while she was at one of those restaurants or bars further down the canal?"

"She's a spring breaker on the last weekend of her vacation. I believe Grill's had open bar for girls last night. She gets drunk and meets her attacker. He rapes her, beats her up, and throws her in the water afterwards." I looked at Ron. "If you visit the bars, then I'll go back to the motel and talk to her friends. I need to contact this girl's family right away."

Ron put a hand on my shoulder. It was tough to look at this girl, the same girl I had seen at my parents' motel so many times the past week. She was not more than a few years older than Emily...killed on a joyful night in town while on spring break. I had a terrible feeling about this.

61

March 2015

"WHAT DO you mean Britney is dead?"

The three other girls staying in the room were barely awake when I knocked on their door and told them what had happened. Leanne, the tall redhead who I always saw Britney with looked at me like I was lying to her.

"We were just with her last night?" Leanne had tears in her eyes. They all did, except Katie.

"So, you were all out last night?" I asked.

They looked at each other, then at Katie, who was still sitting in her bed under the covers. "Well, we were. Katie stayed here."

"I...I wasn't in the mood for partying," she said.

I noted it on my pad, then looked at the two other girls. "So, the rest of you, Leanne, Irene, and Britney, you all went out? What time did you leave the motel?"

"We..." Leanne looked down. She looked guilty of something. Irene and Katie both avoided looking at me as well. Something was very fishy.

"We left around six to go to dinner at The Lobster Shanty," Irene said.

"And was that all of you?" I asked.

Leanne shed a tear and wiped it off.

"We have to tell him everything," Irene said.

Leanne hissed. "I know. I know." Leanne's face suddenly twisted into an expression of fury as abrupt as a gust of strong wind. "It was just Irene, Britney, and me. Katie stayed at the motel." Leanne stared at Katie, like she was waiting for her to say something.

Katie didn't seem to be feeling well. "Why didn't you go to dinner with the others?" I asked.

"I...I wasn't hungry."

I didn't quite believe her. Something was definitely wrong here.

"She had a date," Irene said. "She was going to meet up with one of the boys, with Greg. They were going to watch the moonrise."

I made notes on my pad.

"How do you know about that?" Katie asked. She sounded angry and hurtful at the same time.

"Because..." Irene looked at Leanne, who didn't seem to want to take part in the conversation. "Because...well, it wasn't exactly Greg who sent you that text and asked you to meet with him."

"Who was it then?" Katie asked. She was the one sounding angry now.

"Britney," Leanne answered.

"She borrowed Greg's phone and sent the text earlier in the afternoon, then deleted the texts afterwards," Irene said. "She asked Greg to meet her there, at the spot where you thought you were going to meet him. She told him she would give him a blowjob, no strings attached. No boy would ever say no to that, right? But it was all a show. A show meant for you to see as you came down there thinking..." Irene stopped. She had made her point.

Katie had tears in her eyes. "So, she did this to me to hurt me?"

I was getting a clearer picture of what was going on now. "So, if I'm getting this right, you came down to meet this Greg and found Britney...found him with her instead?" I asked.

Katie tightened her lips, and then nodded.

"Alright," I said and noted it. "So, Britney was with Greg, then what happened?"

"We stayed at the Lobster Shanty and had some drinks, then Britney came there and told us what she had done," Irene said. "I want you to know, she never told us what she intended to do; we knew nothing until after it was done," she said, addressed to Katie. "If I had known, I wouldn't have been in on it."

"So, Britney came to the restaurant and then what did you do?" I asked.

"We grabbed a taxi and went to the port. We started at Milliken's and ended at Grill's, where we could drink for free all night," Irene continued.

"Who did she talk to during the night?" I asked.

"She talked to a lot of guys. Britney always talks to everyone."

"Why didn't you come home together?" I asked.

"It was getting late," Leanne said. "We wanted to get a taxi home, but Britney wanted to party some more. She was dancing outside on the deck by the water with some guy and told us to just leave. She said she would come home later. We were tired and thought the place was getting boring, so we left."

"So, the last time you saw her, she was dancing on the deck at Grill's?" I asked.

They both nodded. Leanne sniffled and wiped her eyes, not caring that her mascara was smeared. It looked like it was left over from the night before anyway. I turned and looked at Katie. I didn't like this story one bit.

"So, what did you do while they were all out partying?" I asked.

Katie looked at me with wide eyes. "I...I was just here. Asleep."

"Did anyone see you? Were you with anybody?" I asked.

Katie shook her head. The two other girls looked at her. The tension was thick in the room. It didn't take a mind reader to know what the two other girls were thinking. I had no idea what to believe. The girl had a strong motive. What Britney had done to her was really bad, but would she be capable of killing her? I had my doubts.

On the other hand, anger and jealousy were hard to control even if you wanted to.

"I need to have Britney's personal information so I can contact her family. What was her last name?"

"Foster," Leanne said. "Her mom lives in North Carolina."

I wrote it down, thinking I had heard that name somewhere before. "Good. Thanks." I got up from the edge of Britney's bed where I had been sitting. "No one touches any of Britney's things. I'll have to have our technicians go through her belongings. I'll ask my parents to give you a new room."

"But, we're going home today anyway?" Katie said.

"Yeah, spring break ends today. We have classes tomorrow," Leanne said. "We're driving home today."

I shook my head. "No, you're not. I'm going to have to ask you to stay for a little longer. We need you here for the investigation. All of you."

62

March 2015

STANLEY WAS ON THE MOVE. Both of his legs could hardly move, but he did it anyway. He had to. This was his chance to escape this hellhole once and for all. He stumbled towards the door, left slightly ajar, and then managed to pull his hurting body into the hallway. He couldn't believe it. He was out of the room. As he passed the door next to his, he heard the voice of someone crying behind it. It sounded like Roy, the guy he had spoken to through the walls in the bathroom. He was begging and pleading.

"Please, stop. I can't eat anymore!"

Stanley had wanted to help Roy out, but now realized his guardian was in there feeding Roy right now, so there was no way he could save him. He had to think about himself. He dragged his painful body down the hallway and finally reached a set of stairs. He almost cried when he saw the ray of sunlight coming through the entrance door at the bottom of the stairs. Stanley thought about Elyse and wondered if the girl was somewhere in the house as well, but then decided he would have to come back for her. He couldn't do this on his own. He had to get ahold of the police somehow. The police would be able to help. It was the only way.

Stanley held onto the railing as he dragged his hurting legs down the stairs, resisting the temptation to scream out loud in pain. He panted and used all of his strength and finally managed to get himself to the bottom of the stairs. He was crying in pain as he stopped to catch his breath. In front of him he could see the daylight through the frosted glass of the front doors.

Freedom. Wonderful, beautiful freedom.

Stanley drew in a deep breath. The smell of freshly cooked food filled his nostrils and he felt like throwing up. If he ever made it out of there, he wasn't going to eat again. Never again. Stanley moved as quietly as possible, making sure his guardian wouldn't hear him upstairs. But Roy was making an awful lot of noise up there, so chances were, no one could hear a thing.

At least that's what he thought. Stanley hadn't exactly accounted for the fact that maybe, maybe there were more people in the house.

"Stop right there," a voice said behind his back.

Stanley froze. All hope was sucked right out of him as he turned and looked into the barrel of a gun.

Damn it.

"Where do you think you're going?" the voice said.

Stanley drew in a deep breath. All this pain. All this...for nothing? No. No. No. He wasn't going to take it. Not anymore. He was done.

"You haven't eaten yet," the voice said.

"I can't...I can't..." He looked down the barrel of the gun, then felt the anger rise like a wave in the ocean.

NO MORE!

"I'm afraid I can't stay for dinner," he said. Grabbing an umbrella leaning against the wall next to him, he slammed it into the person with the gun, forcing both the person and the gun to fall to the ground and slide across the tiles. Then, he sprang for the doors. He grabbed the handles and pulled both open at the same time. He limped heavily, but the prospect of feeling freedom again gave him strength and made him push through the pain. The smell of fresh air without a hint of fried chicken in it gave him the last push he needed to make it into the front yard of the house.

63

March 2015

BRITNEY'S MOTHER flew down immediately from North Carolina and was at the ME's office in the early afternoon. I made sure two officers from our department picked her up at the airport in Orlando and got her to me in a hurry. I had told her over the phone that we believed something had happened to her daughter and we needed her to come down for identification.

I greeted her as she stepped inside. She was a small delicate woman who looked like she had led a hard life. I could sense she was very fragile, and I tried to break things to her gently.

"Maggie Foster," she said, as I shook her hand. It was at that moment, when she said her name out loud that it occurred to me where I had heard that name before. I stared at her for a few seconds, while trying to get the pieces to fit together. They still didn't.

"Let's go inside," Yamilla said and helped Maggie Foster in.

The identification didn't take long. Maggie Foster took one look at the body and then burst into tears. I grabbed her as she was about to fall when she turned away to cry.

"Yes," she said through tears. "Yes, that's her."

"Thanks, Yamilla," I said, and helped Mrs. Foster get out of the

ME's office. There was no reason to stay any longer. I drove Mrs. Foster back to the Sheriff's Office and poured her some water and a cup of coffee. I borrowed Ron's office for our talk. I let her cry for a little while, let the news settle in before I started asking my questions. It was always a delicate moment when interrogating a victim's relatives. It was important to do it as fast as possible while everything was fresh in their memory, but I still had to consider their emotions and the rollercoaster they were going through. It wasn't an easy task. Luckily for me, Mrs. Foster opened the conversation herself.

"Who?" she asked and looked at me for answer. "Who would do such a terrible thing?"

I shrugged. "We don't know yet, Mrs. Foster. But that's what I am hoping to find out as soon as possible. Now, tell me, I have to ask, your name. I remember it from another investigation that we recently took a look at. It could be a coincidence, since it took place in Boca Raton, north of Miami, but are you the same Maggie Foster that witnessed and gave your statement after the shooting in the cinema in 2009?"

Maggie Foster went pale. "Yes," she said with surprise in her voice. "We used to live in Boca. After the shooting, I went back to my family in North Carolina. I lost my husband that evening. My daughter, Britney was seriously injured when she was shot in the arm. I had to get away. There was no way I could stay."

A million thoughts flickered through my mind as I looked at Mrs. Foster in front of me. This could hardly be a coincidence, could it? But how on earth was this connected? The killing of Britney? Was that connected to the shooting at the country festival?

Maggie Foster suddenly looked at me with wide open eyes. "You don't think...oh, my God," she said. She looked like she remembered something. Then she clasped her mouth.

"What?" I asked.

"She called me last night. I suddenly remember. There is nothing unusual in her calling; we talk almost every day, but she said something."

"What did she say?" I asked.

"She told me she believed she had seen the killer in Cocoa Beach. She had seen the shooter in Publix, she told me. She said she wanted to go to the police and tell them the next day...that is today, before they left town. She was so uneasy, because she knew the guy that was initially called out as the killer, the guy that had killed himself and that all the media said was the shooter...she knew that it wasn't him. She knew because she had looked into the eyes of the killer. Right before she was shot, right before her dad was killed. She never told anyone except me. And I didn't believe her. I told her it was nonsense. I was certain it was him and that it was all over. That's what the police told us. It had to be the truth, right? Maybe I just really wanted to believe it. I couldn't stand the thought of him not being caught, of the shooter possibly still being out there. All those years, I refused to believe her. Even last night. I told her she had to give it up. It was over; it was history. I begged her stop ripping up the past. Still, she kept going on about it. How the police had it all wrong. How they had blamed the wrong guy. She knew it could never be him, because the shooter wasn't a he. It was a she."

64

March 2015

COULD OUR SHOOTER BE FEMALE? I found it hard to believe. Usually, shooters in mass shootings were Caucasian males with a death wish. Mass murderers were often characterized as isolated individuals that, over time, had built up aggression towards the society they felt disconnected from.

It did make a lot of sense when I thought it through. Many things about the shootings at the cinema and at the country festival were so different from other mass shootings. There was something about both incidents that rubbed me the wrong way. It didn't seem like the shooter wanted to kill a lot of people. There had been fifteen people in the movie theater; eight were hit and four of them died. With around forty thousand present at the concert, it was quite lucky that only two had been hit. Two certainly weren't many, considering how many people had been there. It was still two too many, but it wasn't a lot.

"Tell me more about the shooting in '09," I said to Maggie Foster. I sensed the memory of what happened back then made her feel very uncomfortable, but I had to know more.

She shrugged. "I don't know if there is much more to tell, other than what I told back then."

I kept thinking about the emails that Shannon had received from the alleged killer. *I'm so sorry. It had to be done,* all of them said. What did this killer mean by that? Why did it have to be done?

"There is one thing that always struck me as odd," Maggie Foster said.

"And what is that?"

"I don't know...maybe it's just silly..." she turned her head away.

I looked at her. "No. Anything will be of help at this point. Please. Continue."

She looked up. Our eyes met. "It's just that...I mean, it may not be important, but we knew all of the others."

"What others?" I asked.

"The three others that were shot in the cinema. I knew them. They weren't our friends, but I knew who they were. It might be a coincidence, but..."

"It might not be. How did you know them?"

"From Britney's school. They all had kids that went to Klein's Jewish Academy. I didn't think about it until afterwards, when Britney told me they had talked about it in class."

"Were all the kids the same age?" I asked.

"No, they were different age groups."

I wrote it all down on my notepad, wondering if we were looking at an anti-Semitic motive.

Maggie Foster looked pensive again. "I wonder..." She paused and looked at me while biting her lip. "It was odd. I don't think we ever mentioned it to the police back then, but...now I wonder if it wasn't only us."

"Only you that what?" I asked.

She tilted her head. "Only us that won those tickets."

"Won the tickets? I don't follow."

"We received a letter in the mail stating we had won tickets to the movie theater to see the newest Disney movie. It was at a lottery at the school. I didn't mention it to the police before, since I didn't think it was important, but now I get the feeling it might be."

I leaned back in Ron's chair and looked at Maggie Foster. There was definitely something there worth moving on with. It felt like we were getting closer now. I still just couldn't quite connect the dots, but I did remember Shannon told me someone had sent a backstage ticket to Joe in the mail and that he thought it was from Shannon, that she had wanted him to be there. It occurred to me the victims might not have been random. I had long had a feeling that neither of the two episodes had been mass shootings. Now it seemed crystal clear to me; they were very thoroughly well-planned killings. This killer liquidated her victims in public, in places she was certain we would see it happen. It was her signature. This killer was making a statement. Like most serial killers, she wanted us to know. And she wanted us to know there were going to be more.

65

April 2009

It DIDN'T TAKE the doctors long to get Elizabeth diagnosed. Through genetic testing, they were able to get the proof that Elizabeth, in fact, had Prader-Willi syndrome, and that was what caused her to eat insatiably and gain weight rapidly, and it explained her behavioral issues as well. It was all very comforting for Dottie to finally be able to put words to her daughter's illness and stop blaming herself. There was no cure for it, the doctors told her, but they did start a treatment with a prescription of daily recombinant growth hormone injections. The growth hormone would support linear growth and increase Elizabeth's muscle mass, and hopefully lessen her food preoccupation and weight gain. At least, that was what the doctors hoped.

And so did Dottie.

It had been years since she felt this relieved, and soon after the treatments started, she could already see an improvement in her daughter. She would still scream for food most hours of the day, but she suddenly seemed to be interested in other things as well. She started reading books while waiting for the next meal to be served, and somehow the books took her away from the constant cravings.

Dottie had learned to keep an eye on her constantly and was better now at limiting her food intake...now that she understood it was a disease and that she wasn't being evil or punishing her when not giving her food whenever she craved it. Dottie started buying healthier food and was very strict with the amount of food her daughter got at each meal, no matter how much her daughter cried. The doctor had helped her find a nutritionist, who knew about the diagnosis, and knew how to handle patients with Prader-Willi Syndrome. Dottie knew if she followed her schedule, it would help her daughter, and that made it easier to be strict about it and endure the screaming fits Elizabeth threw whenever she was denied food.

It was like she had regained some control in her life, and it felt good.

James had moved in with his new girlfriend, and even though Dottie hated the whole situation, and especially this young girl James had chosen in exchange for Dottie, she had decided to accept that this was how things were now...this was their new reality. James had asked to get to see the girls every other weekend, and up until now, Dottie had let him have the three older ones, but kept Elizabeth with her. This weekend was the first time she had agreed to let Elizabeth spend the night at her father's new place, and she was terrified. Dottie had never been away from Elizabeth more than the few hours she was in school every day, and certainly never at night. So, naturally, she was anxious when she packed Elizabeth's overnight bag and made sure her medicine was in there as well.

"Her injections are in the backpack," she said, as she handed over all four girls. "Don't forget to keep an eye on her at all times."

James rolled his eyes. "Take it easy, Dottie. She's my daughter too, you know. I know how to take care of her."

Dottie wasn't so sure he was right. He had refused to acknowledge that Elizabeth had a disease, a syndrome that made her the way she was. When Dottie had told him about the diagnosis, he had laughed out loud on the phone.

"This is what we've come to now? A diagnosis for those who can't control themselves? That is exactly what is wrong with this country. We have a diagnosis for everything. Sometimes people just eat too much, Dottie. That's all there is to it."

His reaction had been part of the reason why Dottie hadn't let Elizabeth spend the night at her father's until now. But he had agreed to give her the injections and make sure she followed her diet. It was, after all, just for a weekend. How much could go wrong in just one weekend?

66

March 2015

"We're looking for a woman."

I threw a glare around the room. Richard and Ron both looked at me. Ann and Duncan were out.

"Say what again?" Richard asked.

Ron was eating a sandwich while standing by the water cooler. He stopped chewing.

"It looks like the shooting in Miami and the shooting at the festival might have been committed by a woman," I said.

"A female mass shooter?" Ron said. "That's rare."

"That's the other thing," I said. "I'm not sure I believe they were mass shootings anymore. Not the traditional kind, that is. I believe she chose her victims deliberately and killed them, then covered it up as a mass shooting...making it more spectacular."

"So, you're thinking it's a serial killer?" Ron asked. He had started chewing again and washed the bite down with his soda.

"That's exactly what I'm thinking."

"And what about the murder of the young girl this morning?" Richard asked. "I thought that was what we were working on? Am I the only one who is a little bit confused here?"

Ron shook his head. "I was lost long ago."

"I think it might all be connected," I said and sat down at my desk. "See, Britney was at the shooting in '09. She was shot in the arm and her dad was killed. She saw the killer. Her mother told us she spotted her here in Cocoa Beach, at Publix of all places."

"So, you think she was killed because she could identify the shooter?" Richard asked.

I nodded. "All this time, we've been looking for a man, and that made the best cover for this killer. If Britney spilled the beans, she would no longer be able to walk around in public. For six years, she has been able to hide without having to go underground while planning the next attack."

"So, how do we catch her now?" Richard asked.

"I have several things we can check up on. First of all, I want you to call all shooting ranges in the area. There was a distinct difference between the attack in '09 and the one this month. The shooter didn't know how to shoot back then, but she does now. It's my theory that she never meant to hit all the other people, and especially the children present in the movie theater, but she hadn't accounted for the fact that she didn't know how to control a firearm like that, and she didn't think about the fact that a bullet ricochets when it hits a wall or a ceiling. That's why we haven't heard from her for so long. She never meant for this many people to get hurt. She just wanted to shoot the people she had planned, and then get out. But more were hit by bullets and that wasn't the plan. She has spent the last several years getting ready, preparing herself for the next kill by taking shooting lessons. She didn't want anything to go wrong this time. Up until now, I had thought that Joe Harrison was just a coincidental kill, that he got in the shooter's way somehow, but I don't think that anymore. I think she killed him deliberately; it was planned. He was sent a ticket, so she'd be sure where to find him after shooting Phillip Hagerty in the crowd. That's where you come in again, Richard. I need you to take a look at Joe and Phillip. What do they have in common? Can we find a link between those two, and maybe even a link between them and the four that were murdered six years ago in the movie theater, then I believe we'll find our killer. I need background info, everything we have on all the victims."

I stopped to breathe, when suddenly, all the phones rang in the office at once. That was never a good sign. Something was up.

67

March 2015

SHANNON HADN'T HAD a drink in several days now and she felt terrible. She had been cooped up inside of that condo for so many days it was starting to drive her nuts. Even though Jack and Kristi did come by almost every day to be with her and bring groceries and occasionally cook for her, it just wasn't the same as feeling the fresh air on your skin or breathing in the salty sea breeze. She opened the windows now and then, but then the photographers took pictures, and she didn't want that.

Weren't they getting tired of this by now? Apparently not. The story was still everywhere, and it made Shannon so angry and miserable. Angela was going back to school after spring break tomorrow and Shannon was looking forward to that. She knew her daughter would probably have to hear a lot about her mother and Shannon feared it would be rough for her. But she would have to get by. They all had to.

"Mommy, can you help me?" she said, coming out from her bedroom with a brush stuck in her hair. She looked so adorable with her hair all tangled up, Shannon had to laugh.

"Let me fix it," she said and grabbed the brush.

Angela whined. "Ouch, you're hurting me."

"Sorry, baby, but this is really stuck. How on earth did you get it so stuck in your hair?"

Angela shrugged. "I don't know. I just tried to brush it."

Shannon sighed and tried to untangle the brush. She felt frustrated, and the more she pulled on it, the more Angela whined. Shannon's hands couldn't stop shaking and it bothered her. Why couldn't they simply keep still? Why did she have to feel this unease inside of her constantly, this anxiety, this feeling that something was about to happen, something really bad that would once again crash her entire world? It was like she had stopped trusting the world, like she was constantly expecting terrible things to happen for her. She hated the feeling that she couldn't do anything right in this life. She felt like a child because people had to take care of her the way they did. She hated it. She wanted to take care of herself, of her daughter...she wanted to...she wanted to *get this damn brush out of her daughter's hair!*

"Mom. You're hurting me," Angela screamed. "Mooom."

Shannon let go with a sigh. "I can't do it," she said. "I simply can't do it. I can't do anything right."

Angela stared at her mother. "Yes, you can. You're the best mommy in the world."

Shannon shed a tear, then hugged her daughter. "Thank you, sweetie. I don't feel like I am right now."

"Maybe we should just get the scissors, "Angela said, hugged her mother, and then sprang to get them from the kitchen.

Shannon sighed with relief. Angela was right. There was always a solution to the problems. Always. It didn't have to all be bad. So what if she lost a lock of her hair? It would grow out. So what if the media wrote all those things about her? They would stop when someone else got in trouble. They would forget about Shannon eventually. The fans would forgive her. Wouldn't they? Of course they would. They loved her.

Shannon stared at her computer on the dresser by the wall. She hadn't opened it for many days. She didn't dare to read what they wrote about her on Facebook and Twitter. People could be so mean.

This too shall pass. Like everything else, it will pass.

Angela returned with the scissors and Shannon cut the brush free from her hair, thinking it was all going to get better soon. It had to. She was going to be all right...they were going to be all right, when her phone rang. Shannon looked at the display. She knew the number. It was her lawyer. She let go of her daughter and grabbed it.

"They found it, Shannon," her lawyer said. "They found the body."

Shannon closed her eyes. Her heart was already pounding in her chest. "And the gun? Did they find the gun?"

Her lawyer went quiet.

Uh-Oh. Quiet isn't good. It's definitely not good.

"I'm sorry, Shannon. They didn't."

68

March 2015

I PUT the siren on as we headed down A1A. Ron was driving. Cars stopped when they heard us and pulled over to let us pass. I was confused as I watched Patrick's Air Force Base go by my window. The call we had received was from the Indian Harbor Police Department. Minutes later, we met Sergeant Bill Gray in front of the gate to Lansing Island. He came out of the small booth as we drove up to the closed boom.

"Where is he?" I asked, as I jumped out of the car.

"He's in here," Bill said and pointed inside of the booth. I looked inside and spotted a man sitting in the chair. The guard stood next to him.

"He keeps saying the same thing over and over again," Bill continued.

"And you're sure he is Stanley Bradley? The same person that was reported missing earlier this month?" Ron asked.

"That's what he tells us," the guard said. "We found him lying in the street inside the community, yelling and screaming. One of the neighbors called for me. I have no idea how he even got inside. He's not on any lists of visitors."

The case had been on Ron's desk for quite some time now. A middle-aged man had gone missing on his way back from Disney World with his granddaughter. The car had been found lying in the ditch off 528 from Orlando by the ramp leading to Cape Canaveral. The two tires on the front wheels had been punctured. When the fire truck arrived, they had only found the granddaughter in the car. She had been unconscious and taken to the hospital. No one knew where the grandfather had disappeared to. Until now.

"Stanley Bradley?" I asked and showed him my badge. "I am Detective Jack Ryder. What happened to you?"

"You need to get my granddaughter," he yelled. "You've got to save her. She's back there."

"As far as I know, your granddaughter is with her mother," Ron said. "She is safe."

"She was the only one they found in your car," I said.

Stanley Bradley looked baffled. "But...but...I thought..." Stanley paused as something settled in him. "They lied to me?"

"Who are they?" I asked. "What happened to you?"

Stanley looked at me. His eyes flickered in desperation. "There are more back there. Roy is there. You've got to help Roy. They're going to kill him."

"Who is Roy?" I asked.

"I don't know. But I talked to him through the wall. He is in danger. You've got to get him out of there."

"Slow down a little, Stanley. Please, answer me this. What happened to you?"

"I was taken. Kidnapped. Held prisoner by this awful woman who kept feeding me, forcing food into my mouth. She did this to me," he said and showed me his legs. They were bleeding heavily from deep wounds and one was badly infected. "She hurt me with a fire poker. So I wouldn't leave. She kept me there for a long time."

"You say she was force-feeding you?"

"Yes."

"And, you say she has more kidnapped people she's keeping

there?" I said, as my hand landed on the shaft of my gun. If I was right, then we had found Daniel Millman and James West's killer.

"Bill, you stay here with Stanley while Jack and I check this out," Ron said and looked at me.

"Better call for an ambulance," I said. "Stanley here needs medical attention. What house did she keep you in?"

"I...I don't know, to be honest," Stanley said.

"I picked him up outside number 222," the guard said.

"It was a gray house," Stanley said. "That much I saw when I got out. It was big. And had big colored windows on the front."

I wondered if we should just take him with us, but I feared for his safety. Besides, he needed to go to the hospital with those legs as soon as possible. No, we had to find the house on our own. I had a feeling it wouldn't be too hard. I had a very good idea who it was we were looking for. Number 219 was awfully close to 222.

69

March 2015

SHE WAS SITTING in the bedroom when she saw him. He wasn't alone. He was with the sheriff. They were running up the street when she found them in the gun's sight.

Bingo!

This time on a Sunday, the streets were usually filled with the children of the gated community, riding their bikes, playing ball, and so it was today as well. As the two officers came running up the street, they told the kids to get inside their houses, and soon the street was cleared.

"I really don't want to have to do this, Detective," she mumbled, as she followed Jack Ryder's every move towards the house. "I am so sorry."

Her eyes drifted across the street towards number 221. The bedroom where they would find the body was the third window to the left. The shooter's heart was starting to pump rapidly now.

One mistake, one wrong move, and it would all be over. She couldn't afford to miss. That's what her teacher at the shooting range in Melbourne had told her over and over again, as she went there every Saturday and practiced her aim.

"If that burglar enters your house and you have him cornered, you only get one chance. You can't miss."

The shooter hadn't missed one shot since that night at the movie theater in Boca Raton. Not one accident. It had been hell for her, knowing all those kids had been hit by bullets. She had realized she had no idea what she was doing. Everything else had been so well planned out. Covering it all up as a mass shooting was brilliant, she thought. It had been her own idea. Inviting the bastards to the same movie theater and getting rid of them all at once, then disappearing. It was the perfect plan. No one would think of her as the suspect. No one would know her motives for doing this before she let them know. She was in control.

But, it hadn't gone as she had planned...all those children that had been hit by stray bullets. It had haunted her for years afterwards. Luckily, none of them died. Only the ones she had wanted to die had died. In that way, it had been a success. But, she had to make sure it wouldn't go wrong the next time around. She couldn't afford it.

The second time, at the festival, everything had gone as planned. She had killed the two men she came for, and then slipped out easily before they managed to block the exits. And even if she hadn't made it out in time? Well, who would look for a gorgeous blonde woman in the prime of her life?

No one.

Then there was the truck. She had been one step ahead of them all this time. She hated that the female officer had to get hurt, but it had to be done. She had to be punished.

"I'm so terribly sorry," she whispered softly.

The killer cocked the gun and followed the two men as they ran up the driveway towards her house, then stopped, looking confused. The handsome one with curly hair pointed at the house across the street. They spoke for a second, then walked across the street.

The killer watched as the detective took out his gun and knocked on the door to the gray house.

"That's it, my little children," she mumbled. "Follow the trail of bread to find the house of candy. Follow the yellow brick road. See what awaits you on the other side of the rainbow."

She sighed and prepared herself. She really hated that she had to do this. She really did.

70

March 2015

I HAD BEEN MISTAKEN. We realized it as we walked up towards number 219 where, Mrs. Millman lived, that it was the wrong house. The only gray house on the street was number 221. I was confused as we made the realization standing in the driveway of Mrs. Millman's house. I had been so certain it was her. I was so sure she was the one we were looking for, that she had killed her husband and maybe James West.

But I had been wrong.

Across the street from her house was the gray house with the big colored windows as Stanley Bradley had described it to us. It was the only one of its kind on this street. There was no doubt about it. It had to be it.

We walked up and I grabbed my gun right before I knocked on the door. There was no answer. I looked at Ron. He nodded. I grabbed the handle and realized the door was open. I walked inside with my gun first.

We had called for backup on our way, and I could hear sirens in the distance, but knew it would take a few minutes before they would be here. I wasn't sure we had minutes if we were going to catch this killer and hopefully save this Roy that Stanley had spoken about.

It was all a very strange story and I didn't like it.

"Hello?" I asked, as I opened the door.

"This is the sheriff," Ron yelled. "Anyone home?"

I walked into the kitchen, but found it empty. Tupperware containers, stacked in towers, with freshly made food inside of them filled the counters. The stove was still hot. A pan with fried chicken was still simmering. It had been turned off recently.

"Someone's expecting company," Ron said, when he looked at all the food.

"Or maybe they're staying over," I said and nodded at the stairs. We walked up with our weapons in front of us, then reached a long hallway with many doors. I opened one door and found a bedroom. It was empty. Then I found another and opened that one as well. Empty too, but someone had been sleeping in there recently. I guessed it might be the owner of the house. It was a big room with views of the river. The bed was a king and the sheets silk. I went through it and into the bathroom that looked big enough to fit my entire living room.

"No one here either."

"How many bedrooms does this place have?" Ron asked.

I walked to the next door, but found it locked. Ron and I exchanged one look before I kicked the door in and we walked inside. There was someone on the bed. The room stank. The air was confined and stuffy. Hardly any light came through the closed hurricane shutters.

"Police!" I yelled and walked up to the bed.

The person lying there didn't move. I hurried towards him. I felt sick. He was lying in his own vomit that had run across his pillow. His eyes stared into the ceiling and his face was frozen in a tortured grimace. It had been a painful death.

"Roy?" Ron asked.

I nodded. "I think so."

"I'll go make sure the rest of the house is secure," Ron said, and left while I looked at the body.

I touched his neck. It felt cold, the way dead people's skin felt when the blood hadn't circulated in it for a while. Livor mortis was starting to show on his skin. The blood had started to pool into the interstitial tissues of the body. It happened between twenty minutes to three hours after death occurred. It wasn't much yet. My guess was he had been dead for about half an hour. My other guess was that his stomach had burst. There were no signs of trauma to his body anywhere. Except for his legs, which were hurt in the same way Stanley Bradley's had been.

To make sure he couldn't leave.

Ron came back and told me we were clear. There was another room next to this where someone had been staying, but it was also empty. Ron called for a second ambulance and asked where *the hell that back up was*, while I opened the shutters to let in the light. I walked back to the bed and looked around, wondering if this was the way Daniel Millman had died, if he had been kept here right across the street from his own home, tortured by being force-fed till his stomach burst. I wondered who would be this sick in their mind, this twisted and brutal, and then I wondered why.

As I threw around a glare that ended at the window, I thought I saw something. Ron was still on the phone, and as he walked towards the window, my eye caught a small yellow spark coming from the window across the street. Before I could react, before I could scream at Ron to get down, the window splintered, and like the snap of a finger, Ron fell to the ground.

71

March 2015

"OFFICER DOWN. OFFICER DOWN!"

I screamed into the radio as I grabbed Ron in my arms. He had been hit in the shoulder and it was bleeding heavily. I tried to stop it by pressing my hand on it, then ripped some of the sheets from the bed into pieces and held them against the bleeding. Seconds later, the room was filled with paramedics, and I could let go of him.

I ran outside and towards number 219, where Mrs. Millman lived, where the shots had come from.

I had been right all along!

I kicked the door in and stormed into the hallway.

"Where are you?" I yelled like a mad man. I was a mad man. I was so angry, on the brink of exploding in anger. "Show yourself!"

That was when I heard an engine start. It coughed once or twice, then roared loudly.

The river!

Why hadn't I thought of it before? I ran through the living room out into the back, then passed the pool area, and ended up at the dock. In the distance, I watched as the speedboat disappeared. The sun was setting over the mainland and I wouldn't be able to keep track of it for long. I had to think fast. I couldn't let her get away with this. I couldn't let her disappear.

I looked around, then spotted a jet ski at the neighboring dock. I made a quick decision, as the sirens wailed in the street on the other side of the house. I ran across the yard, climbed the fence, and hoped they didn't have a dog or an alarm system. I jumped onto the Jet Ski and then realized I didn't have the key. I spotted a shed in the back, ran to it and opened it. On the wall inside was a small cupboard with three sets of keys hanging on it.

"Remind me to give these people a theft-precaution course," I mumbled, as I picked the one with Jet Ski written on it.

I jumped on the Jet Ski, put in the key and pushed away from the dock before I turned the engine on. Growing up in Florida, I knew the routine. The ski roared to life and I darted into the river in pursuit of the speedboat. I caught up on it pretty fast. I sped up and reached the back lower side of the speedboat, then realized I had no idea what I should do next.

"Police! Stop the boat!" I screamed through the wind, but the noise from the two engines drowned it out. "Mrs. Millman, stop the boat!"

I came up on the side and managed to yell the words through the noise, and she must have heard something, because the woman driving the boat turned her head and looked at me.

It wasn't Mrs. Millman.

It was a woman I had never seen before. The realization dazzled me, just enough to let down my guard for one second, one crucial second. Just enough for her to make her move. She pulled the wheel and maneuvered the boat in front of my jet ski and bumped into it. There was a loud crash and I was thrown into the air. Next thing I knew, I fell into the water, the deep dark water.

As I resurfaced, spluttering and splashing, I spotted the woman and the speedboat disappearing as darkness surrounded her as the sun finally set on the horizon.

72

March 2015

I couldn't believe I had lost her. The next morning, as I sat in the office and stared at my screen, I felt like such an idiot. It was like I couldn't get anything right lately. Ron and Beth were both in the hospital. Ron was doing better, they said. He had only been shot in the shoulder and would need a few weeks to recover, but he was going to be fine. Beth was another story. She was still unconscious and they didn't know if she was going to make it. I worried about her children. They were still with her neighbor, but I had a feeling they couldn't stay there for much longer. I had asked Richard to try and find Beth's relatives, a grandmother, something, anyone who could take care of the kids until she came back. If she came back. The thought made me sad. She had to get better. I couldn't bear losing another partner.

I had let Travis Goodman go, since I no longer believed he was our man. I had no idea how it was all connected yet, but had a feeling I was really close to figuring it all out.

Close, but no cigar, like my dad always used to say.

The kids had all gone back to school this morning and it felt good to have something go back to normal when everything else was chaotic. I hadn't spoken to Shannon since Sunday morning. The media was still occupying our condominium and I felt bad for her. I had spoken on the phone with her before I went to bed Sunday night and had told her everything. She had sounded tired and sad. It wasn't strange, since she was in a dire situation, now that they had found the body but no gun. I feared all hell could break loose any moment now. It was really bad for her.

I had gotten myself a coffee and sat at my desk, staring at the many files and papers, Richard had placed there. They were all profiles of the victims in the shooting cases. I stared at them without reading them, wondering about Stanley Bradley and the statement I had taken from him the night before. He had explained, in detail, how this woman had stuffed food into his mouth and threatened to kill his granddaughter if he didn't do as he was told. He had also told me something that had been very interesting.

There had been more than one.

He had seen the other one in the kitchen as he had escaped. She was the one who had been cooking the food, while the other was feeding the victims. Stanley had also spent the night at the hospital and I had planned to send over a sketcher to have a drawing made of these two women. I was certain they were still out there in this area. Mrs. Millman had disappeared from the face of the earth and I had sent her picture to the media in the hope she would show up. I had no idea if she was a part of all this or not, but the shots had been fired from her house, so she had to know something.

I looked at the papers, thinking it was so hard dealing with two cases at the same time. I kept getting them mixed up. I took out the file on the four victims from Boca Raton. Their children had all gone to the same school...that was the connection. Then, I picked up Phillip Hagerty's file and went through it. Phillip Hagerty had two children. They both went to Roosevelt like mine did. Then there was Joe Harrison. His daughter went to a private school in Nashville.

No, she didn't.

I frowned, then looked at it again. The information was wrong. It was old. Angela hadn't been at the school in Nashville for the past month. She had changed schools. She went to Roosevelt like most kids in our area did.

Theodore Roosevelt Elementary School.

"Oh, my God," I said.

Richard looked up from his screen. "What?"

"The killer, our female shooter, works at the school. Of course she does. She is a teacher. All we need to do is to find someone who recently transferred to Roosevelt from Klein's in Boca. That's it Richard! That's the connection."

"I'm on it."

73

March 2015

"I GOT A NAME," Richard said and got off the phone.

I lit up. Finally, we were getting somewhere. Richard approached my desk.

"Natalie Monahan. In 2010, she transferred from Klein's to Roosevelt," he said. "But she isn't a teacher. She's a school psychologist. And get this. I ran her name, she owns a house. She owns *the* house on Lansing Island, where Stanley Bradley and Roy Miller were being kept."

"You're kidding me, right? So, the two cases are connected?" I was blown away by this. I mean, the thought had somehow crossed my mind, especially when I found out the suspects were females in both cases, but I just didn't quite see how it was all fitting together. Who was doing what here? And why?

"The school said she didn't check in this morning and that they haven't heard from her, but I found her on Facebook," Richard said.

I walked to him and looked over his shoulder. I looked at the picture. She looked like the woman I had seen on the boat.

"That's her," I said. "She shot Ron. She was on the boat I followed. Print that picture and let's have it out everywhere." Richard was scrolling through her pictures when, suddenly, it dawned on me. "Stop there," I said. "Right there."

Richard stopped at the picture I had seen and made it big so I could see better. Four women standing in each other's arms, smiling, on a boat. The picture was from an older date. I looked down and saw the description.

TBT. MY SISTERS AND ME. THIS WAS TAKEN IN 2000. TRIP TO MIAMI ON A FRIEND'S BOAT. WERE WE EVER THIS YOUNG? LOVE YOU ALL FOREVER.

I pointed at one of the women. "That one right there. That's Mrs. Millman."

Richard looked closer.

"Take away fifteen years," I said, thinking of the picture we had sent out to the media of Mrs. Millman, with her neat dyed blonde hair. In this old picture, she was a brunette...gorgeous and without the bitterness that life had somehow given her later on. Even her eyes were smiling. It was so far from the sedated emotionless woman I had met with at her home.

"So, Mrs. Sarah Millman and Natalie Monahan are sisters?" Richard asked.

"Correct, Detective," I said with a grin. I was feeling uplifted all of a sudden. I hadn't fit the pieces completely yet, but we were getting there. We were on to something.

Richard printed a series of pictures and got busy putting together something we could give to the media. Meanwhile, I went back to my desk. I called the school in Boca Raton and asked them if they had kept the old files for students who visited the school psychologist in 2009. To my surprise, they had. They had them online and could send them to me. I told them the last names of the children I wanted, then waited half an hour before I received the email. I was quite surprised at the school's efficiency down there. I went down to Roosevelt and asked for the files of some of their children as well. It was a hunch, but I sensed I had to follow it. As I got back, I opened the files and went through them, one by one. All were written by the mysterious Natalie Monahan. It didn't take me long to find the connection between all of them. I made two phone calls to clear something up, then put the phone down as the picture became clearer and clearer to me. I didn't get to tell Richard before the phone rang and I had Weasel from Cocoa Beach on the other end.

"We found your woman," she said.

"Sarah Millman? Where?"

"She was speeding on 520 when Officer Hall pulled her over. He took her in. Recognized her right away."

"I'll be right down," I said and slammed the phone down.

"Good news?" Richard asked.

"Yes. Excellent news. Finally."

74

April 2009

JAMES WEST WAS SO HAPPY. He had all of his daughters over for a visit for the entire weekend. He had missed them all so much, ever since he left the house and his family.

And, this time, Elizabeth had come with them. She had come for the entire weekend for the first time, and James had been so thrilled to see her. Even his new girlfriend, Nicole, had liked her. At least she had pretended to, until Elizabeth threw her first fit and sat down on the floor screaming for food. That was when Nicole had told James he'd better take care of this before the guests arrived.

They were having a party. Nicole was the one who had invited people over, even though James was having the kids for the weekend. She didn't care much; she was only twenty-five and didn't understand what it meant to have kids. James was so in love he didn't care. He let her do whatever she wanted to...as long as she was happy. After all, it wasn't an easy task to have to endure another woman's four children, especially not when one of them was completely out of control like Elizabeth.

James knelt in front of her and tried to comfort her, but Elizabeth still screamed at the top of her lungs.

"I'm HUNGRYYYYY!"

Not knowing what else to do, James slapped her across her face. "Stop that, Elizabeth. You've got to stop that."

Elizabeth cried even louder, acting like a two year-old, hammering her fists into the floor while screaming and yelling that she was so hungry. James slapped her again, thinking this was what his own dad would have done, and it had worked on him as a child. Children shouldn't be in control; they shouldn't be the ones in charge, and Elizabeth had been given way too much liberty to act however she wished. He felt this was his chance to finally make things right with her. This was what should have been done a long time ago. So, he slapped her again.

The girl screamed and the doorbell rang. Nicole sprang for it and opened it for the caterers. When Elizabeth saw the trays of food being carried in, her eyes lit up.

"Food!" she shrieked.

"No!" Nicole yelled and looked at James. "She's not getting anywhere near this food. You hear me? This is for the guests. This is nice food. Expensive food."

James nodded and looked at Elizabeth, who was about to explode in excitement. What was he supposed to do? He couldn't call Dottie, because she would never let him have Elizabeth over again. He couldn't let Elizabeth run around the house on her own. She would only eat the food and Nicole would kill him.

James sighed. It wasn't easy making everyone happy. The three older girls were all getting dressed and were excited about the party that their cool new stepmom was throwing. They wouldn't be anywhere near their younger sister if they could avoid it. He couldn't do that to them. They were finally so happy to be at his place.

"Elizabeth?" he asked.

She looked at him through her tears, but never listened to what he had to say before she stormed into the kitchen and threw herself at the food.

"Noooo!" James yelled and ran after her. He grabbed her by the shoulder, but couldn't pull her almost three hundred pounds off the food.

Meanwhile, Nicole was screaming. "Stop her! James, get her away from the food."

James was yelling at her, hitting her back, trying to get her away, but nothing helped. She was stuffing her face with food.

"Elizabeth, stop! Stop!"

He looked at Nicole's terrified face, while his daughter gulped down the mushroom polenta and shrimps like she was eating popcorn at a movie theater.

"Do something, James!"

So, James had an idea. He knew it wasn't a good one right away, but at least it was something. He lured Elizabeth down to the basement, holding a bucket of ice cream in front of her face, and by promising her she would get it if she followed him. He gave her the bucket and a spoon and let her dig in, while he snuck up the stairs, closed the door, and locked it. He didn't feel good about it, but at least she was happy, now that she had her ice cream, and he would have the entire day with her tomorrow before she went back to her mother's.

"Is she under control?" Nicole asked, when he came back into the kitchen.

James nodded. "Everything is under control." It was hard for him to hide his embarrassment.

Nicole straightened her dress and made sure her hair was perfect. She sighed with relief. "Good. The guests will be here shortly."

James forced a smile. "Great. That's really great."

75

March 2015

"Where is your sister?"

I looked at Sarah Millman in front of me in the interrogation room at the Cocoa Beach Police Department. Sarah Millman looked like answering my questions was beneath her.

"Which one? I have three," she said.

"You know which one I'm looking for. Natalie. The one who shoots people and force-feeds her victims in her house across the street from yours. Or maybe that was you? I'm beginning to think it was you who killed your husband, after all. What about the others? Roy Miller? James West? Why did they have to die? And, what about Stanley Bradley?"

Sarah Millman laughed. "You don't know anything. You have no idea what you're talking about. And you never will."

"Then tell me, Goddammit. Tell me."

"I'm sorry, I can't. I couldn't betray my sisters like that."

"Your sisters? So, now you're saying that they're all in on it?" I asked.

"I didn't say that."

"Well, that's what I'm thinking. Here's how I think it went down. Your sister Natalie worked as a psychologist at the schools. She found the victims. They all had one thing in common. Their children were seeing Natalie on a regular basis because they had trouble at home. They all came from parents who were abusive or neglecting them somehow. It is the same for Don Foster and Brad Schmidt, who were among the four killed in Boca Raton, and it goes for the last two who died here as well. Phillip Hagerty had two children in Roosevelt, who both saw Natalie, and spoke to her about how their dad would come to their bedroom at night and ask them to get undressed. It was her latest case. The case should have been turned over to Social Services so it could be investigated, but it never was. Why? I'll tell you why. Because you and your sisters had a better way of dealing with these things, right?"

"Social Services never gets the work done. They have so many cases, they drown in them. They don't have the time to handle all of them," Sarah snorted. "The bastard deserved both of those bullets, and you know it."

I leaned back in the chair. Sarah Millman was finally talking. "When did it start?" I asked. "Who was your first victim?"

I threw a file on the table in front of her that Richard had pulled right before I left the office. I opened the folder. The picture of a man appeared. Sarah Millman looked away.

"He was your father, right? They found him in the canal in Boca Raton fifteen years ago. Stabbed twenty-six times. The killer was never found. Weird, huh? What did he do? Did he beat you up? Was that why you started this vendetta against parents beating up their kids?"

"Any injustice against a defenseless child should be punished," she said.

"I feel the same way, believe me, but you and I are not judges in a court of law. It's not our job to make that decision, and a smart girl like you knows that very well. So, tell me, what did your father do to you girls to make you believe he needed to suffer this fate?"

"He got one of us pregnant," she almost whispered. I could hear the bitterness and anger in her voice.

I sighed. "He raped one of you?"

"Not one. All of us," she said. "Over and over again. Through all of our teenage years. We came from a rich family and lived in an expensive neighborhood, where people had as many boats as they had cars. There is a perception out there, Detective, that child sexual abuse doesn't happen in those neighborhoods to those kids. But, what people need to realize is that child abuse, whether sexual or not, can happen and does happen to any child in any neighborhood. It cuts across all socioeconomic backgrounds, cultural and religious."

"Who was pregnant?"

"That is a secret between the four of us. We swore to never tell anyone. Not even our own mother knew. We never told her anything."

"How did you manage to hide it?" I asked.

"Big dresses, staying out of her sight. She was drunk most of the time anyway. She never knew. When the time came, right before she was about to deliver, we told her we were all going away to France for a couple of weeks over Christmas break to study the language and the art. It wasn't uncommon among our friends. We all left and went to a clinic that took the child and gave it to someone who wished to adopt it. When we found out one of us was pregnant, we made a pact...a blood pact, where we promised we would never look upon any abuse of children without acting on it. See, we believed our mother, the teachers at the school, and most people knew, but chose to turn a blind eye, thinking it was none of their business. Our father was influential. No one dared to touch him."

"Except you and your sisters. You finished him off. And got away with it," I said.

Sarah Millman was smart enough to not answer me. She knew not to say too much. She knew I would never find proof enough to nail her for the death of her father this many years later.

"So, why did your husband have to die?" I asked. "You have a son together. Did he touch him? Did he abuse Christopher?"

"What do you think?"

"I think he did. I think you found out and sent the kid away to boarding school before you arranged to have your husband punished. Your one sister, Natalie, had already bought the house across the street and she was ready to help as soon as you asked her to. Maybe it was even her twisted idea to force-feed him till his stomach burst. It's quite a painful death. Serves good as a punishment, doesn't it?"

"Sounds like you know more about that sort of thing than I do," she said, careful again to not say too much. But I could tell I was right. I could see it in her eyes. I guessed she had started to take the benzos we found in her house after the discovery of what her husband had done to their son, to calm herself down, and that had left her emotionless when they planned his death. It took a calm and cool mind to plan a death like this.

There was a knock on the door and Richard peeked inside. I stepped out.

"You were right, Ryder," he said.

"About what?"

"I just got off the phone with Stanley Bradley's wife. He had beaten his son too. The boy was transgender, and apparently, Stanley had a hard time figuring out how to react to that. So, he beat him up. The boy went to Cocoa Beach High. Graduated two years ago."

"Let me guess. The two schools share the same school psychologist?"

"It's a city thing. It's run from City Hall. She covers both schools in town."

"So, Stanley and Daniel were also punished for abusing their children. I'm guessing Roy was too. It looks like a pattern. Anything else?"

"Two things. First, I think I finally figured out the signature. The AM. It's all explained here," he said and handed me a printout from Wikipedia. "Second, you asked me to look into James West, who was killed in 2009 in Boca Raton by the same manner as Daniel Millman and Roy Miller."

"Yes, you found something?"

"I don't know if it is anything important, but apparently, he was once married and had four children."

"Okay?"

"One of them died in April, 2009."

"Died? How?"

"She burst her stomach."

76

April 2009

JAMES WEST WAS CRYING. For the first time since he was a child, he was crying. He was at his daughter's funeral. A week ago, she had been alive. But now, she wasn't here anymore.

And it was all his fault.

He should have listened to Dottie. He should have taken her word for it when she told him Elizabeth was sick and that she really couldn't control herself, no matter how much she tried.

Why? Why hadn't he listened?

Because he was a fool, that's why. He was a damned fool, and now he had to live with the fact that he had killed his own daughter.

Elizabeth hadn't stayed in the basement. Of course she hadn't. He hadn't been able to hear her because of the music, but at some point during the night, she burst through the door to the basement and broke it into pieces by her forceful weight. James had been drunk at the time. He hadn't thought about her for even a second, he was ashamed to admit. He had completely forgotten she was down there, and as the night progressed, she became more and more desperate. She was screaming for food and finally managed to break through and find her way to the kitchen.

They didn't find her until the next morning, when Nicole screamed from the kitchen and James woke with a start.

"Elizabeth."

Oh, my God. Oh, my God.

He ran downstairs and into the kitchen where Nicole was standing, frozen, holding a hand to her chest. On the tiles lay Elizabeth in a pile of hors d'oeuvres and Spanish Ham with olives and oranges. She had foie grass smeared over her entire face and piles of empty trays next to her. James gasped and knelt next to her. He couldn't believe it. There had been so much food left...big piles of food, and now it was all gone.

"Elizabeth," he said, grabbing her hand. He leaned over her. He could hear her breath and catch her pulse. She was still alive.

He had taken her to the hospital and told them what had happened. They had examined her and told him Elizabeth's stomach had been distended and she was in severe pain. At the emergency room, doctors pumped her stomach, but her condition worsened. A day passed before surgeons discovered that her stomach had been distended long enough to lose blood flow and become septic, and now it had ruptured. Elizabeth died that night in her hospital bed, and now she was lying in her coffin, and he would never see her again. And, as if that wasn't enough, Nicole had left him, and Dottie told him she was going to make sure he never saw any of his children again.

James had pleaded with her, trying to explain to her that it was an accident...that he had tried his best, but he knew it was a lie. He hadn't done his best. He hadn't listened to his ex-wife; he hadn't taken the time to get to really know his daughter and figure out what was wrong with her. He had taken her for being this monster, this person who lacked self-discipline because her mother smothered her.

But it was all too late to change now.

As the funeral was over, James West drove home to his empty house, where his daughter had eaten herself to death in his kitchen, and continued to cry. He cried his heart out, thinking about how stupid he had been, when the doorbell suddenly rang. Outside stood four young women in their twenties. They looked alike, and he guessed they had to be sisters. At first, he thought they were Jehovah's Witnesses and he told them he wasn't interested, when one of them put her high-heeled shoe in the door as he tried to close it on them.

"Oh, but *we* are interested," one of them said.

"We're very interested in you, James West," another said.

"Especially interested in what happened to your daughter," a third said.

"Who are you?" he asked.

"We're the Angel Makers," the fourth said. "I sure hope you're hungry."

77

March 2015

"Tell me about the child," I said, as I returned to Sarah Millman.

"What child?" she asked.

"The child you and your sister adopted away to another family."

"What's there to tell?"

I sighed and looked at her. I was getting a little fed up with her tough-girl approach to everything. It was getting old.

"She died, didn't she? How did you find out?" I asked, cutting to the chase.

"It was in the paper," she said. "The story of the girl who ate herself to death. We recognized the name and our daughter in the picture."

"Our daughter? So she was yours?" I asked.

"She was all of ours. We all acted like we were pregnant; we all loved her like she was ours, but none of us could keep her, since we were too young. We thought we were giving her away to a family that would take good care of her, better than what we could. But they didn't. They let her eat herself to death."

"So, you killed James West. You force-fed him till his stomach ruptured, just like had happened to your daughter."

"I never said that I did," she said.

"Was it Natalie who shot those people in the theater? That was her deal, right? She liked to shoot. She learned about the parents through the students at her school, then planned their execution. I'm guessing she's the dramatic one of you, right? After the shooting and the killing of James West, you knew you couldn't stay in Boca. It was too dangerous. So, you all moved up here, to Cocoa Beach, where Natalie got a new job and you got married to Daniel, right? You were pregnant and expecting Christopher at this time."

"I had just given birth," she said. "And we were already married when we moved here."

"Okay, so did you all move up here, or was it just you and Natalie?"

"It was just me and Natalie. She bought the house across the street from me with her money from our inheritance after our mother died."

"And the two others?"

"Angelina and Kelly stayed in Boca. They came up here a year ago."

"Right when they heard you were in trouble, huh?"

"My marriage wasn't doing well, no. That's no secret. They came to help me. There is nothing wrong with that. Besides, Angelina had been laid off from her job and needed a place to stay. Daniel was never home anyway, so she moved in here with me. She never married and never had any children. Kelly married, but was divorced after three years. She never had any children either."

"Tell me about the Angel Makers," I said.

"What?" The way Sarah Millman blushed told me she knew exactly what I was talking about. I put the article from Wikipedia on the table in front of her.

"That's what you call yourselves, isn't it? AM, Angel Makers. According to this article, The Angel Makers were a group of women living in the village of Nagyrév, Hungary, who, between 1914 and 1929 poisoned to death an estimated three hundred people, mostly abusive husbands and family members that had become a burden to them or to get hold of their inheritance. Others poisoned their lovers, some even their sons, as the midwife behind it all allegedly told the poisoners, *Why put up with them?* Is that how you and your sisters think? Why not just rid the world of these abusive people?"

"You must admit, they do make a strong point," she said.

"I do. But this is 2015 America and we have a justice system that is supposed to handle these people."

"Maybe we do and maybe we don't," she said.

"Who wrote the emails to Shannon King?" I asked. "Was it you?"

"I don't know what you are talking about."

"No, it couldn't have been you. You're not the one with the conscience. It has to be one of the other sisters. I'm thinking Natalie. She sounds like she is more emotional. Except, of course, I don't know much about the last two, do I?"

"I don't think you know much about anything, Detective," she said with a smirk.

I leaned back. It was getting annoying. I wasn't getting her to say anything useful. Still, I kept trying.

"So, Angela Harrison told Natalie about her father Joe and how he had beaten her once. Something not even her mother knew. But, a few weeks ago, Angela came to school crying and they sent her to see Natalie, to talk to her. She told her she missed her father, but that she was also afraid of him. I read the files that Natalie wrote. Am I right? That's why Joe had to die, right?"

"I wouldn't know," she said.

"I get that one of you killed Britney Foster because she had seen Natalie in Publix here in Cocoa Beach and knew she posed a threat to you, but what about Beth?" I asked.

Sarah Millman looked at me indifferently.

"Bethany Gruber, my partner? Why did she have to get hurt? At first, I thought it was just a coincidence, that you were trying to scare us off, to try and get us to back off, but then I went through Natalie's files at the school and realized that Beth's youngest daughter had problems too. The little girl told Natalie about how her mother drank, right? That was why you tried to kill her, wasn't it? I just don't understand how you knew that Beth would be the one who would open the truck's door."

"I'm sure I don't know what you're talking about, Detective. However, maybe if someone was trying to kill that little partner of yours, they would have set the bomb up so that it would only go off if someone of her size tried to open the door. You know how short and pudgy she is, not like any of the other officers who would have been called to the scene. That's just a guess, of course; I don't even know whether such a thing is possible," she replied nonchalantly.

"But it was all based on a lie. Beth doesn't drink anymore; she's been in AA for a year and is getting better. See, all I did was to talk a little to her neighbor, who told me everything. If you had done a little research, you would have made the same discovery. The file is two years old when everything went wrong at her household and Beth was drinking...right after her husband left her alone with three children. But, not everything is black and white. That's why we need a justice system. That's why vigilantism is a felony. Now, all I need for you is to tell me where your sisters are. They can explain the rest, but I need to find them. First of all, Natalie, I need to find her. Where is she?"

"She's gone, Detective."

"Where?"

Sarah Millman shrugged. "Who knows? She left last night. Who knows where she might have gone to? Maybe it wasn't just her, maybe it was all three of them that left. Who knows?"

"You've got it all figured out, don't you. Why didn't you leave?"

"I have a son, remember? I can't just leave."

I hit my fist on the table. Mrs. Millman hardly reacted. She was probably still doped.

"Where did she go?" I yelled. "Where is Natalie Monahan?"

Sarah Millman shook her head. "Sorry, Detective. There is no way I'm telling you this. You see, that would blow the entire thing, wouldn't it? We're going to be everywhere, keeping our eyes on you. We'll be your lawyers, your child's teacher, and your policewomen. We'll be everywhere, making sure you behave. You should be thanking us. We're doing society a favor. Do you have any idea how many prisoners on death row right now were beaten by their parents? How many were abused by the very same people that were supposed to protect them? It's a disease. And it is passed down to the next generation. Chances are, if your daddy beat you, then you'll do the same to your child, and so on. We are here to break that cycle. Lord knows, someone has to. Now, if you don't mind, I'm not saying another word till my lawyer is here."

78

March 2015

I STOPPED by Shannon's condo on my way home. I had picked the kids up from my parents' place and told them to continue up in the elevator to our apartment with Emily while I checked on Shannon. I felt bad, since I hadn't had any time for her in the past couple of days. At the same time, I felt exhausted after interrogating Sarah Millman all day and not getting much out of her. Her lawyer had arrived and told us everything his client had told us in the initial interviews couldn't be used for anything, since he wasn't present. He was one of those high-paid lawyers that you didn't want to get up against.

I was worried Sarah Millman would get away with everything. I wasn't going to let her. I still had one more card to play, and I was going to do it the next day. Stanley Bradley would identify her in a line-up. If she had been involved in his kidnapping, he could tell me. Meanwhile, I had sent out all kinds of pictures of the three sisters to the media, letting them know we were searching for them, and especially for Natalie Monahan, who I believed to be the shooter at the cinema and at the festival. I also believed she was the one who shot Sheriff Ron before she escaped by boat. Richard had found out that she had been taking shooting lessons at a shooting range in

Melbourne. They recognized her picture when he went down there and showed it to them. She had been going there for years.

I rang the doorbell to Shannon's place and waited. I wasn't going to stay the night, since I had promised Emily I would watch *The Tonight Show* with her and I had promised Abigail and Austin that they could sleep in my bed with me, since they had missed me, and Abigail blamed me for never spending any time with them anymore. It was true, I guess, but I had a job to do, I told her.

"You always say that," she said. Then she gave me that look that I can't refuse. She had a way with her daddy.

There was a fumbling behind the door and it was opened. "Shannon?" I said, as her face appeared. My heart started racing when I tried to look into her eyes. She avoided looking directly at me.

"Come on in," she said, and walked to the living room, where she threw herself on the couch.

I sat next to her with a sigh. "Why do you torture yourself like this?" I asked, trying to get her to look at me. "Where is Angela?"

"Sleeping. I put her to bed early. She was getting on my nerves."

"You're drunk," I said. "Again." I tried to hide how emotional I was, but my voice was breaking. So was my heart. I felt so bad for Angela that she had to see her mother like this. Shannon turned into this completely different person when she drank. She was aggressive and angry.

"Do you even want to stop?" I asked.

"I just took a little drink, alright? That's all. Get off my back." She snarled as she spoke. "It's just this damn thing with the police." Shannon closed her eyes. She was swaying. This wasn't just the result of one or two drinks.

I wondered where she got the alcohol from, but decided I didn't even want to ask. There were many ways to get ahold of it. I felt betrayed, like she didn't care about anyone but herself. I knew she was hurting from the case against her and the massive media coverage, but still. I needed her to be stronger. I needed her to want to be strong. An alcoholic would always find her drinks somewhere. It didn't matter if we tried to keep her away from it; she needed to make the decision to stop. That was how my mother had explained it to me when I had spoken to her about Shannon's drinking a few days ago. That was when I had thought I could simply keep her away from the alcohol and then she would get better. But now, I realized my mother was right. It wasn't that easy. It was Shannon's decision to make. I just knew I couldn't watch as she drank herself into misery and dragged all the rest of us with her.

Feeling all kinds of rage, I got up and walked to Angela's bedroom.

"Where are you going?" Shannon said.

I opened the door and found Angela sitting on her bed, crying. Of course she wasn't sleeping. "Come on," I said and picked her up in my arms, still wrapped in her blanket. She put her arms around my neck while she cried helplessly.

"You can't just take her, Jack," Shannon yelled. "She's my daughter, Goddammit."

I walked towards the front door and stopped. I looked at Shannon. Her eyes were glassy and flickering back and forth.

"She won't be much longer if you keep this up," I said, opened the door, and walked out. As the door shut behind me, Angela looked into my eyes.

"Will she be alright? Will Mommy be alright?" she asked.

I walked to the elevator and pushed the button, my blood pumping in my veins. "She's a grown woman. She'll be fine," I said.

79

March 2015

It took a long time for her to calm down, but finally, Angela fell asleep on the couch between Emily and me while we watched Jimmy Fallon talk to Madonna. She sang *Holiday* with Jimmy Fallon and The Roots. It amused me enough to be able to laugh and relax a little. Emily thought it was boring and called Madonna old. She still stayed for the rest of the show, though, and I enjoyed her company. I even managed to get her to talk a little about what was going on in her life and had her tell me she was doing a concert at the school next week, but also said that she didn't want me there.

"What? My daughter is playing a concert and I'm not allowed to be there?" I said.

"Jack," she said through gritted teeth. "I don't want you there. It'll be so embarrassing. You're *durpy*."

"Excuse me? I'm not cool anymore? What happened? And what happened to daddy? You used to call me daddy?"

Emily looked into my eyes and put a hand on my shoulder. "I love you, Jack, but you're not my dad, and you are not very cool. I will kill you if you show up at my concert."

I looked at her, disappointed. "You really mean that?"

"Yes."

"At least tell me what you're doing. Are you playing an instrument?"

"I'm not telling you."

I looked at Emily with a grin. "Then you know what I must do."

"Jack, don't."

I lifted my hands in the air and yelled *Tickle Monster* before I attacked her and tickled her till she pleaded for me to stop.

"Pleeease!"

"Only if you tell me what you're doing in the concert, and only if you call me dad."

"Alright, alright, I give up," she said.

I let her go and sat back down, laughing. She looked at me like she was mad, but I could tell she was about to laugh too.

"So?"

"Okay," she said.

"Okay what?"

"Okay, *Dad*. I'm singing."

"Since when are you singing? You're singing in the concert? Like, in a choir, or what?" I asked. I had never heard Emily sing one tune in her entire life.

"No." She rolled her eyes at me. "It's just me."

My heart was about to melt. "You're singing solo? And you're telling me I can't be there? That's not fair!"

Emily got up from the couch. "But that's the way it's going to be," she said. "I'm too embarrassed about this to want you there. I told my music teacher I didn't want to do it, but she said I had to. I hate it, so that's why I don't want you to see it. Now, it's getting late, *Dad*. I'm going to bed. Goodnight."

I looked after my grown daughter as she walked to her bedroom. I couldn't believe how big she already was. She looked so much like her mother. I wondered if she ever thought about her. Of course she did. She had been six years old when her mother was killed. Lisa was born in the U.S., but her parents came from Bahamas. They moved to

Florida before Lisa was born. I often wondered if she had any family over there. Maybe some cousins? I would have to take Emily there some time in search of her roots. It would do her good. She needed to know who she was and where she came from. Her grandparents were both dead now, but surely there had to be other family members?

I grabbed Angela and carried her into the twins' bedroom, where I put her in Abigail's bed. I would make sure she made it to the bus the next morning. I would have to stop by Shannon's to get her backpack, but she could borrow some clothes from Abigail. They were about the same size. I would have to pack her a lunchbox as well and a snack. I guessed Shannon hadn't done any of it. I felt so angry with her for the way she behaved. I knew she was going through a tough time, but still. She had a child. She was responsible for another life.

I stroked Angela's hair, and then kissed her on her forehead, shut off the light, and left the room. I grabbed an apple and ate it while looking out the windows at the dark beach. I walked into the balcony and stood for a little while, listening to the waves. I hadn't had the time to surf much the last week. The waves had been good; I had seen them on Facebook on several of my friend's pictures that they'd posted. I felt like the ocean was mocking me, telling me to come catch some of my own. But this wasn't the time. I had to finish my case first. I looked into the deep darkness and thought about the Bahamas. It was right out there, about three or four hours by boat. It was so close.

So close.

80

March 2015

I BOARDED the airplane in Orlando. It was just me. I had made arrangements with a local officer to meet me at the airport in Nassau. It was late Tuesday afternoon. The trip was only one hour and fifteen minutes. I had no idea how long I was going to stay. When I was in the office this morning, I had told Richard to ask our Special Investigative Unit to help him try and trace the emails sent to Shannon once again. Richard had made profiles on all the sisters and found out that one of them, Angelina Monahan, worked in cyber-security. She helped protect big corporations against hackers. She would know exactly how to cover up the email's origins. But one of the IP addresses that came up during their investigation was in the Bahamas, and I thought it was worth a try to look into it. So, I had called the local police in Nassau and had them tell me who owned the house with the address from which it originated. It belonged to an American company called Millman Technologies, they told me.

I hadn't talked to Shannon yet, but my mother had promised to take all of the kids. Emily would help her and my dad out, I told her. Angela wasn't going home to her mother's until I knew she was sober, and so far, she hadn't even called me, so I assumed she was still on a bender. It hurt me like crazy to know she was hurting and there was nothing I could do to help.

"Mr. Ryder?" a smiling man said in his singing English. He had one of those smiles that literally lit up his face.

"Yes," I said and shook his hand.

"I'm Commissioner Ellis, The Royal Bahamas Police Force."

"Nice to meet you."

Commissioner Ellis had a car waiting and we got in. I had told him we believed a person of interest was hiding in the house, and he had agreed to take me there. This was a high-profile case I told him, since it involved two mass shootings and a murder attempt on a sheriff.

"The house is in Lyford Cay," he said. "In Western New Providence. It is one of The Bahamas' most desirable communities to live in. The biggest properties in the exclusive development sell for twenty million plus, and beachfront homes for ten million and up."

I whistled, impressed.

"It is very exclusive, Mr. Ryder. Only for the über-rich. Gated, naturally. It has a par-72 golf course, twelve tennis courts, a full-service marina, dining facilities, a post office, a private international school, and a mile-long private beach. I do hope you have good reason for us to intrude on this place."

"I do," I said, sincerely hoping I was right about this. I had spoken to Ron about it on the phone to get his permission to follow this lead. He had told me I needed clearance further up. I had spoken to the governor, and he had given me the green light for this. Everyone wanted to nail this shooter more than anything. As long as nothing went wrong, the governor told me.

"Make sure nothing goes wrong, Ryder. This entire case makes me sick to my stomach."

I had promised that. It made me sick too. I hated how these sisters thought they had won this. Sarah Millman was still in our custody, but I had a feeling if I didn't do something, then she wouldn't stay for very long. Her lawyer was that good.

The commissioner had brought along four officers. They were sitting in the small van, looking very serious under their beige hats with the red stripe. The weather was glorious; it was even hotter than Florida, the skies blue, the breeze warm. It wasn't my first time here, but it still amazed me how clear the water was.

"We're entering the gated community now," the commissioner said, and looked at me with a serious look, like he wanted to make sure I still wanted to do this. I nodded and looked out as our car was let through the enormous gate and we entered Disney World for the richest in this world, the über-rich, as the commissioner called them, those that thought nothing of dropping a few hundred thousand at the roulette table, or even millions to buy an island. This was a completely different world. At least for me.

81

March 2015

THE HOUSE WAS EMPTY. I was secondary, since I was operating on British soil, so I wasn't let inside before the Bahamian Police had been inside to make sure it was safe. I walked inside and went through all the ten or more bedrooms, but there were no signs of any of the sisters.

I should've known. They're not that stupid.

I walked through what I believed was the master bedroom and onto the balcony, where I could see the Bahamian officers walking through the yard, searching every corner. I felt so tired. I had been so sure that this was the place...that I would find them here. But it was yet another dead end.

I walked back into the bedroom looked inside the closets and found many dresses, shoes, and suitcases, but there was no telling if that was something new or it was just here so the sisters didn't have to bring much when they arrived. I found jewelry on the dresser and a hairdryer in the bathroom, along with several toothbrushes. It looked like someone was living here, but I couldn't be sure that it was recently. I was about to leave, when I saw something on the floor. I picked it up and looked at it. A tag from a dress. I turned it and looked at the name on the back.

"I'm afraid we don't find them here," the commissioner said, as he walked in. I showed him the tag.

"I know that place," he said. "It's in downtown Nassau." He rubbed his fingertips against each other on one hand. "Pricey place."

"Take me there," I said.

The commissioner told his officers they were done at the house, then drove all of us back to Nassau. We found the small store in the middle of town and I walked in, flanked by two officers. I showed the woman behind the counter the picture of the four sisters and she pointed at one of them, Natalie Monahan.

"This one. She was in here yesterday. Bought three dresses."

"Did she say anything about where she was going?" I asked, almost overflowing with excitement. Finally, I had found her trail. I hadn't been wrong about this. She was here. Somewhere.

The woman shook her head. "No."

I was about to leave when the woman stopped me. "But she did say she wanted to dress nicely for a man."

I stopped and looked at her. "A man?"

"Yes, a man," she said with her strong island accent.

"Do you know anything about this man?"

The lady shook her head. "I just sold her some new dresses."

Once again, I was disillusioned. It was getting late and the sun was about to set. The commissioner drove me to my hotel and I checked in. I lay on the bed of the room, watching the local news and dozing off, when the story of a famous American baseball player named Todd Quentin came on. Apparently, he lived in The Bahamas now, since he had retired, but recently he had been involved in a scandal. Apparently, his ex-wife accused him of having locked their son in the basement because he told his dad he was gay.

"According to the ex-wife, Todd Quentin wouldn't let the son come out again until he admitted he wasn't gay and said that he had just been joking. The ex-wife was out of town when the incident happened, but divorced him as soon as she learned what he had done, and today, she decided to drag him to court and demand full custody of their son," said the reporter in her story filmed outside of a building I recognized as the one marking the entrance of the Lyford Cay community.

I stared at the screen and turned off the sound, while trying to straighten out my thoughts.

Could it be? Could it really be?

I grabbed my phone and called the commissioner.

"I need to get back into Lyford Cay," I said. "Yes it has to be right now. It's a matter of life and death."

82

March 2015

Natalie Monahan was enjoying her evening with Todd Quentin. Not because of the celebrity company, but more because she was so excited about finally being able to wipe that smirk off of his face. She had been dating him on and off for months now, whenever she visited the island and stayed in her sister's house. It wasn't his money she was after. Lord, no. She had enough for herself. After their parents died, they had all inherited enough money for them to never have to work again. No, just like her job as a school psychologist, this was her charity work; this was her passion; this was her helping out where society had failed.

"More champagne?" Todd asked with his handsome smile.

He was older than her, by fifteen years, give or take. But he liked his women young, she had learned.

Natalie had played it all out with him. Ever since she had heard the story about him and his son. She had approached him at the golf course and he had asked if she wanted a drink in the bar afterwards. Then, she had let him fuck her in the bathroom, just to make sure she had him on the hook. Now he was caressing her hand and it gave Natalie chills all over her back, especially since she knew what was on his mind. His little sex games had become worse and worse, but she had played along...until now, that was. Tonight, she was going to give him what he deserved.

"Yes, please," she said and thought of the nine mm in her purse. She couldn't wait to see his face when she pulled it out. The question was, how far she was willing to let him go?

"I do enjoy these small meetings," he said and looked into her eyes. He had served her dinner on the balcony overlooking the ocean. It was gorgeous with all the lights in the yard beneath them.

She forced a smile. "Me too."

He grabbed her hand and yanked her forward so hard she hurt herself on the table. "Have you been a bad girl, huh?"

She tried not to show she was hurt. She smiled. "So bad."

"Tell me how bad. You've been playing with yourself, huh?"

Natalie felt sick to her stomach. She hated these little games he played. It was terrible, so cliché. And then there was the sex. How this sick bastard could ever have thought any woman would find that pleasing was beyond her understanding. No, this world, and especially the women of this world, would be happy that she removed him from the surface of the earth. It was in everyone's best interest.

Natalie couldn't help thinking about his son. She had met him at the house once. He was twelve and so vulnerable, and yet Todd had yelled at him and called him a fruitcake. He had even slapped him when he didn't answer him correctly.

She had fought the desire to kill the guy right then. She wanted to wait. It had to be done at the right time. And that time was now.

"Oh, yes. A lot."

Todd Quentin laughed loudly and let go of her hand. He continued to shovel down food with his fork. "I like that," he said with his mouth full. He pointed at her with his fork. "I really like that. You sure are something. You're nothing like all those boring housewife bitches you see around here with all their money, charities, and hats. Oh, how I loathe those hats they all wear."

"Well, I'm nothing like that," she said chuckling. "You're right about that."

He stared at her with lust in his eyes and shook his head. "No, lady. You're fine. You are so fine and so damn sexy. I could ride you all night long."

"I bet you could."

83

March 2015

WE HAD JUST PARKED the van in front of Todd Quentin's mansion when we heard the gunshots. Two shots were fired right after one another.

"*Break my heart again and I'll put two bullets in yours,*" I said and looked at the commissioner.

"What does that mean?"

"It's a song. It means we're too late."

I rushed up the driveway, and secondary or not, I ran inside of the house. The commissioner and his officers were right behind me.

"It sounded like it came from upstairs," I yelled and ran up the carpeted stairs. I found myself, seconds later, on the balcony, where I stopped. Right there on the tiles, next to a table with food and champagne in a bucket, stood the famous baseball player Todd Quentin, holding a nine mm gun in his hand. He was naked from the waist down. In front of him lay Natalie Monahan on the floor. She was completely naked, her dress on the floor behind the chair, her panties next to it. She was holding a hand to her stomach, where the blood was streaming out from a big wound.

Todd Quentin looked at me. He was crying. "I...I...she was about to shoot me. She pulled this thing out of her purse while we were...I thought it was a toy. I thought she was playing a game. But then she said she wanted to kill me. She asked me if I knew what it was like to be hated by your own dad, to be abused by the one person who was supposed to love you and protect you. I had no idea what she was talking about. Then, she cocked it and lifted it to pull the trigger. I had to move fast. So, I did. I grabbed the barrel of the gun from her hand and...I got it and turned it at her, told her to not come closer. But she was screaming and yelling, and then she...she leapt towards me and I...I pulled the trigger. I had to."

Three Bahamian officers were soon all over him and got the gun out of his hand. He was cuffed and taken away. I knelt next to Natalie Monahan. She was still conscious, but only barely.

"Natalie. Can you hear me?" I asked. "Stay with me. Okay? We have ambulances coming."

Natalie looked at me. I could tell she was holding on to her life with everything she had, all the strength she could find. I felt so desperate.

"Don't go, Natalie. We need you."

I heard ambulances wailing in the distance. They didn't sound like the ones I was used to, but I knew it was them.

"Just hold on for a little while longer. I know everything, Natalie. I know your entire story. I know how your father abused you. I know how one of you was pregnant and gave the child away. I know how the child died. I know that you and your sisters made a pact. I need you to tell me the rest, Natalie. I need you."

Natalie opened her mouth, as if she wanted to say something to me, but no words left her lips. I could tell she was struggling to find the strength. Finally, a word managed to come out of her. A small still word I could barely hear through all the noise coming from down the stairs.

"...sorry..."

I looked directly into her eyes as she went into a cramp. Her eyes died first. Then her body gave in and became limp in my hands.

"No!" I yelled, as a paramedic came rushing in and took her out of my hands. But it didn't matter. There was nothing they could do. She was gone.

84

March 2015

I CAME HOME three days later and threw myself on the couch with a loud sigh. I was finished in the Bahamas, where I had gone through all the belongings found in The Millmans' big house, and together with the police there, finished the Bahamian side to the case. Todd Quentin was, once again, facing a media frenzy, since everyone was talking about him, both in the Bahamas and back here in the U.S. Finally, it seemed like they had forgotten about Shannon. At least for a little while. I hoped that gave her the peace and quiet she needed. I had noticed the reporters and photographers were all gone from the entrance to our building, so that was a start. I knew my mother had been taking care of all the children, even Angela, for as long as I was gone, but I had no idea how Shannon had been doing. I feared the worst, to be honest.

The case against the Monahan sisters wasn't closed, and it wasn't solved either. I was told Sarah Millman had been released on bail, and now it was up to me to build the case against her. Stanley Bradley had identified her as one of the two keeping him hostage, so that was at least a beginning. We were going for charging her with the murders of her husband and Roy Miller. The two other sisters would be charged with assisting her and the fourth sister, Natalie, in planning her shootings, but it was like they had like sunken into the ground. Their pictures had been shown everywhere, but still there was no trace of them. I hadn't given up on finding them, but prepared myself for the fact that it would take a long time before we did. They would mess up eventually. They all did.

Beth was awake, Richard told me on the phone. She had gone through a severe skin transplant, but was much better now. She had been asking for me. I promised I would go see her the next day. And, Ron was back, Richard said. He was supposed to be on sick leave for at least three weeks, but he couldn't stay away.

"I think the old wife drove him nuts," Richard said. "She is constantly terrified something is going to happen to him again. She wanted him to quit the force, can you imagine?"

"No. I really can't," I said. "The force is his entire life."

It was the truth. He always said we were his second family. And if anyone loved his family, it was Ron. Both of them.

I was sitting on my couch and had opened the windows to listen to the waves, when there was a knock on my door. I got up and opened it. Outside, stood Shannon. Her eyes were clearer, even though she looked very sad.

"I'm so, so sorry," she said.

I smiled and sighed. "Come in."

"I can't blame you for being angry with me. I don't know what got into me. I feel awful, Jack. I really do."

"So, now you're here to tell me you're sober, is that it?" I asked.

"I am sober. I have been for three days now."

I shrugged. "And how am I supposed to believe that? You said that last week too. So what if you're sober now? You'll drink next week or the week after that. This case isn't over; they still haven't found the gun. It will keep going; there will come more bad news, eventually, in the coming months; they'll write bad things about you again. Then what? Then you'll go back to drinking again?"

Shannon shook her head. I saw a light in them I hadn't seen in a long time. Maybe never.

"I won't, Jack. I really won't."

I rubbed my eyes and leaned back in the couch. I really wanted to believe her, but how could I? I didn't want to get hurt again. I didn't want to stand and watch as she hurt herself and her daughter. I simply couldn't.

"Shannon...I...I don't know if I can trust you again. I don't want to live a life where I am constantly afraid you might slip again. I can't watch you all hours of the day. You need to make the decision that you want to get better. You have to make the decision to not drink again."

She nodded. "I know," she said. "And I have."

"So, how can I trust that you won't drink again in, let's say...in a month?"

"Because I won't. I really won't, Jack. Not for the next nine months."

"You say that now, and then you..." I paused and looked at her. "Did you say nine months?"

Shannon bit her lip and then she nodded. "I don't know how this happened..."

I got up from the couch and put both hands in my hair while staring at her, then took them out and sat down again. Seconds later, I got up again and walked back and forth while my thoughts settled. I turned and looked at her, then sat down again. My mouth was open, but no words left my lips. Shannon nodded. She seemed happy, yet anxious.

"I'm terrified too, Jack, but..."

"Terrified?" I finally managed to say. "I wouldn't call it that."

"What would you call it?" she looked at me. "You do want it, don't you?"

"Are you kidding me? Look around. I love kids. The more the merrier, right?"

Shannon chuckled. I put my arm around her and pulled her close. This changed everything. "And, you're sure, right?"

She nodded again. "I took four tests. Today, I went to the doctor and he told me I was six weeks pregnant."

I shook my head. "Wow," I said. "That is really something."

"It sure is," she said and leaned in against me.

"So, what do you say we move in together?" I asked.

She looked up at me, then kissed my lips. "I would like that. I would really love that, Jack."

I looked around the condo that had been my home for seven years, mine and the kids' home. It had been a time of great happiness when the twins were born and of great sadness when their mother left us. I had cried and laughed a lot in this place. I loved that it was right on the water, but now I was beginning to think it was time for a change.

"Maybe we should get a house together," I said. "One that is big enough for us and all of our children."

Shannon smiled again. "That sounds great. I saw that there was a lot for sale two blocks down. We would still be on the ocean and still in walking distance to your parents' place. We could buy that."

"And build our own dream house. I like the sound of that," I said. I had always wanted to build my own house. "But, there is no way I can afford that on my salary. A lot like that is close to a million, and then there's the house..."

"You might not be able to. But I could," Shannon said.

"Oh, Shannon, I couldn't..."

"Of course you can. We're about to be parents. Last time I checked this is 2015. A woman can buy her family a house and provide for them."

I had a tickling sensation in my stomach. I leaned down and kissed Shannon again. I was just so happy to have her back to the woman I loved. Could we do this? Why not?

"Guess I'm building you a house, then," I said.

She chuckled. "We'll all live in the house that Jack built."

Epilogue

HOP ON THE BUS

85

April 2015

KATIE LOOKED out the window of the bus. Florida's flat landscape raced by as she continued her way back home. At first, the police had asked her to stay until they were done with the investigation of Britney's murder. They had asked all of them to stay, but let the others go a few days before they told Katie she could go back home.

Katie drew in a sigh of relief. It had been scary waiting at the motel for the police to make up their mind if they wanted to charge her with anything. They still hadn't closed the case, Jack Ryder told her, but he didn't believe she had anything to do with it.

"Then, who was it?" Katie had asked.

"That's still under investigation," he answered.

Katie lucked out. She knew she did. She had a pretty good motive. The worst part was that the others believed she had done it. Both Leanne and Irene told her to her face. They were terrified of her, they said. And they had asked for another room at the motel while they waited for the police's verdict. Katie had felt so lonely.

Now, she was looking forward to getting back to the dorm after two weeks in Cocoa Beach. It hadn't quite been the spring break she had dreamt about, but it would still be remembered as something special, she thought to herself.

In the middle of all the chaos, she had somehow found herself. She had realized who she was. She wasn't someone who simply took crap from everyone else...at least not anymore.

Katie smiled when she thought about Britney's face when she had slammed her fist into her pretty nose in the restroom at Grill's restaurant that night. It had hurt like crazy on her knuckles, but it was worth all the pain. Just to get all the anger out that was threatening to burst inside of her. Just to feel the relief of justice being served to the BITCH.

Katie chuckled and spotted a dead armadillo on the side of the road. She had surprised even herself. She didn't know she had it in her. Neither did Britney, apparently. It had been such a thrill just to see the look on her face when Katie attacked her as she came out of her stall in the restroom. Katie had slammed her fist into Britney's porcelain-face again and again, and as she landed, her chin slammed into the toilet. Katie picked her up from the tiles, spat into her face, then slammed her fist into her over and over again till she stopped making sounds.

Katie knew she wasn't dead when she picked her up and carried her outside to the deck on the back side. It was late and there were only a few people left in the bar. No one saw her as she threw Britney over the rail, and no one heard the sound her body made as it plunged into the canal.

But Katie remembered. She remembered every little bit of it. Every sound, every feeling she had felt when giving Britney what she deserved.

Boy, it felt good.

It was even worth going to jail for. But, as it turned out, she didn't even have to do that. She was getting away with it. From now on, no one would ever mess with her again. She looked at her phone and at the picture of Greg she had as the background. Katie knew she had probably lost him. He had been so shaken up by Britney's murder that he hadn't spoken to anyone afterwards. Katie had seen him as he carried his suitcases to the van when the others were let go. He had looked at her with terror in his eyes. That's when she knew she wasn't going to see him again.

Katie opened the phone and deleted the photo. She also deleted Greg from her contacts. He wasn't worth her love anyway. She looked up at the landscape, when suddenly, her phone beeped. She had received a Snapchat. Katie opened it. It was a picture of Katie, taken just as she tossed the body over the railing at Grill's. Katie gasped. So someone had seen her after all? But who?

The picture was gone after a few seconds, and she would never see it again. At least, she hoped. Lucky for her, that's how Snapchat worked. It only lasted for ten seconds, then it was deleted automatically. So was any chat you ever wrote. She wrote back:

WHO IS THIS?

She received an answer and opened it with a pounding heart.

WE SHOULD TALK

Katie stared at the message till it disappeared. Her hands felt warm and clammy. Who was this person? Why hadn't they gone to the police with what they knew? She wrote back.

WHO ARE YOU?

She waited a few seconds before the answer came.

WE ARE THE ANGEL MAKERS. JUST LIKE YOU, WE FIGHT FOR JUSTICE. JOIN US.

Katie stared at her phone till the message was cleared again. She couldn't believe this. Somehow, they knew. Somehow, these people knew what she had done. She realized she didn't feel bad or even afraid. As a matter of fact, she never felt anxious or afraid anymore. Not since that night when she had taken matters into her own hands. She felt strong. Independent. She felt in control. Nothing and no one could touch her now. These people knew her name. They saw her and understood what she had done. She felt like she fit in somewhere. She was famous. Finally.

THE END

Afterword

Dear Reader,

Thank you for purchasing *Slip Out the Back Jack*. It is the second novel about Jack Ryder and his family. I hope you enjoyed reading it as much as I did writing it. I want you to know that Elizabeth's story in this book—crazy as it might seem—is actually taken from real life. Prader-Willi syndrome is real. It is a rare genetic disorder. And it is a real struggle for the families with children who have it. You can read more about it here and watch a video that inspired Elizabeth's story. It's truly amazing what these families go through.

The Angel Makers of Nagyrév is also a true story. Read about who they were here.

We will, of course, hear much more about Shannon's struggle to stay out of jail and, hopefully, Jack will pursue the rest of the Angel Makers in the next book.

Until then, you can check out my other books by following the links below. And don't forget to leave reviews, if possible.

Take care,

Willow

To be the first to hear about new releases and bargains from Willow Rose, sign up below to be on the VIP List. (I promise not to share your email with anyone else, and I won't clutter your inbox.)

- Tap here to sign up to be on the VIP LIST:
https://readerlinks.com/l/415254

Win a signed paperback of your choice from Willow Rose! Just become a member of my Facebook group **WILLOW ROSE - MYSTERY SERIES**.

We'll randomly select a winner from all the entries.

To enter, just tap/click here:
https://www.facebook.com/groups/1921072668197253

Tired of too many emails? Text the word: "willowrose" to 31996 to sign up to Willow's VIP text List to get a text alert with news about New Releases, Giveaways, Bargains and Free books from Willow.

Follow Willow Rose on BookBub:
https://www.bookbub.com/authors/willow-rose

Follow Willow on BookBub

Connect with Willow online:

https://www.facebook.com/willowredrose/
https://twitter.com/madamwillowrose
http://www.goodreads.com/author/show/
4804769.Willow_Rose
http://www.willow-rose.net
madamewillowrose@gmail.com

About the Author

Willow Rose is a multi-million-copy best-selling Author and an Amazon ALL-star Author of more than 80 novels.

Several of her books have reached the top 10 of ALL books on Amazon in the US, UK, and Canada. She has sold more than six million books all over the world.

She writes Mystery, Thriller, Paranormal, Romance, Suspense, Horror, Supernatural thrillers, and Fantasy.

Willow's books are fast-paced, nail-biting pageturners with twists you won't see coming. That's why her fans call her The Queen of Plot Twists.

Willow lives on Florida's Space Coast with her husband and two daughters. When she is not writing or reading, you will find her surfing and watch the dolphins play in the waves of the Atlantic Ocean.

To be the first to hear about new releases and bargains —from Willow Rose—sign up below to be on the VIP List. (I promise not to share your email with anyone else, and I won't clutter your inbox.)

- GO HERE TO SIGN UP TO BE ON THE VIP LIST :
http://bit.ly/VIP-subscribe

Tired of too many emails? Text the word: "willowrose" to
31996 to sign up to Willow's VIP text List to get a text alert with
news about New Releases, Giveaways, Bargains and Free books from
Willow.

Cover design by Juan Villar Padron,
https://www.juanjpadron.com

Special thanks to my editor Janell Parque
http://janellparque.blogspot.com/

Ingram Content Group UK Ltd.
Milton Keynes UK
UKHW011832270423
420877UK00001B/33